FORGET MY FATE

Special Agent Eric Lund is in Northern Minnesota at Camp Midaywin, but he's not vacationing. He's there to investigate a lead on someone who is trying to blackmail a U.S. senator. What he finds is Mr. & Mrs. Fitts, the aged owners of the camp; Verne Anderson, a fellow fisherman; Althea Sharon, an older hiker who is writing her adventures; and Roger Winton and Mart Bryan, two young men who are both interested in fellow-camper Rose Dallam, sometimes writer and wealthy young heiress.

Things take a serious turn when the body of woman none of them know is pulled from the lake. When Rose's half-sister Tevy arrives, Lund has more suspects than he knows what to do with.

"The setting is exquisitely rendered… but the mystery plot is quite intricately engaging as well… a fine send-off for Eric Lund."
—Curtis Evans from his introduction

**Ruth Sawtell Wallis Bibliography
(1895-1978)**

Fiction/Mysteries:

Too Many Bones (1943; Dodd Mead; reprinted by Dell, 1946)
No Bones About It (1944; Dodd Mead; reprinted by Bantam, 1946;
   Eric Lund series)
Blood from a Stone (1945; Dodd Mead; reprinted by Bantam, 1947)
Cold Bed in the Clay (1947; Dodd Mead; Eric Lund series)
Forget My Fate (1950; Dodd Mead; Eric Lund series)

FORGET MY FATE

RUTH SAWTELL WALLIS

INTRODUCTION BY CURTIS EVANS

Stark House Press • Eureka California

FORGET MY FATE

Remember Her: Ruth Sawtell Wallis' *Forget My Fate*

By Curtis Evans

When I am laid, am laid, in earth, May my wrongs create
No trouble, no trouble in thy breast;
Remember me, remember me, but ah! Forget my fate.
Remember me! But ah! Forget my fate.
Dido's Lament ("When I am Laid in earth"), *Dido and Aeneas,*
by Henry Purcell

Ruth Sawtell Wallis wrote the first three of her five published mystery novels—*Too Many Bones* (1943), *No Bones About It* (1944) and *Blood from a Stone* (1945)—during the summers of '42, '43 and '44 while she was vacationing with her husband Wilson Dallam Wallis, an anthropology professor at the University of Minnesota, at Rockwood Lodge, a rural resort overlooking Poplar Lake deep in the Minnesota Northwoods. This idyllic location was situated about thirty miles up Minnesota's scenic Gunflint Trail from the small city of Grand Marais, perched on the North Shore of Lake Superior in the easternmost tip of the state. "There wasn't much work to keeping the cabin and Mr. Wallis fished a lot," Ruth wryly observed to a newspaper interviewer in 1951 when explaining how she got her mystery writing done on these otherwise idle occasions. She added, seemingly somewhat ruefully, that her husband, the father of an adolescent boy and girl from a prior marriage when he had wed Ruth two decades earlier, "didn't marry a writer." Mystery writing was an onerous craft which Ruth had learned only after she had been terminated in 1935 from her own position of employment as an assistant professor of sociology at Hamline University—on account of, she believed, "envy over the dual incomes" that she and her husband had enjoyed "in the midst of the Depression."

Buoyed by superlative reviews for her first three mystery novels, Ruth published a fourth one, *Cold Bed in the Clay* (1947), a biting academic murder story for the composition of which she drew on her experiences during the early Thirties as a teacher at the University of Iowa. Then after three years came Ruth's final mystery novel: *Forget My Fate* (1950), the third book featuring series sleuth Eric Lund, a Special Agent with the Federal Bureau of Investigation. (The other two tales in this series are *No Bones About It* and *Cold Bed in the Clay*, previously reprinted in one volume by Stark House.) For this final detective story Ruth chose as her setting a fictionally rendered version of Poplar Lake's Rockwood Lodge.

The first cabins on Poplar Lake, comfortably resting in a dazzling white and green/gold bed not of poplars but rather aspen and birch, were built in the late nineteenth century. However, the resort of Rockwood Lodge was not established until 1926, by enterprising couples Paul and Jennie Stoltz and Wally and Helen Anderson. The cabins and the lodge, the latter of which was completed in 1932, the year of the Wallis' nuptials, were constructed by hand by the two men, with the assistance of their wives and Helen's sister Inez. (The lodge and two of the original cabins, suitably modernized, are still in existence today.) Not long after their own marriage, Ruth and Wilson Dallam Wallis began summering at Rockwood Lodge. (In the early years they were accompanied by the two children, son Wilson Allen, a future president of the University of Rochester and economic advisor to four American presidents, and daughter Virginia Dallam.) The couple soon became two of the resort's most loyal patrons. Indeed, Ruth charmingly dedicated *Forget My Fate* to Paul and Jennie Stoltz, along with their teenaged son George. Nothing like the events in the novel ever happened there, Ruth reassuringly avowed. To a newspaper she forthrightly divulged: "Of course you drag characters into the book who don't belong [in the actual, real-life setting.] Otherwise you might insult the natives."

And a good thing for the natives too, for there is mystery and malevolent goings-on aplenty at fictional Camp Midaywin, as Rockwood Lodge is called in the novel, including a spot or two of bloody murder. (Grand Marais is Petit Port and the Gunflint Trail is the Wilderness Trail.) Eric Lund, now well into his forties and the proud, picture-bearing papa of a bouncing baby daughter with his beloved wife Janet Carter (the imperiled protagonist from *No Bones About It*), is staying incognito at Camp Midawyn as part of his investigation into a blackmail plot against a sitting United States senator, whose sins might run the gamut "from barratry to bastardy." Just who among the assorted colorful characters at Camp Midawyn has interests other than the strictly piscatorial? And what does a haunting queenly lamentation composed in the seventeenth century by Henry Purcell have to do with it all? Before truth finally comes out, one decomposed human body will be fished from the lake, another human corpse will be discovered gunned down beside it and a beautiful blonde heiress will find herself placed in peril of her very life. Mrs. Ida Fitts, who effectively runs Camp Midawyn (rather than her moony husband Averill), always says women campers are trouble!

Later in her own life Ruth Sawtell Wallis recalled: "I set 'Forget My Fate' right on the Gunflint Trail....The background, correctly and affectionately recorded, turned out to be the best part...." The setting indeed is exquisitely rendered, with the author rewardingly drawing on events from her own stays at Rockwood Lodge (like the aggressive garbage foraging expeditions of importunate black bears), but the mystery plot is quite intricately engaging as well, unfolding impressively in the final few chapters of the tale. All in all, the novel makes a fine send-off for Eric Lund, though in fact it turns out that the author had future adventures planned for her clever detective. In 1951, Ruth and her husband traveled for the first time down to the state of Alabama, where at the Temple Emanu-El in Birmingham Ruth was to speak on the subject of "Writing Mystery Novels" to the local branch of the American Association of University Women. While there, she gave an interview to the *Birmingham Post-Herald* wherein she divulged that she was working on a new detective opus, entitled *Galloway's Gore*. It was never published, however, and it is unclear whether it was ever even completed.

The previous year Ruth told the *Minneapolis Star* that "she had to work really hard on 'Forget My Fate,' writing it over and over. Yet ... through it all she learned much about the technique of turning out mysteries and hopes to hold to a schedule of doing one a year." It appears, however, that Ruth found it too onerous to invest the time that it took to construct a detective novel to her own exactions. Having received much critical praise for her mysteries and taught a two-week seminar on mystery writing at the University of Colorado in 1949 (her successor on the subject the following year was distinguished fellow Minnesota mystery writer Mabel Seeley), Ruth had high standards but sadly little time, involved as she had become with her spouse's scholarly anthropological projects. In June 1949 Ruth amusingly imparted to the *Star* that a few months earlier she had picked up the latest Agatha Christie mystery, *Crooked House*, "only to see announced on its jacket, 'Forget My Fate', by Ruth Sawtell Wallis....At the time her mystery was exactly two pages long." Putting her nose to the grindstone, she finally finished *Fate* in 1950 and then she and Wilson were off to spend the summer in Canada's Maritime Provinces to study the Micmac and Malecite.

Over a decade later Ruth, in her last known reflections on her mystery writing, fatalistically pronounced to Carmen Nelson Richards, the compiler of *Minnesota Writers*: "[*Forget My Fate*] was my last murder mystery. Two more are planned in full detail, but they will not be written and I shall not care, for I have taken part in two quite different books [*The Micmac Indians of Eastern Canada* and *Malecite Indians of New Brunswick*], and two more are in process. They are part of my real life as wife, scientist and another sort of writer." Anthropology's gain was detective fiction's loss, but at least Ruth Sawtell Wallis left readers five fine mystery novels, all of which have now been reprinted by Stark House. Certainly their fate has been happier than that of Purcell's tragic stage Carthaginian queen.

—May 2023
Germantown, TN

Curtis Evans received a PhD in American history in 1998. He is the author of *Masters of the "Humdrum" Mystery: Cecil John Charles Street, Freeman Wills Crofts, Alfred Walter Stewart and British Detective Fiction, 1920-1961* (2012) and most recently the editor of the Edgar nominated *Murder in the Closet: Essays on Queer Clues in Crime Fiction Before Stonewall* (2017) and, with Douglas G. Greene, the Richard Webb and Hugh Wheeler short crime fiction collection, *The Cases of Lieutenant Timothy Trant* (2019). He blogs on vintage crime fiction at The Passing Tramp.

FORGET MY FATE

RUTH SAWTELL WALLIS

TO THE STOLTZES
PAUL, JENNIE, GEORGE
OF
GRAND MARAIS AND THE GUNFLINT TRAIL
*Where Nothing Like This
Ever Happened*

one
WEDNESDAY EVENING. JULY 8

At Camp Midaywin the hour before sunset was a time of waiting. Quiet yellow light lay over the red roofs and pale, peeled logs of the cabins by the lake, slipped through needle and leaf into the crowding woods. In the dense undergrowth, restlessness began to stir the beasts that choose to live in the wild suburbs of man. Mice, ingenious and hungry, planned twilight infiltration of mouse-proofed kitchens. An inquisitive doe moved soundless toward windows she would peep into after dark. Out of a swamp a fastidious black bear heaved himself to reconnoiter garbage cans which at dusk might yield a wisp of lettuce or a lick of jam.

Around or within the cabins human outlanders also were expectant. Waiting for dinner, hoping the walleye would come and take the hook, looking for the mail truck that once a day linked the wilderness lake with the world.

A man, pipe in mouth and carrying a casting rod, opened a cabin door and stepped out onto the stone sill. Long-limbed and lean, with a narrow blond head touched with gray—his body, along with the way he wore his comfortable old clothes, added up to a type one would expect to find year after year at any fishing camp in the North Woods. That was why he was at Midaywin.

Through casement windows behind him the lake shone in bright oblongs, but everything before him was secluded in the green of poplar and pine. To left and right, he knew, bush and tree hid other cabins, two to the north, three to the south, each set close to the water as was his own and each not more than fifty feet from a neighbor. On this July afternoon of the biggest resort season known to the North Woods, four of those six cabins were tenantless.

As the man quit the doorstone, the fine network of scars around his mouth lifted in amusement: could his infallible chief for once have erred in selecting a Special Agent too typical for his assignment?

He turned north into the wooded path leading to the main buildings of the resort. The smile was gone. Crime, even murder, may have its grotesque humor, but there was never anything funny about the kind he was here to investigate; there was nothing comic about blackmail and extortion.

The pines on his left, the thin screen of dwarf poplars on the right ended in a small clearing where, among cedar stumps, were parked three cars, all of humble status. Beside a brash new scarlet example of the most length for the least list price, there was only a bulky old Army surplus Command car and a black Dodge, with New York plates, not fresher than 1940. Yet Midaywin rates were fifteen dollars a day. If there were blackmailers among the owners and guests, they must be ascetic sales-resisters or notably unsuccessful operators.

With a friendly pat on the red false nose of his own car, he passed on to the highway.

This was the Wilderness Trail, sixty miles of graveled roller-coaster, the one road through three thousand square miles of forest from Lake Superior to the border. The east side of the Trail was steep and wooded; the dense overgrowth thinned here and there, suggesting paths to cabins. On the west, beside Lake Midaywin, the gay roofs, flower beds and racked canoes of the camp followed the open shore line for an eighth of a mile. From the opposite wings of the log lodge, dissonance now hurt the air, two sounds, good enough separately, that should never have been combined: the heavy descent of something sharp through something hard, and the tinkle of unknown music from the age of Hearts and Flowers.

The man with pipe and rod grinned in recognition of typical activity: Mrs. Fitts, owner of Camp Midaywin, assaulting wood; Mr. Fitts caressing ivory keys.

He walked out on the dock, squinted into the sun lying low on the water, made a long clean cast, and reeled in.

A voice piped behind him. "Getting anything?"

Without breaking the slow even rhythm of his wrist the tall fisherman glanced around and down. "Not yet."

A squat, youngish man was trotting over the planks. Bright plastic on his rod looked new and so did the red sweater where twin moose nuzzled across his chest. Shading spectacles with a dimpled hand, he scrutinized the progress of the plug now wriggling to shore. As it swung onto the dock, he lowered and held out soft fingers.

"My name's Anderson. Verne Anderson."

A smile of kinship moved the thin, scarred lips of the tall fisherman. "Just a couple of Minnesota Swedes," he said. "My name's Lund."

"What do you know!" Anderson's face quivered. "Only I haven't lived out here since I was a kid."

"Same here," said Lund. "Not since the one year I was at the 'U.' I try to get back once in a while for the fishing."

His River Runt soared and settled lightly on the water.

"You just get here today?" Anderson tested the pin that fastened the oversized Dare Devil to his steel leader. "You're in the cabin next to mine."

"Late last night. And slept late this morning."

"Sun, I guess, woke me up about six o'clock. So I got out early." He poked out a short arm toward the lake. "Just nosing around over there. Got a few strikes and lost one beauty right at the boat. I didn't come in till after lunch. Mrs. Fitts gave me a snack and even that was something. Boy, what a chef she is! Funny she don't have more business. You ever stayed here before? How'd you happen to pick it?"

"Through the tourist bureau in Duluth."

"Me, too." Anderson cast his spoon in a short, loud plop. "Swell place," he added with a peevish eye on Lund's still distant lure.

Lund stared into the ragged shadows of islands darkening the quiet water. Beyond these, the wild cry of a loon rose from some wilder lake.

"It's a lonely spot," he said slowly.

"Well, I suppose it is," Anderson's tone was superior, "if you want a gang around. It suits me."

"You like to get away from it all." Lund retrieved the River Runt and took a tobacco pouch from the pocket of his comfortably worn flannel shirt. "So do I. But there's something about this place. Uninhabited islands. The Wilderness Trail. If a man took ten steps off that road he could be lost for keeps. Not," he laughed ruefully, "a good spot to make a getaway."

"Why'd anybody want to get away?" Anderson's attention was fixed on the dragging, weedy return of his Dare Devil. "The real sport is to still-fish for walleye from a boat, with live minnows. The chore boy's gone to a pond back in the woods to get some. Want to go out with me when he gets back?"

"Swell. But," Lund turned to gaze up the narrow white road, "I'd like to wait until the mail gets here."

"Okay. You know, up here I don't care a thing about getting letters." Anderson cleaned the last green festoon from his triple hook. "Or newspapers. I don't even want to listen to a radio. Camp Midaywin's got everything I want. Quiet. Fishing. Swell food …"

"And a girl," said Lund.

A warm expression rippled Anderson's flat white face. "You seen her?" His voice lowered, "Quite a girl."

"She came into the lodge while I was eating lunch. You wouldn't expect to find a girl like that alone in a North Woods fishing camp."

"Yeah," Anderson pushed a finger into the dimple on his firmer chin. "I was surprised when I saw the place."

Lund gave him a long thin grin. "There's also a boy."

The finger descended to Anderson's reel. "You mean Mart? The chore boy, guide or whatever? He's not in her class."

"Neither are you and I. Anyway, I'm not competing." Lund reached into his hip pocket. "Take a look at this. That's all the girl friend I want."

The leer with which Anderson approached the extended wallet turned tepid.

"Some little pinup." He stepped to the edge of the wharf.

"Of course, you can't really tell from a snapshot." Lund's explanation was aggrieved. "The light wasn't too good. Her hair actually curls all over her head. She hasn't got a big nose. It's a shadow that makes it look that way."

The Dare Devil again landed noisily on the water. "Pretty good just the same." Anderson appraised his performance.

"Not bad for our first. You'd never think to look at her that she's only a year old. You ought to see her try to feed herself maple syrup. Is she," asked Lund with rhetorical pride, "a mess?"

"I'll bet," said Anderson.

"You ought to hear her try to say …"

"Hi," yelled Anderson, "I got something. I got something!"

He reeled frantically, rocking back and forth from heel to toe. The line came in slowly, then stopped.

"Boy, is it something!"

"You're straining your reel," said Lund.

"He isn't fighting now! He's heavy as lead!" Anderson jumped and yanked on his ominously bending rod.

"You'll snap your line!" said Lund.

"He's hanging back. He's gone down deep. He's just laying there." Anderson panted. "Bet I've got a whale."

"You've caught the bottom of the lake," said Lund.

Beside the kitchen door of Camp Midaywin the low sun caught the rim of a pan where an old cat licked up porridge, disdaining the tongue-lashing of the red squirrel that scampered, frenzied, in the tall cedar above the dish. The faintly quivering air smelled of fresh pine chips.

A young man in denims and a blue T-shirt came round the path from the dock. His compact body, not tall, moved in the easy unhurried way that gets long distances in short time. Under the tree he stopped, brown hand on left hip where hung a sheathed knife, head tilted back to jeer at the wrathful red shadow.

"Z-z-z-z," buzzed the squirrel and spat rags of cedar down onto the curly brown hair.

"Go right ahead. You're perfectly okay as long as I haven't got my .22."

And the squirrel was left bouncing on his forepaws, his rear quivering with frustration at the closed kitchen door.

In the middle of the kitchen a clean harsh woman of fifty stood with a wide solid stance, rolling out dough. She took no notice of the young man who passed behind her to the great porcelain refrigerator, took out cheese, ham, mayonnaise, put them on the opposite side of her long work table, and began to slice a homemade wheat loaf. Starch crunched through her white uniform as she rolled and cut. In the pine-paneled lounge beyond the kitchen a sweet vague piano alternately tinkled and groped.

Sandwiches went into waxed sacks, biscuits into the oven before Mrs. Fitts spoke.

"Both men?"

"Yes. I'm taking them over to the Narrows. For walleye. Turning down a good dinner for this junk because the fish phoned them they'd be there at seven-seventeen!"

"You'll have to wait till the mail truck gets here."

"Okay."

"Quite okay with you." A sardonic smile watched the faint flicker of his eyelids. "Look here, Martin, it is not the policy of this resort to deliver the tourists' mail to their cabins."

"No exceptions?"

"Yes. If the tourist is so old and feeble she might trip over a root after dark and break a leg."

Mart looked across at eyes as blue as his and only a little harder.

"Guide Meets Girl," said Mrs. Fitts. "That's sweet, but it don't happen here." She moved off to the cupboards, light on her big feet as a teacher of physical education—emeritus.

"That I don't believe." Mart's tone scoffed her. "This isn't the first summer resort I've been in, you know."

Mrs. Fitts put a giant's chocolate cake on the table between them. "I've hired guides because city girls like to have them around. The guides weren't hired to enjoy the girls."

Mart whistled.

"This particular girl." Mrs. Fitts neatly cut wax paper. "She's not a regular tourist type. I've never had such a ladylike girl around. In some ways she seems young for her age. Why does she want to come to a place like this all by herself?"

"Maybe she likes to be alone. Don't you think a person can be an individualist without being as rugged as you are?"

"She might have run away from somebody. She might be hiding."

"And you've got it all doped out, I suppose, who it was she ran away from, and all that?"

"From the police, maybe. From a boyfriend—probably. Take it easy with your knife in that cake. You aren't gutting a fish."

She reached for the rich, mayhemed hunks, talking, as she wrapped them, more to herself than to Mart's blank face. "I can't make her out. She isn't any Nature Girl, but still she don't seem to be afraid of the mice or the bears, off in that God-forsaken old cabin down the lake. And yet she seems a timid kind of a girl."

"Why did you take in such a suspicious character?" Mart inquired. He added slowly, "Every day you turn away customers—plenty. Including that schoolmarm type, this afternoon."

"That makes your job nice and light, don't it?"

"That's right. So I figure I might have time to deliver a little mail without interfering with my other work."

"It will interfere." Her mouth set tight. "Your work begins tonight."

"My work begins ... I don't get it."

"The work I hired you to do."

"I still don't know."

"You're smart enough to find out without being told." She took a coffee pot from the stove. "And remember about the mail."

"I'll remember not to take the men out fishing before the mail truck comes."

For a moment, while the little lovesick tune sobbed peevishly behind them, the two looked at each other, measuring, learning how far each could push the other. Then Mrs. Fitts and Martin Bryan sat down and in silence drank their coffee.

The music had stopped. The woodland of Midaywin had become so still that a listening ear could catch only a tiny teasing crack, crack, crack high overhead where squirrel teeth husked cedar berries. Then a kingfisher swooped low with a shrill rattle.

Feet sounded on the hard Wilderness Trail. Hands in pockets, pipe in mouth, Eric Lund idled along the road. He had left Anderson squatting on the dock, white cloth hat brim flopped down to thick glasses and squat nose, picking over his big tackle box and dreaming of his evening's projected fishing. He's better at waiting than I am, thought Lund, who was often paid to wait. Probably Anderson's a better fisherman, too. For Lund was quite aware that, in the world of angling, exuberant small boy self-delusion did not necessarily distinguish the tyro from the skilled sportsman. If he were in for a period of professional inactivity, Lund felt he might get a good deal of enjoyment from fishing with Verne Anderson.

And there ought to be plenty of sport. Deep channels between the islands, rocks, and reedy shores: it looked as if Lake Midaywin had everything.

From this pleasing estimate—which is every fisherman's opinion of every lake before he has tried it—a voice suddenly called Lund.

"A beautiful evening to you, sir! A beautiful, beautiful evening."

The gust seemed issuing from the rocks and trees of the Trail's steep eastern side. Or from the base of the cliff itself. It took a second of adjustment from his long squint at the lake before Mr. Lund was fully aware that the biggest pile of gray slabs, crowned by a rakish little poplar tree, had been heaved up by man, and fitted at ground level with a rough door.

At this door, now ajar, a stout, elderly man with a head of hair as rough and gray as the rocks was gazing with rapt eyes at the sunset, while hips, elbows, and wrists, hitching, bending, poking, attempted to maintain the delicate equilibrium of a watermelon, three cartons of milk, and a two-quart jar of pickled cucumbers. The further—and to the spectator—more crucial problem of maintaining his trousers at a point no lower than the present level beneath his paunch seemed to concern him not at all.

"Oh," said Lund. "Good evening, Mr. Fitts."

"Beautiful evening," corrected Mr. Fitts softly through his sparse teeth.

"That's right," agreed Lund. "Nice clouds behind that island over there ..."

"That isn't—" Mr. Fitts' breath drew in sharply as the melon leaped over the pickle jar. "That isn't," he repeated, "an island. It's," with a certain agony shared by Mr. Lund, he bent to retrieve the melon without quite releasing the three gurgling cartons. "It's a ..." unbelievably he had done it. "That's the mainland. A long point, about a mile across at its greatest width. And beyond it lies the Dark Arm."

His own arm rose in drama and again the melon bounded, fortunately to the feet of Mr. Lund.

"I thank you, sir. I will take it, if you please. I cannot burden a guest—yes, the Dark Arm. Some people—and Mrs. Fitts is one—refer to it as the old Lumber Camp Bay. But when you see it, you will know why I have named it the Dark Arm."

"What do you call this bay here?" asked Lund.

"Bear Cub. A merry little name, isn't it?"

"Yes," said Lund. "Although cubs do grow up. Do you have much trouble with bears?"

"Come here." The pickle jar beckoned and the melon lurched. "See these scratches on the door? Bear claws. Trying to get in to the meat."

"Deep," agreed Lund, with one eye on the obviously weakening bottom of the milk carton balancing on the gesturing elbow.

"And look here. Kneel down. Oh! Sorry if it got you in the ear. See those tooth marks? Porcupines. And another scratch. Another bear."

"I see." Lund removed a sloshing carton juggling on his shoulder, and rose. "I'll say you have trouble with bears. Have to shoot them?"

"Trouble? Shoot? Oh, no, never, Mr. Lund." There seemed to be tears in Mr. Fitts' kind, not very bright eyes. "One must love the Wild Life. How can anyone kill it? Or," he sighed, "how can anyone want to hook a fish?"

"I wonder," said Lund.

"It is the same in all phases of life." Mr. Fitts shook his thick gray head. His voice grew dreamy, his arms slackened perilously. "What this world needs is—tenderness. In my music I try to convey that message, but so few really understand. Tenderness," he added softly, "yes, that is my mission, to bring tend …"

Down the road at the Midaywin lodge a hand-bell was being rung and by no weak hand. The effect on Mr. Fitts was startling. His fingers fastened efficiently over the ill-assorted solids, his eyes cleared and brightened, his abdomen retreated slightly, and while his trousers did not actually rise, Lund felt that they would probably carry him decently home.

Before the bell could be sounded a second time, Mr. Fitts, slow and sure as an old porcupine, was on his way. The bell rang a third and last time.

"Mrs. Pavlov, I presume," murmured Lund.

He stood for a moment, looking back along the Trail for a sign of the mail truck. He then closed and latched the heavy cedar door of the root cellar, a process evidently not included in Mr. Fitts' conditioning, and continued his stroll. The road now mounted a ridge. Trees and deep undergrowth hid the lake, and the air felt suddenly cool, blowing over ferns and low beds of white bunchberry flowers. Solitary iris in the ditches were a surprise of blue.

This was the kind of country where Lund had been born, not a place for blackmailers. Nor, in this case, would the distant victim have been more suited to the scene: a Senator who, Lund was certain, had not set foot off pavement for twenty-five blameless years. Unfortunately the Senator was fifty-three. The extortion letter which he had brought, raging, to the FBI mentioned a date—1923—and the sum—$20,000—demanded for silence. The exact offense which the writer threatened to reveal was not stated, but the Senator had no doubt that the information was full, genuine, and fit to end his public life. It could be, he swore, anything from barratry to bastardy. He named the fellow-members of the rum-running crew he had defrauded; all of them were dead. Most of his women he had forgotten; none of them had ever complained. No one who knew him well, he boasted, would have written the letter; they would have known he would fight. So now it was the job of Special Agent Eric Lund, climbing the Wilderness Trail in northern Minnesota, to carry on that fight.

The hilltop was the mere rim of a roller-coaster drop into a loop so deep that an approaching car was completely hidden from Lund. A monster gray nose thrust at him and he leaped into the bushes at the left as a tank truck, riding the bumps with care, swerved past.

Where Lund had left the roadway, there was no ditch. Grass and low bushes grew around a flat rock and a small graveled plane, just large enough to park a car off the highway. No recent evidence of a car was there, but the slight flattening of grass and leaves suggested the entrance to a path seldom used. He took a few steps off the highway and looked down through birch and pine. Yes, there was a steep path, barely discernible, rocky and nearly overgrown.

A few more steps and he saw a red-brown roof tight against the hill. Trees rose above and beyond the roof, and through the boughs he could see the waters of Midaywin. The lake must come almost to the cabin wall. A little farther down the slope and brown upright boards appeared, chinked with oakum, and to the right a tiny clearing still holding a bit of sun on clover and tall grass. He descended farther and saw a woodpile and a small dock.

A girl sat motionless on the dock, back straight, head half-turned toward the hillside and slightly bent, hands resting flat on her knees. The poise of her small head, the close-brushed short brown hair, the soft green jacket closed at the throat and wrists, seen in this secret way, charmed even the dispassionate eye of Eric Lund.

On one upturned palm a pale-yellow fluff vibrated gently, disappeared, returned. The yellow, Lund now saw, was striped with black, and only one end was fluffy; at the other was a very sharp black nose. The girl was feeding a miniature chipmunk.

All round her, birds made a high steady cheep. There was no other sound, as Lund took a last step and looked down more closely on deep peace.

Or was it? Tiny rodent eyes stared, fearful; teeth clipped too fast around the edge of the nut, and every few seconds the little creature froze, listening probably for an approaching rival. If a stray breeze riffled a lock of the girl's hair, he was off into the bushes, then back to the terrible lure of a peanut.

And the girl, too, was tense. Even when the chipmunk left her knee, she did not relax a muscle, and nearly as often as the little animal's, her eyes shifted with an almost imperceptible motion of her neat head.

To Lund the evident tension was natural. A girl alone in the woods. A girl waiting to hear the distant approach of the mail truck, or, it could be, aware that someone might come to spy upon her hiding place, as he was doing now.

Noiselessly Lund turned and retreated up the slope. So this was where she lived and where he would return. For however incomplete the plan of his stay at Midaywin might yet be, one feature had been added. He would have to spend a lot of time watching that girl.

two
WEDNESDAY EVENING. JULY 8

The first sunset red stained Lake Midaywin as the girl left the woods and followed the treeless shore to the lodge. Under the deep overhanging roof of the central section, the four men watched the slim green-clad assembly of feminine lines and arcs pass the root cellar, the dock, the canoe rack, coming lightly toward them through the soft evening.

Verne Anderson, arms akimbo and short legs apart, stared openly; with equal concentration old Mr. Fitts from his bench against the log wall, hands resting on belly and belly on knees, ogled kindly.

At his feet, Mart Bryan, kneeling to adjust Anderson's broken pack strap, cast one look over his shoulder and turned squarely to his task.

We're a commonplace bunch, thought Eric Lund, none of us in that girl's class. She's high-bred, well-kept, and those slacks are tailor-made. No more than the other men had he been born to such nice judgments, but Mrs. Eric Lund had.

"Hi! Look, here comes Miss Rose Dallam, the Sweetheart of Lake Midaywin!" Unhampered by nature or nurture, Anderson was trotting toward her, falling in step beside her, slipping a wide white hand around her elbow.

The girl's sharp little shrug of withdrawal relaxed into polite acceptance of his not too offensive familiarity.

"The beauty," Mr. Fitts was murmuring, "of untouched nature...."

Yes, Lund agreed, she was quite lovely, with the light even tan of her skin almost the color of her hair that was cut and brushed as if it were carved out of marble.

Glasses and short dimpled chin bent near her ear, Anderson used the low confidential whisper that carries far. "How'd you like to go fishing with me this evening?"

Rose Dallam's small head turned quickly toward Mart's young obdurate back.

"Mr. Lund, here, and I are just going across the lake to pick up a few walleyes," Anderson went on in his absurdly chummy manner. "How about coming along?"

"Wouldn't I be one too many in the boat?" She still looked toward Mart. "Wouldn't it be harder for you to fish?"

"It might at that." The Anderson fingers pressed a little. "Might be harder to keep the old mind on the end of the line." He surveyed her accurately from demurely collared throat to tiny-waisted bolero. "You'd add just a little weight for the feller who has to row us while we troll. Kinda hard on you, Mart? What's your idea, Lund?"

Only Lund responded. "By all means come with us, Miss Dallam. We invite you to inhale the fumes of my foul pipe and share our mosquitoes. And shudder at our curses when we lose fish."

She shrugged off Anderson's hand gently and smiled up at Lund. "It sounds awfully attractive."

"There's one attraction you left out, Lund." Anderson added it peevishly. "You could give the young lady a chance to admire the picture of your kid."

"I'm afraid I might do just that," said Lund pleasantly. "Miss Dallam, you are warned."

"My dear," piped Averill Fitts, "have you yet seen your most charming neighbor, Mr. Beaver?"

Rose shook her head. "But the pile of sticks he's bringing for his house is getting bigger every day."

"You may never see him. Some night, though, you'll probably hear the flat slap of his tail when he dives into the lake. —I hear," Mr. Fitts began with a rising note of proclamation which shivered to a weaker key as he stumbled over Mart and the pack-sack. "I hear the thunder of the Wilderness Express."

"Thank God," said Anderson. "'Cause when it's gone, we can get going fishing. Come on, sweetheart, let's you and me watch the Super Chief pull in."

But Mart came between him and the girl, standing close. "I was going to bring down your mail."

She met steady blue eyes and a jaw squared with a lot more determination than seemed necessary. "Were you?"

"If you don't want me to come again, you'll only tell me once."

"Is that a threat?" She too had quite a tough little chin. Abruptly, Mart turned away and she put out her hand, just brushing his arm. "Mart! Tomorrow?"

He looked back at her and very slightly nodded, as, lumbering after its own noise, the Wilderness Express blazed into view.

No sleekness or speed detracted from the vehicle's one conspicuous merit, a coat of bright red paint of that naïve shade suggestive of circus wagons. To Eric Lund, whose urchin days had been highlighted by Ringling street parades, all such big scarlet flanks should be ornamented with figures from unnatural history, resembling manatees crossed with woolly mammoths and labelled "Behold Behemoth." In this respect the present van did not altogether disappoint him. Each side bore beneath the legend "Wilderness Express" a great white heart bisected by a bleeding arterial highway, and the subscription "Straight Through the Heart of the Woods."

Stopping very neatly alongside the Midaywin party, a shock-headed young driver swung off his seat, raked his cap farther over one ear, and casually handed the mail to the nearest person, who happened to be Lund. At the exact moment when the bus halted, Mrs. Fitts strode out of the lodge, her course not diverging by one big toe from the straightest line between the kitchen door and the Express's front wheels. Her eyes, however, shifted sufficiently to note, evidently with some amusement, the person of Rose Dallam who alone remained close to the house, and to include in a silent command the presence of her husband and her hired man, both of whom moved to her side.

"Hi, Mrs. Fitts! Got a surprise for you. Wait till you hear … Hey, wait a sec." The driver turned his head and shouted up to the passenger bench crudely accommodated behind his own seat. "This is Midaywin. Come ahead! Here's where you get off."

Stooping his head to avoid the top of the truck, a passenger appeared, paused on the step, and met the upturned faces of Mrs. Fitts and the four men.

He was young, dressed in town sports clothes—pale tweed jacket, bow tie, coffee-colored flannels—his thick black hair cut in sharp lines around a face languid as with fatigue or illness. He glanced down at the little group and an expression sudden and live passed from eyes to mouth.

Who is it he knows? Lund wondered. But the stranger greeted no one. No one spoke to him. For a long moment he stood motionless, while his face seemed to grow whiter and the shadows darkened under his eyes.

Then he got down from the bus, and his voice, well-bred and a trifle lordly, stated, "I should like to have a cabin for a day or so."

He said it only to Mr. Fitts, for with an impatient jerk of her tight-knotted hair, Mrs. Fitts had motioned the driver to the rear of the truck and was now listening to his story told with large gestures and loud laughter. Mart, not amused, was unloading luggage and crates of lettuce and canned goods from the opened freight compartment.

"I shall have to consult my wife," Mr. Fitts frankly admitted and waddled off eagerly.

The dark young man leaned with a tired, quite natural grace against the garish old Express, uninterested eyes halfway between the shadowy corner of the porch where Rose Dallam waited and the bench where Lund and his fishing partner had withdrawn to sort the mail.

"It's a good thing you don't care about letters, Anderson," Lund didn't attempt to conceal his interest in the thick envelope bearing his own name. "Want to break down for once and read the Fitts' Duluth paper?"

"I might take a look at the sports section," Anderson said and carried it into the lodge.

Mrs. Fitts called curtly to her approaching husband, "Yes. If it's only for a few days. Put him in the Honeymoon," and returned her attention to the bus driver's narration.

With a low bow before the indifferent young stranger, Mr. Fitts fell into the most exalted role ever assigned him, and led the guest down the path to the cabins.

"You have some mail tonight," Lund held out a woman-size envelope and a copy of *The New York Times* to Rose Dallam.

Standing in the shadows by the wall, her head resting lightly against the logs, eyes fixed vacantly ahead, she did not at first hear him. Was this self-effacement or was she deliberately shutting the scene from her mind?

The rear door of the truck banged down and she gave a slight start. With one last laugh the driver mounted his chariot and heaved away. Mart picked up a pigskin two-suiter and a rod case, and without a glance toward the lodge, he also took the cabin path.

"Oh, thank you," Rose Dallam's eyes, full and gray under sharp, short brows, seemed to ask forgiveness for her daydreaming. The brows contracted slightly as she glanced at the letter. For a moment she hesitated, looking toward the lighted window behind her, where Anderson crouched beneath his newspaper. "Good night, Mr. Lund," she said and set off down the Trail toward her isolated cabin.

Well, the fishing party might be off or on, but, Lund reflected, as he watched the small, proudly carried figure move alone between the still bright lake and darkening woods, it was Anderson's party, not his. Again, the air was quiet, and now satisfyingly scented with frying steak, announcing that Mrs. Fitts had strode direct from truck to stove.

And something else had been added to the scene. In the clover patch by the roadside where Mart had gathered up the stranger's luggage, three bags remained: overnight case, wardrobe and hatbox, all of matched pastel pink.

Mr. Lund regarded these unsuitable intrusions with highly professional curiosity. He took a step toward them, breathed in the succulence from the kitchen, and turned abruptly indoors. While he was paid to watch, he was also permitted to eat.

The dining lounge of Camp Midaywin, fundamentally sound and pleasant with walls and low ceiling of oiled logs, great fireplace, strong red-cushioned chairs, black bearskins and mounted bucks, had too many tortured diamond willow trimmings on buffet, smoking stands and lamps, and from each electric wall bracket dangled a weasel's tail. Not, Lund felt, the expression of Mrs. Fitts but of her tested ideas of tourist taste. He chose a table by one of the three casement windows overlooking the lake, slit open the envelope the bus had brought, and spread out the photographs it contained.

"That's an adorable baby." Mrs. Fitts deftly set a crisp bowl of melon balls flagged with mint between the glossy snapshots. "Cute curls. She's got a pretty mouth, nice and small."

Eric Lund wiped what felt like a silly grin off his face, and then, remembering it was in character, quickly replaced it—not a difficult operation.

"Your first," stated Mrs. Fitts.

"Yes."

"You waited a while!"

"That's right." He flushed slightly around the gray hair at his temples. "We've been married ten years."

"Wife's younger than you are."

"Yes, ten years." It sounded monotonous. "I wanted a little more security before we had a family." Of course, they didn't have it now; security to the Lunds didn't mean a raise, but it had never been Janet Lund who had been cautious or afraid. "A lawyer gets a slow start," Lund went on, "unless he's got a father who can take him into partnership. My dad died in Minneapolis when I was a kid. I had an uncle in Watson, Massachusetts, who had always been interested in law, and he got me a job while I was going to night school."

Mrs. Fitts's cool red face looked approving. "Mr. Anderson, you want to come and eat with Mr. Lund?" she called toward the chair shrouded in newsprint.

"You betcha," Anderson emerged.

"I'm awful sorry," she said to the two, "but I guess your fishing trip is off. Unless you want to go out alone. I've got to send Mart off in the car. About a guest we were expecting tonight. Nothing serious but it has to be attended to, and I can't go myself, at dinner time, with a new guest just come."

"That's all right with me," said Lund. "This way we don't miss one of your grand dinners."

"I'd just as soon stick around, too," Anderson added. "I been on the water a lot since morning. I don't want to rush things too much on my first whole day here."

"You're being nice about it. I know how you men feel about your fishing. It won't happen again."

"Well, I guess I'll just eat, and hit the hay." Anderson yawned toward the pictures of little Miss Lund.

"Same here," said her parent, pocketing them.

The motor of the Command car raced loudly. Thereafter they worked on steaks in a comfortable silence broken by Mrs. Fitts' light comings and goings, the clink of Mr. Fitts' dishpan, and the occasional champs of Mr. Anderson.

It was the hour when shadows of rocks and trees move out across the water, crowding and narrowing the surface between the shore and the nearest island. Once, for a few moments, the men watched an orange spot move at the distant shoreline as a doe drank among lily pads.

"Gosh, they're pretty animals," said Anderson. "I don't see how anybody could bear to shoot them. I couldn't stand to shoot anything, anyway. Could you?"

"There's no sport in it for me," answered Lund. "No, I guess I won't go down to my cabin just yet. I want to call up my wife."

Alone in the lounge, he turned off the overhead lights set in a swinging wagon wheel and stretched out on a vast settee in front of the fireplace to wait through the struggle over the precarious twenty-party line of the Wilderness Trail to the Lake Superior town of Petit Port (local name: Pettyport), and on to Long Distance at Duluth. Two tables, he could see, were still set for dinner, each for a single place, and separated from each other by the long diagonal of the room, one at the left of the main door, the other at the right of the windowed wall.

One table for the missing owner, surely female, of the pink luggage? And one certainly for the elegant young man with the pale, driven face, the apparently unexpected guest. He was taking his time about coming to dine. What was his relationship, if any, to the others at Camp Midaywin? Or, as a matter of fact, of any one person to another? Lund's job here seemed to concern one person only, but it was never safe to assume that there was nothing below the surface, no organization, no pattern for future crime, or no additional victims. All but his chief suspect might be innocent or all might be criminals together, from the gentle, charming Miss Dallam to the ineffectual Mr. Fitts.

Midaywin might turn out to be less comfortably dull than he had expected. So, with the seasoned operative's canny ability to get sleep while he could, Lund's head sank into the pillows.

For a time he had slept deep and dreamlessly and then faint pink images began to trouble his darkness—odd sensations because he seemed to smell rather than see them. With an enormous effort he pulled himself upright and stared into a blinding light.

Around him the room had darkened and through the windows water and sky were gray. Beyond the glare that still confused him, someone was standing in front of the corner casement. It was a woman, half silhouetted, hair piled in short curls, high round breasts, and throat and shoulders veiled in white organdy ruffles from which perfume, rich yet delicate, was carried by the breeze. Her face was dim to Lund and his own, he knew, on which her table lamp was concentrated, was as clear to her as that of any grilled suspect.

As he got to his feet, the woman clasped her hands suddenly between her breasts and her gaze seemed to shift beyond and behind Eric Lund. He turned quickly and saw that the door leading to the Trail had opened.

Standing with his hand still on the latch was the dark young man from the Wilderness Express. He was looking toward the woman and his lips were smiling. It could be the uncertain lighting of the room that made his eyes seem full of hate.

"Mr. Lund!" Mrs. Fitts shouted through the office door. "Here's your Minneapolis call at last. You better come quick."

At midnight only one building in the camp was bright. From his own dark house Lund could see light from Anderson's windows, piercing the poplar leaves that concealed them by day, and Anderson propped up in bed, reading a magazine. On the dock that Lund shared with the small cabin to the south, there was a mass of shadow. The new man had been standing there for some time, apparently staring at the stars and listening to the jumping pike.

A quarter mile to the north, Rose Dallam woke in terror from a dream of something striking water, and sat up with a loud-beating heart. Everything was still. "The beaver," she remembered, and fell asleep, smiling.

Mrs. Fitts at the root cellar, getting out the bacon that Averill had forgotten to fetch for breakfast, heard the splash, and thought that another dead tree had fallen into the lake. She was too tired to notice that the night was windless.

three
THURSDAY MORNING. JULY 9

At five in the morning, when a cold cloud of mist lay over Lake Midaywin, and cedars were wet and dark around the lonely cabin, a red squirrel on the rooftop spotted invasion. Imprudence overriding fear, he sounded the alarm that woke Rose Dallam.

"Shut up!" Prone beneath the Hudson Bay blanket, she muttered against her bare arm that clasped the pillow.

The fierce zizz of the squirrel, like a magnified mosquito, went on and on.

"Keep it up. I don't care. You're too big to get through the holes in even these senile screens." She drew her arms out of the chill air, ready to return to sleep.

Then, as the squirrel's challenge ceased, she knew what he had defied.

Faint, felt at first rather than heard, steps sounded on the path that twisted, narrow and hidden, at the edge of the lake.

Up on her elbows, eyes wide, she caught the sound of a body brushing against boughs. Kneeling, leaning forward to the window beside the bed, she could see someone, vague, undefined, approaching through the trees, and felt sudden warm excitement. Each evening, sitting on the dock, she had watched Mart coming with the mail, seeing first, not a whole person, but between the bushes and low cedar boughs broken triangular glimpses of his blue shirt, his face and hair, human colors, vivid and alien to the brown and green nature that hemmed in her days.

Now, through the light mist with the cold raspberry smell of the cedars, a white shirt appeared and above it something bobbed up and down among the greenery like a big scarlet fruit.

A dozen yards from the cabin there emerged full and clear the figure of a girl. In white blouse outlined by the straps of a pack-sack and pedal-pushers of sleek black, she advanced with light shank movements and constant birdlike tweaks of her red-capped head.

A girl. Chill from the floor boards invaded Rose Dallam. Prancing through my woods. And at this ungodly hour. With a tart hope concerning the prostrative properties of tree roots not unworthy of Mrs. Fitts, she flung on her blue robe and sprang to a defense position at her latched door.

Immune to imprecation, the light unwanted feet passed the length of the cabin and came round the corner. The strange girl leaped upon the doorstep and stared through the screen. Her slim body blocked out the early morning light and dimmed its own details.

"Oh, oh, oh!" At the sight of Rose, she sent up bubbling gasps, and put her left hand to her forehead where pale formal curls framed the red beret. "Oh, you must let me in." The clear, sweet tone broke in her throat. "You must give me a cup of coffee."

Her right hand seized the door handle. The screen moved outward a half-inch, but there the old hook held.

"I haven't any coffee," Rose said firmly. "It's too early."

"I kno-ow." The shattered intensity of the voice was frightening. "But I've come so far. Alone throo-ough the woods. Oh, please, you must help me."

"What do you want me to do?"

"Let me in and make me some coffee. I'm most aw-fully cold." She stepped backward from beneath the eaves and held out her arms in appeal. The stronger light showed deeply tanned limbs, rounded and graceful, flat dark eyes, the line of her throat.

Rose put her hand on the door hook. Reluctant, but compelled. It was neither horror nor despair that produced those tragic tones in the stranger's throat. The throat was corded, the curls were gray: an old throat, an old woman.

"Come in," said Rose Dallam in the proper voice of a young gentlewoman to the aged.

"Oh, thank you." The woman flitted through the opened door, speaking now in firm fluted tones. "I had to come in. I was tiptoeing down the wee path, and when I saw this wee house, I had to tiptoe over the doorstep. Isn't this a sweet, sweet place?" She clasped her hands against the low V of her white shirt. "The darling, rustic cupboard, the holes in the linoleum! …"

The rather blank black eyes gloated over the small old box of a room: walls shrunk at the seams and patched with beaver board, oil lamps on oil-cloth-covered table, the two-burner Pyrofax plate, a self-important little pot-bellied stove. Bright spots of new color shone from the dust jackets of books, the green leather carrying case of a phonograph, the keys of a typewriter, from the striped Hudson Bay that Rose was pulling from the second and unused bed.

"You don't live here alone?" She could be admiring bravery or hoping that a lover was hidden under the mattress.

"Yes, I do. In this exquisite North Woods slum," Rose, helping her to slip out the pack straps, breathed high luxury perfume from flesh that felt really cold. "Curl up on the bed. I'll put your pack"—it was an extraordinarily light pack—"here by the door, and get the fire going."

"It's a new pack-sack," the owner again croaked. "I need it for my adventures, and this is the first time.... Not the first time for adventures, of course, just for this particular kind. You know," her voice dropped to a secret level, "I'm going on such exciting trips. I'm going to sleep under haystacks, and in caves and I shall try to sneak across the Border. You see, I'm a writer."

"Oh," said Rose, her face toward the stove. "What fun."

"It is, rather— Oh, what are you doing with that can? I must see how you do everything so I can put it in the diary of my adventures. I want everything to be accurate, not just romantic."

"Keep your head away," Rose spoke sharply. "I'm pouring in kerosene to start the fire."

"Oh, oh, oh." Retreat to the bed was complete. "Won't it explode in your face?"

"It didn't. Sorry. It would have made quite a nice adventure for you."

"Yes, it would have." The fingers now holding a cigarette quivered with cold.

Rose neatly measured coffee. "Have you got a lot written already?"

"I'm starting tonight. You see, I've just started to have the adventures this morning."

"Where did you start from?" Rose was shivering out of pajamas and into wool slacks and shirt.

"From a camp almost hidden from the world." The woman inhaled deeply. "With a lovely, windy sort of name. Midaywin."

"You're still there," Rose's young voice rebuked fantasy. "I didn't see you at the main lodge, last evening. Did you drive up late from Petit Port?"

"No, oh no, my dear. That wouldn't be adventure. I hiked."

"All thirty miles of the Wilderness Trail?"

"Actually, I hitched. Hitches are wonderful. Don't you hitch?"

"No, I'm not the adventure type. Isn't it said to be dangerous?"

"Hitching?" The face with the strange mixed elements of youth and age thrust forward; the tone again broke in the tense throat. "Oh, my dear, that's why it's so exciting." She paused. "Of course, I take precautions. I wear this red hat so that I won't be mistaken and shot for a deer. And I don't wear red shorts on account of bulls."

"You should be safe." Rose drove a brush harshly through her hair. "This is a game refuge, you know. No hunters or farmers allowed." Then kindliness breaking through, she added, "But you do meet such nice animals. Yesterday I saw a timber wolf on the Trail."

The woman seemed suddenly to glow. "Everyone always talks to me about wolves. On account of hitching. My dear, the men … Last night … And there was that frontier guard in Jugoslavia or perhaps on the Nepalese border. And one doesn't encounter that sort of thing just on hitches, my dear. At little inns … way up here in the forest. And once in the hills behind Vence …" Her bare arm indicated airy heights. "I tiptoed across the threshold at twilight, and out of the shadows a man spoke to me, a handsome creature and frighteningly psychic. Before I even spoke he knew my name was Althea. Such fascinating types at Midaywin. For my adventures, the article, you know. Those scars around the mouth, amazingly criminal."

She paused to take a hard drag at her cigarette, her cheeks bright as the red-striped blanket in which she huddled on the bed.

Rose not caring to sort out the jumble of characters and continents, said drily, "The coffee is done," and moved over to the table that held the typewriter.

"Let me help you," the woman Althea was on her feet. "Let me lift it for you." Her voice and manner were as direct and clear as Rose's.

"All right. Put it anywhere on the floor. Cream and sugar?"

"No, indeed, my child, not at my age." The surprising honesty of the words was echoed in her straightforward but no longer staring glance as Rose returned to the table with the pot and cups.

"You're awfully good to me," she added, as Rose handed over a yellow cardigan to replace the awkward blanket. "I was really frightfully chilled." And then they silently drank.

"Thank you," she said when Rose refilled her cup. "My name is Althea Sharon. Mrs. Sharon."

"I'm Rose Dallam." Pity struggled with distaste as she watched the woman's eyes, expressionless in contrast to her constantly moving head and hands, fix upon her and then shift slightly to the dethroned machine.

"Are you a writer?" she asked.

"Yes," said Rose, startled, and wished she hadn't.

"Really a writer?"

It wasn't an affront; only a sad little confession of her own self-delusion, and Rose responded with equal candor, "I've only published one thing."

"Oh, my child." Excitement mounted again and the old throat quivered. "What did you publish it in?"

"In *Manhattan*. It was a short story, just a sketch."

"Don't you know that's terribly hard to do?"

"I know," said Rose ruefully, "that it's awfully hard to do again."

"I must have seen your story. I never miss *Manhattan*. When did it come out?"

"In June."

"My dear, how thrilling. Do you get fan mail, and go to literary cocktail parties?"

"No, I didn't rate a cocktail party."

"But you did get fan letters?"

"A few."

"Oh, do let me see them. What kind of people wrote to you?"

"There are a couple that the magazine forwarded to me up here. You can see them if you like. You won't thrill. One is from a Colonial Dame who hopes I am a cousin. The other is from a cruder character who wanted advice."

"Oh," Mrs. Sharon set down her thrice-emptied cup, "you can tell me what I need to know. Does one make a lot of money?"

"One might."

"Do you?"

Rose got up from the table. "Mrs. Sharon, I have to see Mrs. Fitts." From the stand between the beds she picked up a little pile of envelopes. On top lay the letter that had arrived, last evening; the two beneath it she held out to Althea. "You may have the letters. I don't want them. I'm sure Mrs. Fitts will be up now and getting breakfast."

Again something old and pathetic in Mrs. Sharon's face touched Rose slightly and she added, "We'll walk up to the lodge together. It was fun having early coffee with you."

But, following the bobbing red hat and fancy movements of the sleek shorts and sleeker legs, and receiving icy showers from branches Althea blithely parted, Rose found it unbearable to hear the woman chirp about the features of the wee path, which included several wee deer droppings, and the sudden wriggle of a wee snake, the latter an adventure Mrs. Sharon did not court.

She stopped dead in the track two feet wide and full of roots to plead, "Couldn't you drive me the rest of the way in your car?"

"My car's in Petit Port. I didn't drive it up the Trail."

"What a strange thing not to have done."

"Aren't you reversing yourself, Madam? My bright idea of adventure was to park myself in the woods and keep myself there till I wrote something or other. Turn sharp left around that rock and we'll be out on the highway."

High up on the east bank of the Trail dew gleamed on the red roof of the Midaywin bunkhouse and on blue bathing trunks dangling from a limb. The suggested male outline inspired a new perk to Mrs. Sharon's sandalled feet.

"Who," she again fluted, "lives on that most romantic crag?"

"Mart Bryan. The guide."

"Don't you think he's a most beautiful boy?"

"He looks normal. Which is your cabin, Mrs. Sharon?"

"It's up there." They had almost reached the main lodge as she fluttered the hand clutching Rose's letters toward a thin path that climbed from the opposite side of the Trail to the continuation of the ridge where Mart's bunkhouse stood. "You can't see the roof from down here—Mrs. Fitts told me," her voice was grieved, "that mine was the most adventurous cabin in Camp Midaywin. But now I've seen yours. Mine has two rooms and electric lights. You wouldn't like to exchange, would you?"

"No, I wouldn't," said Rose.

"Coffee?" Mrs. Fitts, drinking hers, standing at the broad black range, put neither smile nor frown on a face where red veins looked as if she had just broken them by a dawn treatment of Old Dutch Cleanser.

"No, thank you," said Rose Dallam. "I've been drinking it for an hour with a lost traveler. I feel like a St. Bernard who's been sharing the flask."

"Mrs. Sharon," Mrs. Fitts said, not asked, and waited for Rose to state her business.

"My sister—" The girl was nervous. "I've asked my sister to come up here."

"Your sister?" A gleam of curiosity lighted Mrs. Fitts' cold eyes. "So you've got a family. You give the impression, you know, that you'd made yourself."

"I—I have most of the usual features. A father and a stepmother, and a sister. My half-sister, really."

"You live with them when you're at home?"

"No, I've always lived with my grandmother. My mother's mother. Until she died this spring."

"Your mother and father divorced?"

"My mother died when I was born."

Mrs. Fitts lowered her eyes to her cup. "This sister you've asked up here. She's younger than you are."

"Yes."

"How young?"

"Twenty."

"'Bout three years younger. She much like you?"

"No," said Rose, and smiled faintly. "Tevy's big and beautiful and gay and awfully popular."

Mrs. Fitts' narrowed eyes were not altogether unkind. "How you going to like that? Isn't she going to be a lot of trouble to you?"

"I like my sister."

You do, said Mrs. Fitts' smile, and you don't. "I don't much like to have girls here. They give me plenty of trouble. There isn't enough going on around here of the kind of things they like to do, and that leads to the kind of trouble I don't want." She added slowly, "Guide trouble."

Rose returned her straight look, her eyes bland; but hot color was rising in her cheeks.

"You're all right." Mrs. Fitts went on with hardly a trace of malice. "You're a smart, sensible girl. You aren't looking for a mess of glamour. But there are plenty of girls that think bad grammar is cute, and that pants that smell of fish are super-he-man."

She slid a pan of crisp fragrant rolls from the oven. "Sit down and eat and I'll tell you about a couple of those girls." Mrs. Fitts put butter and pin-cherry jelly between them on the table, and sat down, now brightly smiling. "There was Dorothea Dodd. Her folks stayed with us for five summers. She fell for a guide who worked for Aspen Lodge up north of here—he still does. She stayed quite a while with him in his shack on Wild Rose Lake. Finally he sent her off with fifty cents and said he didn't love her anymore." Her bright teeth smiled and bit into a roll.

"Alice Hill was a schoolteacher up here on her vacation. She married Elmer Oftedahl and spent two winters camping out in the cook-house of an abandoned CCC camp. Elmer was doing a little trapping. Alice had two kids."

"I don't think my sister …" murmured Rose and pecked at her roll. "Anyway, I mailed the letter, asking her, last night."

"When would she be coming? I shan't stop her, you know. The cabin is yours for a month. I'm just warning you. And I'd like you to promise to say nothing about it. I don't want these other folks thinking they can have company."

"Probably she won't want to come. I wouldn't expect her for at least a week, if at all. She lives outside New York."

"Why wouldn't she come? You better change your mind about coffee. I've got time for one more cup before the tourists start hollering for theirs."

"Tevy isn't this kind of outdoor type. It's Elizabeth, her mother, who wants her to come. My father is an invalid. He was—in an accident. The pain makes him rather irritable and he worries a lot about Tevy. If she were with me for a bit—it's something that might help the situation."

Man-situation, thought Mrs. Fitts. "You aren't exactly the type for up here, either. How'd you happen to come?"

Rose hesitated. "My father used to come up to the Wilderness Trail when you had to do it by cart. I've always wanted to see it. And my grandmother once stayed with friends on the Canadian side of North Star Lake. They told me about you."

"You wrote that in your letter. The Vandenburghs." She wasn't satisfied. "I've been around here a good many years. What was your grandmother's name?"

Again Rose hesitated. "Mrs. Edgar Warren Bridge."

The name was as thoroughly an American property as Mrs. John D. Rockefeller and the sudden flush of Mrs. Fitts' face acknowledged it. "I remember the summer she was here. She wouldn't have rented that tumbledown cabin."

The girl laughed as she carried her dishes to the sink. "No. Thanks for a superb breakfast."

"I owed it to you," said Mrs. Fitts. "You've already looked after one of my boarders," she spoke in a still crisp but insinuating tone. "You knew Mrs. Sharon in New York, didn't you?"

"Heavens, no. She was out exploring and came across my hideout."

"Huh?"

"She found the primitive features of the cabin completely charming. Of course, I do. But if my sister Tevison comes, Mrs. Fitts, I think she'd like fewer mosquitoes."

"And so would you. O.K., when Mart ices you, I'll have him do a chinking job."

"Hi," called Mart.

"Hello," Rose sped across the cabin to open the screen door.

"Better put some papers down or I'll track up your clean floor."

"It doesn't matter."

"Put them down. This is dripping."

"Oh," she made a quick path of *The New York Times* across the room from the outer door to the enclosed porch that fronted the lake. "I should have done it before you came. And now you have to hold that ton of ice."

Mart said nothing. He trod across the papers to the porch, eased his load gently into the top of the little old ice box, and took the pick from his belt. The few chips that he made were pure grace notes. No cut could have been a better fit.

"Terrific technique," said Rose.

"Not too bad," he turned to her admiration with a self-mocking smile. He went on looking at her and humor left his red-brown face, the hard outlines blurred by an obvious feeling. "That's quite an outfit you've got on."

"You like it?" She glanced down at the gold sport shirt fastened high under her chin, the taupe shorts, the wide orange sash that wrapped her small waist.

"You must be expecting company." Voice and face were suddenly hostile. "I was kind of surprised to find you alone today."

She was astonished. "I shooed Mrs. Sharon out hours ago."

"I don't mean Mrs. Sharon."

"I don't know what you mean."

"So I have to tell you? Okay. The new guy."

"The new—"

"Maybe not new to you. You know who I'm talking about."

"The man who came on the 'Wilderness,' last night? I'd never seen him before. I haven't seen him since he got off the bus."

He still looked at her in that hard way. "It looks as if he might have come up here to be with you."

"Does it?" She was angry. "And Mr. Anderson looks like a boyfriend of mine? And so does Mr. Lund? At least I know their names."

"I can tell you the new guy's name. Roger Winton."

"Thank you."

"Where are the holes that need chinking?"

"Most of the big ones are at this end." He followed her outside to the hillside wall of shrunken cedar uprights filled with oakum, loose and dry.

"The whole shack ought to be pulled down," he said. "It could be done with three yanks and a half a dozen jumps in the right places. Want me to try?"

He put strong hands on each side of the crazy doorframe.

"Don't." She rushed behind him, caught at his shoulders. "Mart, don't. I love it."

He turned swiftly and her hands fell away from him. The relaxed warm look was in his eyes again.

"Okay," he said. "I chink," and picked up a sack lying by the doorstep. "Any more holes you can see?"

"Yes, up high. You can only see from inside. Come in and I'll show you." She crossed to her bedside and tilted back her head to gaze up at the gable over the door. "I'm not sure.... I see three or four spots of sun up there the first thing every morning. I'd better occupy the position." She lay down on the bed and stared toward the roof. "There they are. Big enough for a king-size mosquito."

Martin moved to the back of the room and, hand holding a hammer on hip, also contemplated the general direction of the ridgepole. "I can't locate them."

"Come here."

He came up to the bed and squatted till his eyes were at the level with hers, still looking toward the gable. "There," she pivoted his head slightly to the right.

"I see them." He got up and took a step away. But then he turned and stood looking down at Rose's head still on the pillow. He said quick and low, "Doesn't your hair ever get mussed up?"

"Of course," she laughed up at him. "You should see it when I wake up in the morning."

His face flushed deep.

"I'd sure like to, baby," said a loud voice from the doorway.

four
THURSDAY. JULY 9

Verne Anderson stepped cordially into the cabin. The gleam of his glasses and the spread of his pink baby mouth aimed at the guilty faces of the innocent, in what he doubtless considered a comradely leer.

"What I wouldn't have broke up if I'd have known! But seeing that I've already put my foot on the bed, can I borrow Martie to get me a bucket of minnows?"

Rose had sat up too quickly, but now, erect on the edge of the bed, hands folded in her lap, she quietly regarded the intruder who shifted feet and raised a fat hand as if to remove his fishing hat.

"You'll get your minnows as soon as I finish the job here." Hammer in hand Martin walked toward him, daring innuendo, and Anderson, tugging the limp hat farther down to his eyebrows, felt a concrete shoulder move his pulp aside. The screen door slammed.

"Hope you aren't sore at me, Miss Dallam," Anderson didn't look as if he believed that possible. "A girl like you can't expect to hide from the men. How about that glamour boy that got here last night? Has he found his way down here yet?"

"Someone else asked me that question." She was too angry for strict accuracy. "I told him that the glamour boy would be as likely to come here as you would. The answer meant: No."

A forefinger settled into Mr. Anderson's chin dimple. "You're a very smart girl," he said and did not smile. "Or aren't you?"

From the outer wall Mart's hammer tapped through a silence, and when Mr. Anderson spoke again, it was in a smoother manner. "Miss

Dallam, you had to be more than smart to write that piece in *Manhattan*. That was brilliant."

"So you've been chatting with Mrs. Sharon."

His tone sounded surprised. "Gravel Gertrude from Park Avenue? No, Miss Dallam, even if I don't look it, I can read more than just the comics." He raised a plump hip to rest on the too high table. It slipped off and he settled his back philosophically against the wall. "There you sit, the most perfect little lady I ever saw, and yet you can sure dish out the poison on paper. 'Profile of a Hero.' Did I ever get a kick out of that?"

"Did you?"

"Yes, a thousand times, yes. And how about the rest of your public? Get some reactions? Or did it just happen to hit me right?"

"I've had a couple of fan letters since I came to Midaywin, but they weren't particularly about the story. From people I don't know. They wrote mainly about themselves. I suppose that's typical."

"Typical fan letters? You should start a file."

"I've just emptied this one."

He laughed. "Good kid. I mean you aren't exactly swell-headed. What's that?" He cocked his round head. "Sounds like oars."

He squinted out the window at the gleaming lake. "Yeah, it's Lund. Let's go see how he's making out."

From the tiny pier which thrust out far enough to clear the line of bushes and leaning trees, a boat was clearly visible, the rower moving slowly parallel to the shore, pipe in mouth and trolling rod held between his feet.

"Hi, feller," Anderson called, "don't you know this lake's all fished out of Northern pike?"

Mr. Lund raised a blade in salute. "Good morning, Miss Dallam. Sure I know, but it's always fun to try." He headed a little out into the lake.

"Mr. Anderson, I'm ready." Martin, not looking at Rose, joined them on the dock.

Anderson stared at the boat where Lund was now standing to cast toward shore. "He won't get a thing," he scorned, "in this place and at this time of day."

Mr. Lund seemed to be having some trouble in retrieving his lure.

"You've caught the bottom of the lake," shouted Anderson. "Look out or you'll snap your line."

Mr. Lund, now sitting, was turning the boat with the right oar while his left hand held his bending rod high. Suddenly the line ran out at a sharp angle from its original course. Lund put the oar in the boat and took both hands to the rod.

"Has he really got anything?" Anderson asked Mart. Mart nodded. "Something pretty fair," he said without enthusiasm.

"Hi, hi!" Anderson teetered on the edge of the dock. "He sure has!"

White foam rose from the lake as the fish broke water, then dived deep, still hooked by Lund's lure.

"I bet he's caught a whale. Play it! Play it!" Verne Anderson stumbled along the path shouting through the bushes at the fisherman he could no longer see. "Don't let him break your rod. Don't lose your oar overboard. Let him run. Play him, feller, keep on playing him."

He panted out of Rose's sight, and Mart, unhurried but making better time, soon passed him.

Stroking slowly and easily, Roger Winton, the dark young man, whom Mart had named to Rose, paddled down Bear Cub Bay. He felt rested after a day spent mainly in lying around the cabin and thinking over the whole affair. What he had come to do would be far too easy; as for the added complications, arrangements could be made. But the element of sport was definitely absent. If he were too bored and dropped it? No, for peace of mind, he must go on.

The shore line curved sharply, and following it round the bend, he was suddenly aware that he was not bored at all.

For there on a small dock, not twenty feet from the canoe, he saw a girl, beautifully brown, beautifully made, in a wet green and white swim suit, the trunks brief and the bra molded over pretty little breasts. When he paddled toward shore, she looked directly at him and there was something sweet and shy about her eyes.

"Am I invited to land?" The lordly tone was tempered by pleasure.

The girl began to wrap a dark green beach coat over her shoulders. "Have you another paddle?"

"Yes. Security measure. Are you being very thoughtful of my safety?"

"No," she laughed. "I thought perhaps you might let me paddle with you for a little. It's … It's …"

"Such a lovely day? Yes, right now."

"I'm quite a strong swimmer."

"Madam, you have nothing to fear. I am all cautious rectitude—in a canoe." He ran the nose of his craft carefully to the bank and stepped out with the slow grace she had noted the night before. "Get in. Here's your paddle. Weapon or tool, as you prefer."

"I didn't mean …" she bent her head, tying the lime-green scarf that belted her coat. "What I meant …"

"Was that if I upset you, you would rescue me. You are a nice, nice girl."

She took the paddle and for the first time looked closely at him. His features were boldly molded and the charm was in the contrast of long lashes that softened the reckless glance and shadows beneath the large eyes.

As the canoe headed again toward the northern end of Midaywin, the girl in the bow caught the man's rhythm and they slipped along over dazzling water, well out from the rocks and fallen timber of the shore. A panorama of woolly clouds unrolled above the highest tree tops of the mainland and floated out above the lake, a frieze of grotesque, bloated Nikes.

"I like this place," he said as they rounded the irregular curve of Bear Cub Bay. "The place," he added, "better than the people, until I found you."

"Thank you, sir. I rather like them all."

"The men are all right," he said indifferently. "The Mr. Lund who caught the fifteen-pound pike for the first time in history, and his fishing partner, and the typical landlady's husband. But those women terrify me."

"Mrs. Fitts, yes. The other gentlewoman," she turned her head to smile at him, "would love to write you into her adventures."

He said grimly, "I don't like women who write."

"I've decided I don't either."

"Darling, I love you. What's your name?"

"Rose Dallam."

They didn't speak again until they had passed along the mainland shore opposite Rose's cabin. Between the long point and a ragged island cut a dark, choked passage.

"My God!" he said.

"Yes. They call it Hag's Nook."

Into the crooked watery lane rocks had fallen on rocks, trees had crashed from the island's thin soil, and now in the ruins of her blitzed house, a hag of a cedar, half-drowned, raised bare threatening claws in midchannel.

"It's exciting," said Rose. "Let's try to go through."

"I thought you were such a sweet sensible girl. So thoughtful of me. And how about Mrs. Fitts' canoe?"

Through the passage from the open lake a sudden cold gust swept the water off the ugly rocks and the witch arms rubbed against each other with arthritic creaks.

Rose pulled her cotton coat over her bare knees. "You're so wise. Let's go home."

From the dock, she said, "Thanks, Mr. Winton."

"Have I told you my name?"

"Mart did."

"Yes? Miss Dallam, would you consider calling me 'Wint' and having dinner with me at the lodge tonight?"

"I can't. I really have things to do here."

"Tomorrow for dinner? 'Wint' is quite a short name. You should have time to say it today."

"I might do both, tomorrow," she called and ran shivering to the cabin as the sound of his paddle died away.

five
THURSDAY. JULY 9. EARLY EVENING

Beneath the lighted sconces with the dangling weasel tails, Eric Lund and his fellow guests were finishing a dinner whose size and lateness indicated the priority accorded in the North Woods to the consecrated fisherman. Tonight, the two devout who had returned to Midaywin, tardy, ravenous and scratched from long hours of tramping a trout stream fifteen miles down the Trail, were Verne Anderson and Lund himself. Anderson, cocky and good-natured, had brought back three small speckled trout; Lund, nothing but the hope that he had firmly fixed his identity as another expatriate Minnesotan back on the old camp ground.

Now, as he emulated Anderson's silent wolfing of pineapple upside-down cake, he watched for the first time the two who had arrived the previous night: the aging woman with the deceptively young curves, and Roger Winton. Something in the past twenty-four hours had changed Winton. There were still dark smudges beneath his large eyes, but the eyes themselves were brilliant and the pale cheeks had taken on a slight flush of sun or excitement. There was no languor in his pose or movements; like the other men, he ate with quiet avidity, and the impolite but quite unemotional manner in which he ignored Mrs. Sharon's conversational oblations, indicated that the hatred Lund had seen directed at her, last evening, might have been produced only by the lodge's uncertain lighting.

The woman, making her pathetic offerings from man to man, seemed to expect a little more response from Winton than from Anderson or from Lund himself, but it was hard to assess the degrees of hope and despair with which she advanced topics and/or propositions for the evening. She had quavered something about canoeing in the starlight and the men couldn't have been more uninterested; her bubbles about haystack sleeping and kindred adventures—"for my writing"—burst in heavy silence. Lund, seeing the defeated tightening of her reddened lips, was sorry for her and for the old illusions as cracked as her voice, but he didn't like her eyes. They reminded him of something he saw too often in his work, the dry dark eyes of a corpse. Hoping he had a kind expression on his face, he reached in his pocket for the baby snapshots. At least by exhibiting them, he could cover the weak bid the poor woman was now making.

"And when my adventures are over for the day and I've written them all in my notebook," she was saying to the men's bent heads, "I have one more fascinating occupation before I go to sleep. I shall sit up alone in my bed and read the private papers of another writer."

Anderson raised his round face and demanded through masses of whipped cream, "What writer?"

Althea's cheeks flushed at his interest. "Rose Dallam. You didn't guess she was a writer, did you?"

"I didn't know you were friends," said Anderson, swallowing, but not wiping his mouth.

"Oh we're not, really. I met her only this morning, but writers instinctively trust one another."

"So?" said Lund who had heard different.

"She handed over her diary to you?" Winton mocked, but he too was interested.

"No, no," Althea's voice rose, excited by the male attention. "She gave me some fan letters she had received. Just a very few, of course. She is only a beginner."

"Why'd she do that?" Anderson, openly sceptic, was asking Lund's question for him.

"Why?" Mrs. Sharon hesitated, her eyes gone blank. "Oh," she rallied, "she wanted an opinion about them from a more experienced woman."

"Huh!" said Anderson.

Althea Sharon's voice trembled. "You don't believe me." A veined hand slipped into the deep V of her blouse, and fumbled there.

"Falsies?" asked Anderson and winked at Winton.

"Certainly not, young man," it was an honest elderly shriek. "There!"

From a deeper dive, the hand came out, holding two envelopes. "See. Both of them addressed to Miss Rose Dallam." She waved them in front of Anderson's flat unresponsive face.

"Mrs. Sharon!"

None of the four at the table had heard Mrs. Fitts' rubber-soled tread. She spoke smoothly, she smiled, but it would have taken courage to argue with her. "Mrs. Sharon, you've got a date to go out on the lake. You'd better be getting some warmer clothes on right away."

"Oh," gasped Mrs. Sharon, "oh yes." She got up and stood for a moment, looking regretfully at her hard-captured audience.

"Sorry I seemed to doubt you, sweetheart," said Anderson with a sudden smile.

"Good night, Mrs. Sharon," Winton rose courteously.

"We'll be seeing you," added Lund.

"Yes, oh yes," her face brightened and she skipped off across the room, followed by Mrs. Fitts. Through the open door of the lounge they could see her climbing up the path to her cabin, still waving the letters in her hand.

"Another cup of coffee?" Winton held out the pot toward Eric Lund.

"You're addressing a Swede," said Lund. "Two more. Preferably three. Same for you, Anderson?"

"You fellows," Anderson's smile had become a grin, "must've been surprised to hear that our little Rose is a writer?"

"Yes," said Roger Winton, "although I really had no reason to be. I only met the girl this afternoon."

But it had been quite a meeting, thought Lund, noting Winton's heightened color, as he added his own word of surprise.

"I'll show you something." Anderson walked over to the table by the fireplace where were piled old examples of every mass magazine from *Field and Stream* to *Home Crocheting*. "I took a bunch of this stuff back to my cabin to read last night." He shoved the stack apart and pulled out the fourth from the top, a dog-worried copy of *Manhattan*. "You ever read this sheet?" He brought it back to the dinner table.

"Not often," said Winton, lighting a cigarette.

"My wife reads the pictures to me," said Eric Lund.

"That's a clever little magazine," Verne Anderson sat down and licked his thumb. "There was a time when it didn't mean a thing to me, but in the last few years I've become quite a reader."

"Oh?" Winton regarded him with bright derisive eyes. "I would place you as a writer."

Anderson placidly turned pages. "Here it is. 'Profile of a Hero.' Swell title."

"Is it a story?" asked Lund.

"Kind of. Not much happens in it. It's about a fellow who's been away from home a while and comes back and don't get asked to some party or other. Either of you fellows read it?"

"No," said Winton, "but I'd like to."

Anderson didn't relinquish the magazine. "Quite some little writer," his glasses shone over the open page. "Full of that stuff they say the British have so much of. I forget the word."

"Compassion?" suggested Roger Winton.

"Hell no! Let's get out of here. The Fittses will want to clean up." He shoved back his chair and thrust the rolled-up *Manhattan* into his hip pocket.

"Hell!" he exclaimed, as the three parted on the path in front of his cabin. "I just thought of the word that describes Rose Dallam's style of writing. Understatement, that's the word. Nice and quiet, but you could tell in every line, she wished the hero was dead."

Rose Dallam sat waiting on her dock. It was long after eight o'clock, but here by the lake there was no darkness. In water nearly white, she saw great floating fluffs of pink and pearl; half-way across the still surface, reflected trees came out to meet these reflected clouds. Slim white stems of birch and black cedar trunks were alike topped with foliage of strange golden green. Suddenly at the nearest curve of shore, the pattern was broken.

A shiver ran through Rose, sharp and not cold, as the nose of a canoe came into sight. In the stern was a lone paddler, Mart Bryan.

Relaxed, a little disappointed, she gave him a small wave of the hand as he jumped to shore and pulled the canoe up alongside the dock. He dropped down beside her. One arm around her shoulder held her rigid, the other hand pressed over her mouth, and turned her head to face the cabin. Out of the woods a big rust-brown doe stepped into the glade and paused, staring straight at them. Her lifted nostrils snuffed at the still air a moment before she bent to crop white clover around the woodpile. Then up came her head and again she stood snuffing softly, the great spread ears like deep coral wings. Reassured, she returned to the grass, while Rose and Mart, his chin on her head, rested tense against each other.

"Ec-cho!"

At the shrill cry from up the lake, there was a snapshot vision of matchstick legs and a long white tail. When "Ec—cho" answered from a far island, the deer was gone, deep in the woods.

"Oh," sighed Rose and moved slowly out of Mart's arm. "She's the loveliest creature I ever saw. But couldn't she see us?"

"They have poor eyesight," he said, "unless something's moving, and they can't smell you unless they're downwind. But nothing gets by their ears."

"Ec-cho." The second syllable, a croak, was not returned.

"I better get going," said Mart. "Here's your New York paper and a couple of letters addressed to you. I found them open like this on the path up to Echo's cabin." He left her to a somewhat polyandrous contemplation.

Darkness came with mosquitoes, sending her to half-safety behind the ancient screens. In lamplight the rickety little cabin looked too large, too empty—too lonely. Well, all this illusion would certainly end if Tevy came.

Tevy here. Her bright-colored big beauty crowding this place. Even her easy lighthearted kindness would probably be on a scale to scare away the chipmunks. She didn't like to sit and read and she wouldn't want to listen to Rose's kind of music.

On a small table at the foot of the bed the phonograph stood open with a record in place. Rather ferociously Rose jerked the crank around and around and started the machine. A short whanging of the turntable, a few sharp harpsichord notes, and then a woman singing:

Oh, Death, how long!

Dark music, dark voice, and now the words.

Thy hand, Belinda. Darkness shades me....

No. Rose snatched the tone arm from the record. How could she feel hostile even for a moment to Tevy who had been least equipped to take the blow? Their father was what he had made himself long ago. The whole course of the affair was inevitable, once it had happened to him. Rose honored him for it, and so did Elizabeth, the keen generous woman, big like Tevy but not beautiful, in no way suiting the stereotype stepmother. But Tevy had been so gay and young and afraid of nothing. At school she had been the girl everyone wanted for a friend, and then, a year and a half ago, she had returned from the Christmas holidays and was utterly ignored. Darkness shades me. Of course Tevy must come. Anything would be better for her than sulking beside her father or making a hero of Jim East, a man Elizabeth justly called "that blight of our lives." Here at Midaywin there would be something to fill the hour so dangerous to leave empty. Something, someone for Tevy. Roger Winton. Mart.

A sharp jealous point pricked Rose, and in shame she hid the hurt from herself, covering it deep with the remembrance of the happiest Christmas of her life; of an evening by the fireside with her father and Elizabeth, Tevy asleep upstairs, and then the visitor at the door for the few repulsive minutes that had seemed quite irrelevant to the fate of the Dallams.

With the chill of that memory, there now crept through her nerves the tension she dreaded each night. She was listening to the darkness of the woods. The little sounds strange and indefinable. Patter like rain or dead leaves falling in a still clear air. Thuds against the screens like a heavy old beast. Sharp snaps barely audible. Hush, she wanted to tell the mosquitoes, I must catch these other sounds whatever they may be. Staring out from a bright room, of course, did no good, and when she went outside, it always seemed the place she knew by day, black but in no way fearful. Then she would hear the plop of a small fish jumping for flies and go back into the cabin, reassured. But after a while, nerves tightened again and would not believe that mice ran over Pyrofax tanks, and moths, not bears, bumped into windows.

Yet she wasn't really afraid of bears or brigands or the brown mice that sometimes skidded across the linoleum. She was, she admitted, possessed by the most childish of all terrors: the fear of being alone in the dark. Tonight, after the long day of intruders, small sounds for the first time took on a human threat. A frog dived with a plunk like the lure on Mr. Lund's line, and every crackle of wood in the stove was a footstep on a twig.

At nine-thirty, a more definite thump brought her trembling to the door. Roger Winton stood on the other side of the screen, his white face and black hair dramatized by a dark red shirt open at the neck.

"Don't say I shouldn't be here. I couldn't keep away. Do I come in? Or do you come out and gaze at the stars?"

"You ought not to be out in the woods without a flash. You might break your neck."

"Thanks, Mommie. What about you, living in the woods all by yourself? Don't you get frightened? Lonely?"

"Not particularly. I'm too busy teaching myself to cook and clean house and build fires, and all sorts of things I've never done before."

"Some kinds of learning need cooperation. I'd be glad to help."

Rose took up a coat and a flashlight and said sternly, "I'm going to see you home."

"All the way?"

"All the way to the lodge. Mrs. Fitts will be glad to take you the rest of the way."

He stood aside to let her out on the doorstep, and followed her path of light up the hill.

"Mrs. Fitts," he remarked, "is a really understanding woman. She christened the cabin I've got 'The Honeymoon.' It's the only cabin with a double bed."

They reached the hilltop and the highway, white on this moonless night, in contrast to its dark rim, lying under a thick-starred galaxy like a celestial Wilderness Trail.

Then they heard the cry. A scream and the echo of a scream.

six
THURSDAY NIGHT. JULY 9

A dog down the lake toward Petit Port had begun to howl at twilight. Now it was after nine, fully dark at last, and the dog had stopped.

Through the woods from the extreme south boundary of the camp, Eric Lund moved smoothly along the rough cabin path. No light or life showed in the first two cabins, still unrented, nor in the 'Honeymoon,' whose tenant, he suspected, was not at home.

The lamps Lund had left burning showed plainly and purposely the whole interior of his own cabin next door, but Neighbor Anderson's was as dark as might be expected of a man who had tramped a trout stream from noon until half past six.

The light in the office wing of the lodge was too dim to obscure the gray ribbon of the Trail, flat along the lake and curling up the hill to disappear between dark lines of trees.

Suddenly, high in the woods across the road a woman screamed. The long shrill cry ended and another followed, hollow and drawn out. The sound came from the direction of Mrs. Sharon's cabin and it was, Lund judged, her voice. Slipping the powerful flash from his hip pocket, he ran up the steep notched slope. The last vocal production sounded fake, but the first had been full of fear.

At the top of the ridge, Lund's torch found a small house built with a screened porch to overlook the lake. A huge gash had been torn down this screening and through the gap peered Mrs. Sharon's wild black eyes. Seeing Lund's light she reached one hand to her gray curls, the other to the neck of a pink robe. The neckline plunged and a screech came out of her ropy throat.

"It's all right, Mrs. Sharon," Lund said loud enough to be heard above her din.

"How do I know? You may be an enemy." She let out a weak bleat.

"I didn't tear out your screen. What happened?"

"Oh!" She molded pink stuff around her breasts and leaned into the beam of light. "That horrible hole. Those awful fingernails."

"Turn on your light, Mrs. Sharon."

"No. No. You might shoot me."

A low male voice said beside Lund, "If I had my .22!" and then louder, "It's okay, Mrs. Sharon." Mart stepped up to the porch. "Bear got your screen? We'll fix it."

"Here, Mart," Mrs. Fitts arrived with something under her arm. "I knew it was a bear after the way Smith's dog's been yowling all evening."

To Lund's enormous admiration she handed over wire cutters, a small paper sack of nails, and a roll of screening. "We'll have you safe from the mosquitoes in a minute."

"A bear," croaked Mrs. Sharon. "A bear! Shoot him, oh, shoot him!"

"No, ma'am! Soil's too thin to bury him. Too much trouble to tow him out to an island and hope for a prevailing east wind while he rots."

"And, Mrs. Sharon," a gentle old voice now joined in, "bears do no harm. One must love the Wild Life."

"Some little adventurer." A snigger came from behind Mr. Fitts.

"Oh, Mr. Anderson, it is, isn't it?" Althea Sharon quavered. "Won't you all come in?" She switched on a lamp at her side and a large room walled in knotty pine came into view. "Do all come in and let me give you a drink."

"Follow Anderson, the leader. Uh, oh! Here comes everybody else."

"What happened?" It was Rose Dallam, with Winton, holding her arm against his side.

Everyone told her as they trooped into the very fancy cabin. To the amusement of Lund, always looking for contradictions, Mrs. Sharon waved away Mrs. Fitts's determination to help, and dropping all the coy pink flutter, bossed and partnered Anderson at ice chopping and mixing with neat speed. Averill Fitts made a speech about the more natural and nourishing properties of cocoa before accepting a stiff drink.

Winton refused, saying, "I'm on the wagon."

"Alcohol give you hives?" Verne Anderson wore a mean little grin.

"No," Winton relaxed on a chintz-covered settee, "but I have highly personal allergies." He dropped a long fine hand from the back of the bench to the back of Rose Dallam who sat straight, hands folded around her glass.

By the door, highball in one hand, bag of nails in the other, Mart Bryan gave Winton a contemptuous stare.

"I haven't had such Scotch since the baby came," said Lund.

"You won't again till you've got her married off," said Mrs. Fitts. "You'll be an old man then."

"Right," said Lund, doing a little rueful arithmetic.

"What an evening," Mrs. Sharon sang herself into attention. "What an evening for my writing." She had perched quite gracefully on a table edge, her pink robe falling back from a naked knee that had been too evident all day to be a great treat now, and anyway, all the men were looking at Rose Dallam. Except Mr. Fitts who was looking at the glass, nearly full, that Rose had set on the floor.

Whatever went on here, it was focusing on the girl. Lund knew she'd had plenty of visitors today, and she was now getting some expressions of very mixed regard. Mart's seemed the simplest to interpret: attraction and jealousy. Winton's strong desire was so lacking in tenderness as to appear slightly hostile. The most interesting was Verne Anderson whose crude admiration of the previous evening was now tempered by ironic amusement.

Nor was there much sweetness for the young lady in Mrs. Sharon's well-ripened face as she sang on, "It all began with the lovely hour on the lake. Under the stars. In a canoe with Martin."

It sounded to Lund as if the reticent Miss Dallam had giggled. Mart Bryan evidently thought so, too. With a glower for her, he downed the rest of his highball, slammed the door, and began to nail.

"But that," said Mrs. Sharon, "was the end of beauty. I don't like being all alone in the woods, surrounded by bears."

"Then," Mrs. Fitts suggested, "don't leave an open box of chocolates on the porch, right slam up against the screen. That's asking them in."

"I didn't mean to." The gray curls shook childishly.

Mrs. Fitts responded with unexpected gentleness. "The bear came and went pretty fast, didn't he? He won't come back. Even if he did come, he wouldn't touch you."

"No?" A stubborn, wounded tone came into Althea's voice. "Perhaps not, if it were the bear who came to the front porch, but the one that was at the back door scratched me."

Verne Anderson guffawed.

"Nonsense," said Mrs. Fitts.

"It hurts," said Mrs. Sharon. She got off the table, walked not without dignity to the center of the group, and thrust out her right arm.

"Oh," gasped Rose Dallam.

Across the back of the slim, high-veined hand ran a ragged red gash. "I did not," she declared defensively, "cut it on the window screen."

"Tell us where you got hurt, Mrs. Sharon," Eric Lund encouraged her. From his first minute in the cabin he had been waiting for someone to ask that question.

"Right where I told you I did. At the back door."

Everyone was around her now, saying "too bad" and "how?" and "when?" and following the swishing pink robe across the living room to the dark room beyond.

"It happened just a little while before the other thing. I was almost asleep, but I heard … I got up and went to the door. The screen door. It was latched and the wooden door was open. I put out my hand and," she shuddered, "it clawed me. And just then the bear—the other bear—tore out the porch screen." She paused on the threshold of the second room.

"I'd better turn the lamp on, hadn't I?"

"Didn't you turn it on when you heard the noise outside?" Anderson asked her.

"No, I—didn't."

"How oddly courageous of you." Roger Winton had found the lamp and as he spoke light flared up, making everyone blink. "Didn't you call out and ask its name?"

"No, I didn't make a sound. Not the first time."

"Did you smell it?" Eric Lund stood with his back square across the screen door.

"Smell?" Mrs. Sharon's delicate nose lifted in disgust. "Of course not. Why?"

"Because," Mrs. Fitts put herself close to Lund and the door, "nothing smells like a bear except a bear."

"Or possibly wolves," Winton murmured to Rose Dallam, who had picked up some cotton and a small bottle of alcohol on the dressing table.

Eric Lund turned away and bent his long narrow head over the screen door to see what he had expected to see: around the doorlatch a neat oblong of screening had been cut on three sides and pushed in. A person in the dark room, putting out a hand for the door knob could easily get such a gash as Mrs. Sharon bore. Why didn't the woman say so? He straightened and looked at Mrs. Fitts. Let her make the next move.

For a moment she did nothing. No one else moved; if they had ideas about that door, they didn't express them.

Then Rose Dallam said kindly, "Will you let me clean your cut, Mrs. Sharon?"

"I'll do it." Mrs. Fitts strode across to Rose. "Well," she turned to old Althea, shivering in her flimsy robe, "you've had quite a nice little adventure, haven't you? Better get into bed and write it up before you forget it. The rest of you," she ordered "can go."

Rose Dallam went.

"Yes, yes," Althea croaked eagerly. "I have, haven't I? But some strong soul will have to stay with me for the rest of the night." Her eyes fixed pleadingly on Roger Winton. "You really understand me, Mr. Winton. Will you guard me?"

"If you need me," Winton told her politely. "I should be glad to."

"He talks like a gentleman," Verne Anderson teased, "but you never can tell how loud those high-nosed guys will snore. You better choose me, Mrs. Sharon. I don't. Or so I've been told by experts."

She looked doubtful. "I'm sure Mart doesn't. I must have someone I can trust." Not, her eyes said to Eric Lund, a man with scars around his mouth.

"Dear lady," Averill Fitts, who had not left the living room, advanced to the threshold with Rose Dallam's empty glass in his hand, "it is my duty and privilege as your host to stay."

"I'm the one who's staying," said his wife.

Only Mr. Fitts actually scuttled out the door, but the other three men were close behind him.

"You through with your work, Mart?" Mrs. Fitts called out into the darkness.

Mart Bryan appeared, square and dogged on the doorstep. "Where's Miss Dallam?" he demanded.

"Gone home." In the circle of light from the doorway Mrs. Fitts looked with clear meaning from him to Anderson to Winton and did not exclude Eric Lund. "She's gone home alone. To bed. Like a good girl."

seven
FRIDAY MORNING. JULY 10

"That's the old Lumber Camp Bay. That long narrow streak. With 'Dark Arm' embroidered across it."

Mrs. Fitts pointed above her cedar buffet where, tacked on the logs of the lounge wall, stretched a yard of folk art: emerald poplin shore, royal blue lake, islands of green felt, appliquéd in orange silk, and guarded by cross-stitch moose and rabbit of equal charm and dimension.

"I put that 'Dark Arm' name on the map to please some tourist types. And Mr. Fitts." Her harsh smile flattered the superiority of Anderson, Winton and Lund. "You can only get into the bay through the Narrows. The passage between Mystery Island and the point of the mainland's too shallow."

"Hag's Nook," murmured Roger Winton, with drama.

"That name I didn't put on." Her glance demoted him. "Over where the lumber camp used to be is where we'll have the picnic tomorrow night."

"That'll be swell." Anderson traced a fingernail along the orange silk shoreline of Bear Cub Bay. "Now, how about telling three serious types like us guys the spots where we can catch the Big Ones?"

Mrs. Fitts' face took on professional optimism. "Walleyes run the whole channel. They pick them up almost any place along the drop-off. You might talk it over with Bill Gregg this noon. He's fished every lake around here for years."

"Guide?" asked Winton.

"No. The Sheriff of Midaywin County. Mart's uncle. He's coming up the Trail for a day's fishing. From Pettyport. He'll have his lunch here."

"And investigate our housebreaker?" suggested Eric Lund.

"He isn't a game warden," snapped Mrs. Fitts and walked off to the kitchen.

"No," said Lund who had not referred to the bear. He exchanged looks, amused and baffled, with the other two men. "How about some fishing right now?" he asked them.

"Count me out." Verne Anderson's thumb raised a tiny tail of colorless hair from his fat nape. "I'm going down to Pettyport to find me a barber." He squinted at Winton bending forward to light a cigarette. "Your hair must grow awful fast."

"It does," said Winton, coolly. He flicked the match to the floor and smoothed his thick black crop.

Lund spoke in a slightly break-it-up-boys manner. "Okay, then, Winton, you and I fish? And how about asking Miss Dallam to come along?"

"I'll get her."

"Maybe I'll wait and go to Pettyport this afternoon," decided Anderson. "I've had a date to take that girl fishing for two days. I'll pick up my tackle at the cabin and be right with you."

It wouldn't be quite that quick; for blocking him in the doorway loomed Althea Sharon togged out in her adventure kit.

"Oh Mr. Anderson," her burble was so unbroken that Lund suspected her of being fresh from a night of Nembutal. "I'm off. Today I'm going to tiptoe across the border."

"Got your water wings?" asked Anderson.

"N-o-o. You mean fly?"

"I mean, lady, the border's all lakes in these parts."

"Oh," she said, slipping off her knapsack and cocking the red hat. "But couldn't I get a hitch in a boat?"

"With a customs guard, maybe."

"Oh, yes! You know, in Jugoslavia I took him by the arm and I said, 'Do you know that you're the handsomest man I ever saw?'"

"I can hardly wait to hear what happened."

"He put me in his jail. Overnight." She picked up her knapsack. "But, oh dear, I really ought to try for a hitch in the other direction today. Or else wait here for the mail before I set out on a long adventure."

"Say listen, Mrs. Sharon," Anderson dropped his kidding tone for a husky confidential note. "How'd you like to come to town with me right after lunch? You come on out...." His hand around her arm, they passed out of sight and sound.

"What do you make of that?" Lund asked Winton.

"God knows. You would really wonder why any man would go after that hag."

"She'd be surprised to hear you say that."

"I who 'really understand' her?" Winton's smile, sudden and rather charming, did not linger. "My God, what I brought down on myself!"

He lowered his voice and leaned toward Lund. "The night I got here, it was rather dark when I came up from my cabin for dinner. There was just one light over on that table. And here was the lady very neatly outlined against the window. Well, you know the form and figure. In that light she even looked like a blonde. I handed out a little come-on. She came."

He grimaced and paused to light a cigarette. "Miraculously before she had me flat on my back, in plunked Madame Fitts and snapped on the overhead lights. I'm still suffering from the shock of revelation."

"She's hard to take," said Lund. "I wouldn't care to try it in a boat. I'm not betting on Anderson's being able to shake the lady."

But, a quarter hour later when Verne Anderson sweated across the lodge dock, lugging a sloshing minnow bucket, he was alone. "None of you taking minnows? You're going after Great Northern. Those snakes'll hit anything you throw in. Now you take walleye … Gosh, I hope these fellers are lively!" He poked sluglike fingers among the shiners. "Yeah, they'll do. So you guys got two boats in the water already. Well, Rosebud, you come with me and I'll show you the scientific way to do it."

"May I go with you, Mr. Lund?" asked Rose. "I haven't seen the pictures of your baby yet. And I have seen you catch a huge fish."

"Size don't always count," muttered Anderson.

"He's right," Lund told her. "Those walleye Anderson hopes to outwit are prestige fish, the kind you ship on ice to show the boys back in the office. Northern Pike haven't much class, but when they come out of these cold deep lakes, they're fine eating and they always put up a swell fight. Get in, Miss Dallam, and we'll go after the big ones."

"That makes it you and me, Anderson," Winton looked angrily at Rose. "Set your weight in there and I'll shove off."

"I think this is about the right trolling speed," Lund headed the boat down the bay, and nearer shore than Winton's. "Hold the end of your rod up and the spoon will ride all right. If you snag a rock or a fallen tree, just sing out and we'll go back and get you loose."

"This is easy," Rose tossed out her line baited with a red and white Dare Devil. "Why did Mr. Anderson worry about whether his minnows were alive? Before the walleye ever meet them, won't they be hooked to death or drowned?"

"Miss Dallam, I'm afraid you aren't very reverent toward magic and ritual."

"Perhaps I could learn. This is my first fishing trip."

"How long have you been at the Camp?"

"Ten or eleven days. I got here on the 29th of June. I was the first one here. I came even before Mart did."

They relaxed into a pleasant outdoor silence, eyes rested by the greens and browns of the shoreline. Above the treetops, the red dot of Mrs. Sharon's cabin marked the ridge and farther on shone the smaller spot of Mart's bunkhouse. Aided by a light west breeze, the boat rounded the sudden curve of shore that shut off the sight of Camp Midaywin from the lower end of Bear Cub Bay and approached in slow rhythm the big pine-plumed boulder beside Rose's dock.

The girl began to sing in a light true voice:

> *When I am laid in earth....*
> *Remember me. Remember me, but ah! forget my fate.*

"I like your voice," said Lund, "but haven't you picked a rather low-spirited song?"

"I'm a rather low-spirited girl," she smiled at him. "I've lived so much with my grandmother and her gay old cronies. My sister Tevy is different. She's so full of life." She let out a bit more line. "Actually I sing Dido's Dirge because I went to the kind of school where one minors in Seventeenth Century music."

"And what do you major in?"

"Riding to hounds."

She swung around carefully on the seat to face the stern and her trailing line. Lund smiled at the small straight back and wished he knew all the factors that had gained him her delightful company. Across a short expanse of water he could see his rivals, anchored along what they hoped was the edge of the irregular, treacherous drop-off, Anderson in the bow of the boat crouched motionless above a line doubtless weighted with a lunk of lead and the prize among his minnows. Now and then Lund could hear water gushing into the lake when Winton leaned over the side to freshen the bait bucket.

"Mr. Lund," Rose spoke in a tight quiet voice, "I think I have a fish."

The rod in her left hand was jerking up and down.

"I'll say you have. Let him have some line to run with but keep your thumb tight on your reel. He's making a big splash. You've got to tire him out or you'll never land him."

"Thank you," she said.

Lund, maneuvering the boat for the final act, was amused by her self-possession and her very capable performance. "You don't need coaching."

The fish broke water close to the stern of the boat. "Is he very little?" she asked.

"He's swell. Head him toward me if you can. He's about ready to give up." Pink sail-like fins, long spotted brown body lay flat on the water. "Hold up your rod," he shouted. "He's taking another dive."

But that was the last. A minute later Lund held up the big panting pike for his captor to admire.

"I like him," said Rose. "How much does he weigh?"

"Ten pounds. Can you reach me the pliers? You got him on all of the triple hooks."

"Ten pounds I don't believe."

"Well," said Lund, running the stringer through the jaws, "maybe I don't either. But I'm just an honest dumbbell like you. He's probably about six pounds and that's no small fish. He's what a real fisherman calls a ten-pounder, and if you tell anybody yours was six, they'll think it was four and a quarter."

"Hey," yelled Anderson. "Whatya got, Lund?"

"Miss Dallam got it," Lund held up the pike. "A ten-pound Northern. Now," he told Rose, "I'll bet he'll quit waiting for the walleye and try to beat your record."

"Sure enough."

With Winton at the oars the boat was heading into the bay, Anderson bent over his tackle box. "Head over there," his commands came over the water. "Make for that big pine about a hundred feet in front of them. Right near Rose's cabin."

"Let me row for a while, Mr. Lund," Rose insisted. "My fish ought to have a twin for you in this wee lake. 'Wee,' you understand, is not my word."

"Strictly from Sharon."

"Poor fey soul. Do you know that she considers you 'frighteningly psychic?' I quote."

"I don't recognize me."

"But she told me, yesterday morning, that you knew her name before you'd been introduced. One quick, keen glance and you knew all."

"I did?"

"Certainly. She described … She described you accurately."

"Public Enemy 110?" Lund touched his scars. "Don't let that bother you. I recognize variations on an old theme." He was glad Rose Dallam, being such a lady, would be unlikely to ask for examples; for he was not now in a position to tell her that women frequently thought he had been bitten by the late John Dillinger.

From the other boat now drawn ahead of them, but farther from the shore, Winton's voice commanded, "Sit down!"

"Aw, this is perfectly safe." Anderson stood far up in the bow, reeling in his line.

Winton's reply did not reach Lund and Rose. He leaned over the water, one hand on the side of the boat, the other submerging the bucket. At that moment Anderson moved one foot forward and cast toward shore.

There was a terrible sound of smitten water as the boat went over. For an instant Rose's hands froze on the oars. Then she rowed steadily, not daring to turn her head.

"I'll take the oars," Lund's voice was even and normal as he moved forward to the center seat. They swung around and now she saw the other boat. It had righted itself and was rocking in the light shore breeze.

"The men?" Rose's voice sounded very small. Everything around her seemed hazy and swaying like the empty boat.

Their own boat drew alongside and now she could see a hand clinging to the foreward end and Winton's dark head, wet and spluttering.

"All right?" Lund asked quietly.

It couldn't be all right. She couldn't see Verne Anderson anywhere.

"He must have hit bottom." Winton breathed rather heavily. "He's dazed."

Things cleared and steadied for Rose. Winton's right hand, she realized, was gripping Anderson's hair, holding his head just above water. Anderson's face looked blind and slightly blue. He spat water feebly.

"Catch hold," Lund extended an oar toward him. "Hang on till you get your breath and I'll pull you over to the boat."

"I'm all right," Anderson gasped. He let go Winton and took the oar strongly enough. "I hit my head on the bottom, I guess. I feel kind of dizzy, and I can't see so good."

He again transferred his hold, now to the side of the boat opposite Winton, little rat-tails of water-darkened hair spilling drops along his almost featureless face.

"You've lost your glasses," said Winton.

"Golly, that's right. I got another pair in my cabin." His face brightened and he began to climb into the boat which swayed ominously. "I thought I was knocked blind."

"Don't try climbing into the boat from the side," Lund said. "You'll never make it. It's taken on a lot of water. Try at the end while I steady it."

"You first," said Winton tersely.

"No, no," said Anderson. "I'm okay. Thanks, feller, for hanging on to me."

"Get in!" commanded Lund.

The boat, its equilibrium doubtful, heaved as Winton scrambled over the end and sloshed into the bottom. "Oars are still in the boat, thank God."

"Throw him that coffee can back of you, Miss Dallam, so he can start bailing. All right, Anderson, I'm holding it steady now."

With more effort than Winton, Anderson got himself aboard. "It was my boots. They held me down."

"I was in luck. My loafers fell right off," said Winton. There was no reproach in his voice. The cold plunge seemed to have cleared a weight from his spirit and he looked positively lighthearted.

"It was a dumb stunt to stand up. You told me not to." Anderson, weak eyes closed against the sun, shook his head regretfully.

"Don't worry." Winton tapped his knee lightly with the bailer. "Everything's in order now."

"Here's your bait bucket," Lund held it out on an oar. "Fortunately it floated. It's a swell bailer. As soon as you get enough water out, you'd better go straight to shore. Anderson is shivering in the breeze. You'll get to your cabins quicker by road. Miss Dallam and I will keep on fishing. For your rods and other stuff."

For the first time since he had embarked at the lodge dock, Roger Winton paid attention to Rose Dallam. She was sitting a few feet from him in Lund's boat, remote, a little pale. "Did I frighten you?" His voice, warm and low, added, "dear."

"Not much, Wint. Mr. Lund had everything well in hand."

"Mr. Lund had?" Emotion, of which amusement was at least a part, flashed over his face. Then, "Better keep bailing, Anderson," he warned.

Drenched and dripping though he was, he looked remarkably handsome as he rowed away to Rose's dock.

"Is it shallow in front of your cabin, Miss Dallam?" Lund added heavy lead to massed triple hooks on her line.

"The bottom goes out pretty gradually at the left of the dock, but there's a deep drop-off just under that boulder to the right. Mrs. Fitts told me always to go up to the lodge beach to swim."

"Right. We'll go over the area where the boat upset and see if we can pick up Anderson's rod. Not much chance, and not much sport, but the girl who caught a whale on her first try should be willing to help the unfortunate."

"I've caught enough for one day. I don't want to crowd my luck." Rose smiled and waved toward shore. "There's a welcoming committee on my dock."

Two figures, Mrs. Fitts and Mart Bryan, had come out of the woods and were watching the inglorious arrival of Winton and Verne Anderson.

"They could easily hear the boat upset at the lodge, the sound and the echo. Mrs. Fitts will be relieved that everything is all right. This is a dangerous country." Lund turned the boat back over the course. "How does your line feel?"

"Dragging along the bottom, I think. Now it's free. The water's a lot deeper right here."

"You may be in that hole at the edge of the rock. I'm too close to shore."

"Wait. There's something on my line. It feels queer."

"Keep your line taut and don't pull hard."

"It isn't fighting like a fish and it isn't a dead weight." She sat intent, her cheeks pink again, her eyes shining, already skillful with her rod; the girl would make a fine fisherman.

"Whatever is on that hook is helping me. I can't keep my line tight. Mr. Lund, can you see …"

Eric Lund saw it, just below the surface of the water in the last second before it emerged, a buoyant, light-colored bundle. There was nothing he could do to shield Rose Dallam from the sight of the thing that she had caught.

The line lay limp on the water between the rod in Rose's hand and the spot, fifty feet away, where the hooks clutched folds of drenched white cloth printed with small green spots. Arms and legs lolled into the lake. The head was half out of water, the bulging mouth wide open, the hair peeled far back from the blue swollen forehead.

Rose Dallam had been right when she said there was no dead weight; this was the corpse of a woman which had lain so long in the lake that it was ready to float.

eight
FRIDAY AFTERNOON. JULY 10

On shore it was Mrs. Fitts who first saw the mass of human waste mushroom out of Lake Midaywin. Verne Anderson at her side blindly dripped and shivered, while Mart and Roger Winton upturned the heavy boat on the dock. She had time to be thankful that the body was not that of a camp guest and that Bill Gregg was on the way, before the others, too, were staring at horror.

"The Sheriff will be here right away," she said, noting that none of the three men looked about to be sick. "As soon as I heard a boat upset, I phoned down to Smith's in case we'd need help. The Sheriff had just stopped off there for coffee."

Out on the lake Mr. Lund was pulling toward the dock, talking quietly to Rose Dallam, helping her to keep calm while she wound her line taut. The girl's voice replying came clearly over the water.

"Yes, I think so. The dress."

Mrs. Fitts turned to the cold, quaking Anderson. "Get to your cabin as fast as you can," she ordered, "and put on some dry clothes. You don't have to wait for the Sheriff. Averill's in the lodge kitchen. He'll get you hot water and a drink. We don't have to add pneumonia to our troubles."

"Okay," chattered Anderson. "Th-thanks." He slogged off along the path close to the lake.

"You better go, too, Mr. Winton," she said, but he shook his head, his eyes on Lund's operation. He had taken off his wet shirt and the sun was fast drying his body, so she said no more until they heard the hillside stones and bushes yielding to a man's rapid descent. "Bill Gregg. Thank God."

From the moment of their meeting, throughout the five tense days he was still to spend in the North Woods, Eric Lund shared Mrs. Fitts' attitude toward the sheriff of Midaywin County. Gregg, like his nephew Mart Bryan, was short, compact, square-shouldered. Small wrinkles cut deep into the red-brown skin around his eyes and beneath the brim of a jaunty old hat, his hair showed gray. His brief, quick words pleased Lund who was grateful for the unguarded frankness with which the sheriff stated his first findings to the group. This was a ticklish spot for Lund. He could, of course, have revealed at once his own position to Gregg and have received all the information the sheriff was soon to possess, but the risk of thereby warning the blackmailer and his or her potential partners was too great. For the moment Lund must appear no closer to the law than anyone else at the camp, while he watched each person's reaction to the dead woman.

In the short time that Gregg kept them all standing around the rotting corpse on the dock, none seemed more than superficially involved. Winton's denial of recognition was as quietly definite as was Lund's. Althea Sharon, arriving at the scene with old Averill, showed only tepid interest in an adventure not her own. As for the nature lover, he had displayed more distress over the threat to shoot the bear.

"Did you ever see this woman, Mart?"

The boy turned his eyes from anxious regard of Rose Dallam to answer his uncle. "I might have. If I did, Mrs. Fitts did, too."

Mrs. Fitts gave a quick glance down at a face inflated beyond individuality, "I—think so."

"Her dress," Rose Dallam said again. The two women looked at each other and nodded.

In the lounge the three told the sheriff their brief story. Two days earlier, on Wednesday afternoon at about one thirty, a woman driving a small blue sedan had stopped and asked for lodging. Lund, the only guest to lunch in the lounge, had recently left for his cabin. Verne Anderson was out fishing, Mr. Fitts in his room napping; Mrs. Sharon and Roger Winton did not arrive from Petit Port until evening. Rose, carrying the heavy sack of groceries she had just purchased in the kitchen, was walking slowly up the Trail toward home.

Mrs. Fitts had told the woman in the sedan that she had no accommodations. Why? Well, that type just didn't fit into the woods. She was a heavy woman over forty, very neat, with rimless spectacles and wearing a silk print bolero dress with a Peter Pan collar too young for her. That kind got nervous and complained, and this particular one had curls like cast iron and a deep worried wrinkle above her nose. It was the absence of these two features and also of the glasses that made Mrs. Fitts not quite positive of her identification of the drowned corpse.

The woman had spoken very little. To Mrs. Fitts' suggestion that she try a place farther up the Trail she had assented in a thin voice and had driven slowly away. Patching a canoe near the main dock, Mart Bryan had seen the sedan leave the lodge and pass him. Except to agree that the driver was fat-faced, middle-aged, and female he could add nothing.

Rose Dallam had seen a little more. She had climbed the short hill and was about to turn off the Trail when the car caught up with her and crawled past. The driver stared at Rose, and at first the girl had thought she was about to speak. Her left elbow lay on the open window frame, a white sleeve with irregular green spots like leaves. As Rose started down the path to her hidden cabin, she took a last look at the car which was still moving very slowly. The woman, she thought, was just turning her head front as if she had been glancing back at Rose.

"That's all you saw of her? Miss Dallam, didn't you hear anything later?" Gregg looked hard at the girl. "That body went into the water close to where it was found. Bodies don't drift until they rise to the surface."

It was then that Mrs. Fitts told what she had heard late Wednesday night, and Rose exclaimed, "The beaver!" and looked ill.

"Bodies don't sound like beavers," said Gregg.

"But I've never heard a beaver. Mr. Fitts had told me, that evening, that there was one around. Anyway, I woke out of a sound sleep."

The men had all been in their cabins and, Mrs. Fitts assured Gregg, too far away to hear—all of which Lund knew was true.

"Wednesday midnight to Friday noon," Gregg got up and set his hat on his grizzled curls. "I guess that would be time enough. Water's fairly warm at this time of year. A fat body tends to rise quicker, and this one had quite a little help from Miss Dallam. Well, I'll see what information I can pick up along the Trail. Stick around till I get back."

Everyone relaxed when he had gone. Old Averill announced that Anderson was sound asleep after a large dose of Mrs. Sharon's medicinal Scotch, wondered if she would care to extend the treatment further, and went with her to get the bottle.

They were still together at noon when Gregg came back, the Fittses and Mart Bryan making the coffee and sandwiches that no one thought he wanted, Althea dozing, Rose and Winton quiet and close on the couch before the dead fire, Lund smoking his pipe and wanting action.

The sheriff came in, light, quick, less worried. In the short time he had learned a lot. Right away he had found the blue sedan parked in a small clearing on the right-hand side of the Trail. The spot was an eighth of a mile beyond Rose's path, around a bend, and the car was headed back toward Midaywin. The car belonged to a Drive-Yourself outfit in Duluth. It bore the same registration number that a woman, like the one who had stopped at Midaywin, had written on a registration card at Totem Cabins, five miles up the Wilderness Trail. She had given the name of Miss Edith Brown and her address as simply Duluth. She had paid for a week in advance, had bought a few groceries and said she would "come and go," as she had friends along the Trail. That was the last the Totem owners had seen of her, although they thought they had heard her car drive out around nine or ten on Wednesday night. It hadn't been back since.

Gregg had taken the resort owner and his wife to see the body and they had said it was Edith Brown; they were positive it was her dress. Then Gregg had gone back and itemized what he found in the cabin. It wasn't much help. A small overnight bag had been emptied of a plain nylon slip, bra and pants, Lucite toilet articles all very clean, mass-advertised cosmetics, stockings and bedroom slippers, a three-piece blue gabardine suit and a cloche hat—all without labels. The woman could have cut them out to hide identity but Gregg said he favored their origin in the "Monkey Ward" wish book.

Three things had really interested him. In the garbage dish were the half-smoked stubs of a dozen cigarettes; on a shelf by the cot were fifty little yellow capsules in a plain glass vial, like sleeping tablets sold illegally; in the closet, with the city suit, and where no North Woods clothes hung, there were some fancy pajamas—a red jacket, big black pants with butterflies all over them, and a top that was just a couple of red roses. It looked as though Edith Brown was plenty upset before she went out on that night drive, but not as though she planned on suicide by drowning—not when she could have swallowed the sleeping tablets and put on the pajamas to be found in.

"What do you think did happen?" Lund asked him.

Bill Gregg returned his straight look. "I should say she died by accidental drowning."

"I think you have the right idea," Lund answered him. "I'm a lawyer, you know." It would be a hopeless job to get evidence of any kind of foul play that would stand up in court; for the presumption at law, that any body found in water died by drowning, places the burden of proof on the party claiming a different cause of death. In this case, what other cause could the sheriff claim? Or what cause had a special agent of the FBI to suggest? Only knowledge that where blackmail exists there may sometimes be murder.

Gregg nodded. "It looks like drowning. Mouth open, a little foam in the nostrils; not much, though. The hands aren't clutching mud and stuff the way they usually are, but the head and neck are dark the way you'd expect. I'd say 'normal' drowning if the woman had hit her head or something and was unconscious when she fell in the water. You didn't hear her yelling. Anyway, the Pettyport ambulance is on the way and we'll have an autopsy that will settle the question. I've got to locate her people. The car rental company will have the address." He added to Mrs. Fitts, "I'm glad it wasn't one of your guests, Ida. You've had a perfect safety record all these years."

For the second time he was gone, and now the coffee and sandwiches became at least acceptable. Anderson, flushed and apologetic, came up from his cabin asking what he had missed, and was answered half-heartedly. Everyone was tired and wanted to forget. One by one they began to drift out of the lounge.

"You still want to go to town with me?" Anderson asked Mrs. Sharon. She eagerly accepted and they set off together.

Only Lund and Winton remained, Lund again deep in speculation, Winton looking more relaxed than at any moment since Lund had first seen him on the step of the Wilderness Express.

"Hey, fellers," Anderson, puffing distress, burst back into the room, "I can't get my car started.

"I get plenty of spark," he explained as Lund and Winton followed him out to the car park where Mrs. Fitts and Rose were watching Mart probe the Dodge's exposed old arteries. "She kicked over once or twice, and then she went completely dead."

Through the dirty windshield Lund saw Mrs. Sharon beside the empty driver's seat, her face bearing an expression of complete detachment from the world.

"Fuel pump seems to be working all right," Mart raised a black-streaked cheek. "I can't find a thing wrong with the connections. Points are okay."

"Don't you know a lot about cars?" Anderson asked Winton.

"Not a damned thing about their insides." Winton slid an arm through Rose's.

"Mart'll find out what's wrong," stated Mrs. Fitts.

"Local hero will rescue," Winton murmured to Rose, who did not answer.

"My guess is it's your gas line," said Mart. "Gas must be running out somewhere."

"I don't smell any," Anderson's white nose sniffed like a rabbit.

"You wouldn't out here and with the car on the level," Mrs. Fitts told him.

"I can't find any leak on this side," Mart let down the hood. "Want to lift up your side, Mr. Lund? Thanks, I'll get it now."

"How about right here?" said Lund.

"I think you've got it," agreed Mart. "Want to see, Mr. Anderson?"

"That's the sediment bowl," Lund explained. "It catches the foreign particles in your gas line. The metal frame's holding it together but it's cracked just enough to spill out all the gas as soon as you start the engine."

"I didn't know they made them of glass anymore," said Mrs. Fitts.

"They don't," said Mart. "You've been lucky if you never had one break before, Mr. Anderson. The bowl's so exposed on this particular model that it's easy for gravel to get up under there. It must have happened just about as you drove in here or you'd have stalled on the Trail."

"Golly, I remember now. There was an awful thump just after that last thank-you-ma'am. Just before you turn off at the mail box. That must have done it." Anderson added anxiously, "What do we do next? Get a tow car way out from Pettyport?"

"No, no." Lund turned the cap screw at the bottom and lifted the bowl fragments from the frame. "You can take these to a garage and get a new bowl the same size. Get in my car and I'll drive you down."

"Can you take her, too?" He waggled a thumb toward Mrs. Sharon. "I'd kind of hate to disappoint her."

"Sure," said Lund. "I'm taking anybody who wants to go. How about you and Winton, Miss Dallam?"

Winton put his hands lightly on Rose's shoulders. "Let's," he said.

"Be with you in a minute," said Lund. "I want to call up a friend of mine who's staying in Pettyport. Maybe I can meet him in town."

The clang of the Dodge's hood, slipping from Mart Bryan's hand brought Althea's red-capped curls to the car window.

"Oh," she trilled. "Now we're off." She still looked tranced, and the fate of the car as detailed by Mrs. Fitts seemed utter news, and strangely troubling.

"Go in his car?" she regarded the shiny Chevrolet and its owner with dubiety.

Throughout the thirty jolting miles of woodland, Mrs. Sharon maintained her unnatural quiet, sitting between Anderson and Lund, not once turning to interrupt Winton's murmurs to Rose Dallam. Even the dart of a fawn across the highway brought forth only one weak "wee."

The narrow Wilderness Trail widened at last to a paved highway, woods were replaced by stumpy pastures, and then suddenly below them lay the blue shining drama of Lake Superior. At the foot of a steep street of pleasant houses, jetties enclosed the small harbor of Petit Port. On the east gleamed the white column of a lighthouse; to the west lumber barges hugged a pier.

Along the breezy street paralleling the shore—one side neatly packed with shops, cafés and service stations, the other open to the endless blue water—Lund discharged his passengers.

"We'll all meet at the garage in an hour," he told them and drove there alone with Anderson's broken sediment bowl.

Thereafter, in his course about town, he saw Mrs. Sharon's red hat through the windows of the post office and later at the bank, glimpsed Anderson's round pale head in the shop of the only barber who hadn't locked up and gone fishing, and, at a small stand among the fishing boats drawn up on the beach, smiled at Roger Winton mooning handsomely over Rose Dallam while she bought smoked trout.

In front of the Trading Post, a red-haired young man with a boyish pug nose and a most determined chin suddenly shouted, "Lund!"

"Pete!" Special Agent Lund shook hands with Special Agent Larson. "We've got to make this fast."

"I trailed you Wednesday, Rik. That Dodge is registered to Mrs. Frank Johnson, Cambria, N.Y. It's a town of about 5000. That's all, to date. You're in a foul spot to operate; over that kind of road and with that twenty-party telephone line. But there's a good private phone at the State Conservation Camp about three miles south of your place. They'll call you down there in an emergency."

"Good. Walk around with me and I'll show you the Midaywin bunch. There may be some action by tomorrow. What would be my excuse, or theirs, for coming to town?"

"The Saturday night dance at the Harbor Bar. You'd love it, Rik."

"Like hell," said Lund. "If we come to town, we might stop first at the post office."

"I could be working there alone and late."

"Go around and see the sheriff," Lund said as they strolled slowly, companionably, back past the bank, the barber shop and the fish stand on the beach. He told Pete about the corpse of Edith Brown. "You'll probably have to tell Gregg who you are, but keep me out of it a day or two longer. This drowning may not have a damned thing to do with us, but I want first class fingerprints just in case. Now I'd better rejoin my fine friends from Camp Midaywin."

Back at the garage he found those friends standing around a majestic black car. Anderson, the latest to arrive, was saying to Rose Dallam, "Golly, how'd you ever happen to have a Lincoln?"

"Because I always have," she answered the simple truth. "You wouldn't," Winton asked her, "consider taking this elegant beast into the wilderness?"

She hesitated. "Not quite yet."

So it was in Lund's Chevrolet that they all headed for Midaywin after a stopover at the newest and most chrome of local bars. Rose ordered sherry, Winton a coke; Lund took beer.

"Double Scotch for me," said Verne Anderson.

"And me-e." Althea Sharon's throat quivered in anticipation. Then, the stringy muscles tense in her neck, she contradicted her order. "A sarsaparilla," she said demurely.

As she spoke, a letter she had been holding as usual too lightly fluttered to the floor. All the men bent to retrieve it. It was Eric Lund who without apparent glance picked up and returned the envelope.

That it was not addressed to Mrs. Althea Sharon was no surprise to him, but "Mrs. Alberta Dahlquist" was not the name he had expected to see.

nine
SATURDAY EVENING. JULY 11

From the Wilderness Trail to the Dark Arm of Lake Midaywin, on a sunny summer afternoon, is a journey of contrasts. Straight out from the Fitts' dock the boat goes through the Narrows between Collins and Mystery Islands and into the full sweep of the lake, wide spaces of glaring water to the south and west, with shimmering green dots of trees on the scatter of islets.

The boat turns sharp north around the point of Mystery and passes along the island's length. Then comes the ugly gap with the drowning rocks and the witch tree clawing the sky; after that, mainland begins in a flat white ledge on which a red mink poses or a merganser mother rallies her brood. Now the shores begin to creep toward one another until there is only a long tongue of water between, and at the tip they meet in a cul-de-sac to bound the Dark Arm.

Here in the narrow bay, evergreens grow to the water's edge, so dense that by six o'clock in the evening it is completely dark under the boughs. Dead trees thrust out into the somber water like brittle old bones, and on the living trees all low branches have been killed by winter ice. Iris, young and blue, suggest funeral flowers.

But it is the opposite shore which more strongly repels. There the forest has been wrenched apart, and in weeds and coarse grasses, squalid and desolate, huddle three black tarpaper shacks. By the dock a single tall cedar is dying at the top in a red plume that matches the rusty smoke vents.

On this dock, on this early evening in July, Mr. Averill Fitts, surrounded by his wife's picnicking guests, told a ghost story.

"Do you believe, Mr. Fitts," Mrs. Sharon asked, notebook rested on raised bare knee, "that the old lumberman who haunts the dock is a good spirit or is he evil?"

"Only an evil man would have destroyed this beauty."

"Only a fool," said Mrs. Fitts, "would've thought there was enough good timber to feed a sawmill. No wonder he killed himself."

"It's all so weird," Mrs. Sharon shuddered ecstatically. "Oh, what do you suppose lurks inside those quaint old buildings?"

"Bodies," suggested Winton in sepulchral tones. "Sorry! I'd forgotten Miss Edith Brown."

"What an amazing adventure," the adventuress quirked her gray curls toward Roger Winton, "to sleep all night in one of those little black houses!"

"With the ghost?" asked Eric Lund.

"Porcupine droppings," stated Mrs. Fitts.

"Ugh." Rose Dallam handed the orange she had been peeling to Althea. "In storm or shipwreck, I'd rather take a chance under that big cedar. Or under one of Mrs. Sharon's haystacks."

Winton's long graceful fingers began to strum an invisible guitar as he chanted:

> *Under the greenwood tree*
> *Who loves to lie with me…*

Althea, misjudging his aim, wriggled with delight, and Mart Bryan, lolling on the dock behind Rose, sat up suddenly, unconsciously playing with the handle of the target pistol hooked over the belt of his blue jeans.

"Hey," chuckled Verne Anderson, "how about with Little Boy Blue?" He waved his pudgy paws in imitation of Winton and croaked out:

Under the haystack, fast asleep.

Mart said distinctly, "'What's dumber than a dumb Swede?'"

"'A bright Irishman,'" said Lund, grinning. "End of quote. There's one of your little friends, Miss Dallam." He gestured toward a chipmunk hovering and sniffing at the edge of the group.

"How did you know about my boarders?"

"I'm a spy."

She laughed. "They're fun. I started with one and now I have four, all competing fiercely."

"Like your four young men, my dear," said Mr. Fitts, graciously including Mr. Lund, aged forty.

"They aren't mine. I don't feed them." Rose flushed.

"We too have appetites," said Roger Winton.

"Chipmunks have more." She had taken enough of this. "But life for them is just one long who-will-bite-whom. You should see the scars. They've inspired the only poem I ever wrote:

Squirrels
Have quirrels."

Althea Sharon's jealous old voice shook. "Are you going to publish that, too, in *Manhattan?*"

There was a moment of complete silence in which all the men looked hard at Rose: Anderson smug and smiling, Winton with the grieved expression of one who does not like women who write. Mart's blue eyes widened and then he bent his head and returned to twisting the gun handle. None of them was more interested than was Eric Lund.

The first to find words was Mr. Fitts. "My dear child, you are a writer. Dare I hope that you will someday compose a lyric for one of my tender little songs?"

"Miss Dallam," in desperate attempt to pull attention back to herself, Althea grabbed the first thread dangling in her cluttery mind, "somebody has stolen your two fan letters. They disappeared before I had even peeped at them!"

"You dropped them," Rose irritably broke a second short silence.

"Mart found them and gave them to me. I'll give them back to you." She got up, brushing an orange seed from her knee. "I'll hunt them up tomorrow."

"We've had quite a few writers staying at the camp in the course of the years." Mrs. Fitts' tone lumped them in a low category.

"Oh, Mr. Fitts," began Althea, "let me write your lyrics. Oh, may I try?"

No longer the center of ambiguous interest, Rose turned away from the group and stood for a moment facing the strange water and the green-black shore.

"So you're a writer." Mart had swung round on the dock and was looking up at her.

"I'm not really."

"It's nothing to be ashamed of," he said gruffly.

She sat down between him and Eric Lund. "I'm not ashamed of what I did. But I can't seem to do any more."

"When did you appear in *Manhattan?*" Lund asked.

"The June 25th issue. But they accepted it six months ago, and I haven't done anything since. Anything that was any good. I'm not sure I want to be a writer. But I am sure I don't know enough."

"Are you still worrying about your lack of education?" Lund teased her.

"Just like me," Mart mocked her sincerity.

She looked at him very seriously. "I could be," she said.

"I'm taking off in about three weeks," he said abruptly, staring straight ahead of him.

"Don't you," she spoke timidly, "like it here?"

"There's angles to this job—but that isn't the reason. I'm starting in at the 'U' second summer session. I'm kind of old. It's taken a while to save up. Now I'm going into Forestry."

"Oh," she said.

"You're old, I suppose, like Miss Dallam," suggested Lund.

"Twenty-three. But my education isn't exactly like hers!" He gave Rose a hostile look.

"She hasn't had the kind she wants." Lund thought tears weren't far from her eyes. "I know a little about the sort of school she went to. I started life a roughneck and I'm still one. But I've learned a few things, having married out of my class."

"That don't ever work out." Mart turned deep red. "Sorry."

"No one need be sorry for me. After ten years it's still working swell."

"How about a little target shooting to settle your suppers?"

There was enough of command in Mrs. Fitts' voice to bring them all to their feet, but it was a tired voice. Tourists had always shot at targets at her picnics and it was easier for her at her age if things went on in the same way tonight.

And so she produced .22 caliber cartridges and an eighteen-inch homemade cardboard target for Mart to nail to the crude gray laths supporting the black tar paper of the smallest shack, which stood apart from the other two and at the water's edge.

"Do we shoot at fifteen paces?" asked Lund.

Mart nodded, slipping the target pistol out of his trousers. "And one clip each. Mrs. Fitts thinks that is enough ammunition."

"Wait, wait," cried Althea. "I must look inside the house before you shoot it down."

"With a .22?" Mart began to pace off the distance across berry vines and high grass.

Mrs. Sharon darted out of the building. "There's nothing left inside!"

"You've had luck," said Mart. "That was the horse barn."

"Let me see the weapon." She grabbed for the long-barreled Colt. "What do you use it for except targets? What do you kill with it?"

"Partridge, in season."

"And what out of season?" She let go the pistol and pulled the notebook from the pocket of her shorts.

"Midaywin County chickens," said Mart.

"What are they?"

"Same bird. About the best spot is in front of that old log, Mr. Lund. We can toe the mark easy. How many of us are shooting?"

"Not me," Anderson was firm. "I can't stand using any kind of gun."

"How clever of you!" whispered Althea Sharon, not very softly.

"Five of us, then. Not the Fittses." Mart indicated the elderly couple packing dishes on the dock.

"You first, Miss Dallam," suggested Lund. "Did they teach shooting as well as riding at your fancy school?"

"Oh, please let me," Althea begged. "It would be so magical for my adventures, if I hit the bull's-eye with the very first shot."

"It would be a miracle," said Winton. "I'd guess that when we're through there won't be a dozen holes anywhere on the target."

"That's an optimistic estimate," said Lund. "Here you are, Mrs. Sharon."

She grasped the pistol fearfully. "Could you kill a person with this?"

"It's possible," Lund affirmed. "Yes, if you were near enough and had quite a little luck."

She seemed not to hear, lost in an elaborate and ineffectual display of sighting the target. "Oh," she cried suddenly. "I can't hit the bull's-eye. Because there isn't one."

Verne Anderson grinned at the inch-round black ball in the center of the cardboard and back at Althea. "What there isn't any of," he slapped her on the back, "is your glasses. You shouldn't have left them at home. Better sit over here with papa and take notes."

"And you'll tell me what to write down?"

"Sure." He settled on the ground by one of the two shacks far back of the target barn and leaned cosily against her shoulder—which was, after all, receptive, and he could count on her grabbing him whenever a cartridge went off. "Want to have a little bet on who's the best shot?"

"Oh yes. I choose Mr. Winton."

"Your hero. Okay, bet you a buck. My money's on Mart."

But after each of the four had taken one shot at the target, Anderson changed his mind. "It's Lund."

"But Mart hit the target, too. And Roger Winton almost did. Rose," she giggled, "hit the barn."

"They all will, before they're through. There goes little Wintie's right now. Mart's, too."

"And Rose's again. Oh, Mr. Lund pretty nearly hit the middle, didn't he?"

"Yeah," Anderson was grinning. Mart and Winton, having perceived Lund's superiority, were competing solely with each other—Mart relaxed and with an easy edge, Winton with an almost desperate determination. "And all for Rosy-posy. And doesn't she know it!"

"She does seem overexcited," Althea quavered. "And she is a very poor shot."

"No, she comes pretty close to the target most every time. She's handled a gun before and she isn't trying too hard. She's having fun."

Mart, thought Anderson, was the only one beside himself who noticed that Lund pointed the Colt and shot direct without sighting. "This is their last round," he said.

Lund's bullet punctured the target a quarter-inch from the black. Winton, his score even with Mart's in target hits but not in centering, shot wild, and swore. Mart coolly put his just below Lund's.

"Too bad to end with me," said Rose Dallam, and scored the single bull's-eye.

"But that doesn't make her the best shot, does it?" asked Althea unhappily.

"No, no, it was just luck," Rose comforted her. "Mr. Lund got six hits and Mart and Wint got four and three, and I got only one out of my ten."

"Was her bull's-eye luck the way you said it would be luck if anyone really killed someone with that pistol, Mr. Lund?"

"Well, similar."

"And now do let's all explore. There must be something in the other wee buildings."

Anderson stumbled to numb feet and pushed open the door against which he had been leaning, revealing a bare, uninviting bunkhouse, bunk frames in place and an old mattress spilling hay on the floor.

Farthest from the dock and on rising ground stood the cook shack. Rough bushes had pried between the steps, and within, porcupines had justified Mrs. Fitts' opinion and had also left identifying quills hooked in the edges of holes they had gnawed through the flooring. Two long tables and a battered muffin pan were the only human remains, except for what was on one wall.

"Pin-ups," said Rose. "What fun."

"Better let me censor for you," suggested Anderson. "Lumberjacks ain't ladies."

Althea sped forward and the rest followed.

"I think these were rather ladylike," said Rose. "Here are 'Five Little Sweethearts of the World.'"

"And Claudette Colbert with all the best points missing."

"In 'Zaza.' Gosh, these have been here a long time."

"Boy, they sure weren't Communists if they liked to look at this one." Mart had found the full-page rotogravure of three dull people in evening dress, thin, toothy parents and a dumpy daughter, captioned: A Well-Brought-Up Girl Makes Her Bow.

"I was at school with her," remarked Althea unspecifically after a close squint at mother and daughter.

"Now this," called Anderson, "is more like it."

He was planted before a picture featuring bleach, breasts, and long female legs. "'His Last Cheese-Cake,'" he read, "'At Luigi's.'"

A girl was laughing with her big mouth open wide, and beside her at a restaurant table was a young man with a moustache and a lot of wavy hair.

"There's some smaller printing underneath the picture. Please read it to me," Mrs. Sharon begged, "I have to copy everything down."

But Anderson's brief interest had ended and he was back with the "Five Little Sweethearts," and Winton and Mart, too, had moved toward the door.

"All right," said Eric Lund. "Tell me if I go too fast. 'Dashing Dan Galloway and friend. Less than an hour after this shot was made, the FBI closed in on Galloway, notorious bank robber and forger, said to be related to a prominent New York family.'"

"Oh, how thrilling. I remember. His picture was just everywhere! He must still be in jail. Please read it again."

Slipping past the three men near the door Rose Dallam left the shack. She wanted to be alone. The robber's cheesecake girl had reminded her of Tevy, though only because she was blond and looked so gay. And the man, Rose was sure, wasn't in the least like Jim East who certainly was not in prison. When her sister came—if she came— in ten days, a week, ought she, Rose, to say: Tevy, I'm sorry about *Manhattan?*

Across the Dark Arm she stared into the dense menace of the forest and shuddered. Her father, health shattered, will inflexible, the strain on Elizabeth's kind strength— No, there was nothing she could say to Tevy because she had nothing to regret. She turned from the black shore; and through a gap in the massacred forest where the late sun still shone, saw Mart Bryan coming determinedly toward her with the straight look, hard yet warm, which had disconcerted her the day he chinked the cabin.

"Your ears!" Excited, she laughed. "They're just like the doe's."

His hands went up to the rather outstanding members. "What the devil—"

"You know. When we were on my dock. The doe's ears were such a wonderful pink. But I see now, it was the sunset shining through them. Yours are just as red."

"And just as big, huh? Now, that hair is really going to get mussed!"

He caught her hands and held them behind her, his left arm around her and his right hand tousling her molded locks. She was struggling against his teasing hand, against her desire to put her cheek against his.

Suddenly she was wrenched backward. She was no longer close against Mart, but neither was she free.

Roger Winton held her right arm in a searing grasp. His face was terribly white. "What in hell are you doing to Rose? My God, who do you think you are?"

Mart's blue eyes were hot and angry, his jaw hard-set. "Let me go," Rose wrenched at his grip. "You're the one who's hurting me."

Winton let her free and she raised her other hand around her aching arm. "Mart didn't do a thing to me. It was all my fault. I—I teased him."

She stood between the two, daring either one to say another word.

Winton drew a deep breath. The rage in his dark eyes died down to smoky resentment. "My mistake. Sorry, Bryan." His tone was perfunctory.

"All right," Mart was curt.

Winton moved closer to Rose and laid a finger gently on her reddened arm. "Honey, if I hurt you, I can't bear it," he murmured.

"Fortunately, I have more fortitude," she laughed and turned to Mart who would not smile. "Oh, let's skip the whole thing. Here comes my girlfriend with the other lads. I hope they haven't been beating her up. She would love it."

"Oh, Mart," Mrs. Sharon's bare legs skittered ahead of Anderson and Lund. "Oh, tell me if there's something more to see. I mustn't miss anything."

"You've had it," said Mart.

"But where does the road go?" she pointed to the dead end of the bay where at the center appeared a trail, narrow and clogged underfoot with raspberry bushes.

"That's where they used to skid the logs down to the water," Mart explained, as Lund and Anderson joined them. "They did most of their cutting way back in."

"And where does the trail at the right go?" asked Lund.

"You've got good eyes, Mr. Lund. It runs about a mile across the point and comes out on the highway at Bear Cub Bay, about a quarter of a mile beyond the cabin Rose has."

"It doesn't look as if it got much use," said Lund.

"No. Maybe a dozen times a year, mostly in deer season. It's pretty rough going.... I think Mrs. Fitts wants us all to take off. We'll have to start if you expect to get to that dance by ten."

Mrs. Fitts loaded her boats as neatly as she did her lunch baskets. Anderson in the front of Mart's boat for the weight, Rose and Roger Winton on the middle seat. She took her place in the stern of the second, ready to run the motor, with Averill at the bow as ballast and Lund beside Althea Sharon to grab her by the shorts if she started springing around.

"It'll be dark when we get to the camp. You be careful of the shoal water around the point of Mystery, Mart. No fruit skins around on the dock? I hate to leave rubbish. I'll go out first."

Mr. Fitts raised an oar solemnly in air. "Farewell, unhappy spirit. Ghost of a wretched suicide, we leave you alone to haunt the scene of your sin."

"Oh," Mrs. Sharon shuddered against Lund, who, though no believer in ghosts nor brooder over dismal nature, nevertheless was quite glad to leave the strait waters of the Dark Arm.

Again they crossed the open body of Midaywin, cool under the great night sky, passing cautiously through the channel of the Narrows, cutting straight for the camp. Now the motor was silent and the oars felt awkwardly forward for the dockside.

Suddenly light glared in their eyes. Looking up, blindly at first, they recognized the searchlight on the dock and beside it saw a dim figure.

"Who's there?" shouted Mrs. Fitts. "You turn that light out of our eyes, so's we can see!"

The beam shifted slightly to the left and now the figure was clear. It was a girl, tall, hands deep in the pockets of yellow slacks, head flung slightly back and bound pirate-fashion in a black and white scarf that matched her open-throated shirt. Her vivid smiling face, in spite of its effrontery, was full of allure.

"Well," said Mrs. Fitts, "what do you want?"

"Oh, sorry about the light." The girl had a pleasant resonant voice. "I didn't plan to dazzle. My name is Tevison Dallam."

ten
SATURDAY NIGHT. JULY 11

My sister Tevison is so full of life. Yesterday morning Rose had said this to Eric Lund and it was what he thought tonight. The girl glowed with color laid on by nature and by bold skillful strokes of her big, comely hands which were now tying the boat to the dock for bewildered old Averill Fitts.

"Your sister certainly didn't expect you this soon," Mrs. Fitts said cordially. "She'll be along in a minute in the other boat."

"I'll take off the motor," said Lund, setting about it.

Mrs. Fitts gave him a grudging look, part acknowledgement, part resentment of his skill. "You know something about boats."

"Small boats," he amended, and did not explain that a good many of them had been police launches dragging for the drowned.

He lifted the heavy motor to the dock while Mr. Fitts breathily boosted Mrs. Sharon up beside Tevy Dallam. Althea's slim shoulders were drooping like an old woman's and the valiantly upheld breasts sagged. No one at this moment would have misjudged her age, as had Roger Winton and Lund himself on that earlier night when light had glared upon them. Foolishly, uselessly Althea had competed with Rose's gentle youth, but she wouldn't fight Tevy. She gaped at the tall young girl and trudged away, followed slowly by Mrs. Fitts. And Tevy, oblivious of their coming or going, erect and hands again in yellow pockets, and the charming, slightly insolent tilt to her exotically-coifed head, smiled out at the dark lake and the putt-putt-putt of Mart's approaching motor.

Lund had hauled the first boat on the dock and Mr. Fitts had waddled off, laden with oars and gasoline can, before the second engine was still. In the sudden silence, "All right, Mart. I'll row in," came Winton's voice, and then Rose cried out,

"Tevy! I can't believe it!"

Tevy Dallam sauntered to the edge of the low dock. "I can't quite believe it myself." She was excited. As the boat drew awkwardly alongside, she reached for Rose's elbows and swung her aloft.

"Tevy, you roughneck, set me down. Show Mr. Lund that you were born a lady. And this is Mr. Anderson."

With a quick clowning of the shy *jeune fille*, Tevy hung her head and held out her hand to Lund and to the bounding Verne Anderson.

"Boy!" he cried, as he landed on the dock. "Is this fun! I'm going to enjoy this!"

"But how could you get here so soon?" Rose was asking. "I didn't write the letter till Wednesday night."

"This is the air age. Or have you forgotten up here? Darling, that Wilderness Express! But I flew all the rest of the way and so did your letter. I thought you liked surprises. I do."

"Of course. Only I thought you'd have to shop or something."

"I bought bales of fashion. But not shopping. With a check the size you sent, one merely points to the best and says, 'I take all.'"

The second boat was heaved up on the dock, and Rose said, "Tevy, this is Roger Winton and Martin Bryan. My sister."

It was impossible that two young men wouldn't be attracted by Tevy Dallam and these showed it in their own ways, Mart slightly redder, Winton a bit whiter.

"Hello," said Tevy. She shook hands with Winton and turned to Mart. "So that's your name. Martin Bryan. I thought we'd met before. But if that's your name, we haven't."

"No," said Martin positively, "we haven't."

"You should know," said Tevy, pleasantly, and dropped it.

But Lund was not convinced nor, he observed, was Rose.

In a tight, hostess-type voice she asked, "Have you had dinner, Tevy?"

"Heaps. From your icebox. In vittles you do yourself well. But, darling, your cabin is a highly original choice."

"How did you ever find my cabin?"

Tevy laughed. "By elimination." Her thick-lashed eyes teased each of the four men. "I prowled all your cabins. I know all your secret vices. For instance," she focused slowly on Eric Lund, "you have four pictures pinned up with trout flies. They're all of the same girl."

"Ha!" roared Verne Anderson in relief. "Lund and his bambino."

"What interests me," said Lund whom professional caution rendered safe from any revelation, "is how you knew I was the doting parent?"

"Those two kids?" she waved to Mart and Winton. "No. And there's a big girl, you may remember, in one of your pictures," she nodded at Anderson. "Definitely not the type to be his wife."

"Miss FBI," said Anderson without mirth. "How soon are we starting for the dance?"

"I'll help you carry the stuff to the lodge," said Wint to Mart. "Save me a dance, Miss Dallam Junior."

"Do you want to go, Tevy?" Rose asked. "It's just a rowdy North Shore Saturday night. All the way back over the Trail to Petit Port. You must be terribly tired."

"Who goes?"

"Mr. Lund's invited us all. Mart and Wint and Mr. Anderson. To go in his car."

"I'd love it," said Tevy. "I'm never tired."

Eric Lund, member of an organization frequently described as tireless, regarded her with total envy. "It's nine o'clock," he said. "Can you be ready in half an hour?"

To his considerable surprise, the girls kept their word, appearing under the bright light by the gas pump as Mart finished filling the car—two sweet feminine figures, with soft cotton frocks, burnished hair, inviting perfume. Even Mrs. Fitts, writing down the amount of gas, seemed to find them pleasing, but not so Althea shivering beside her in shorts and sleeveless blouse.

"I think I should go if they do," she said, her words throbbing in her throat.

"It's Mr. Lund's party," Mrs. Fitts explained firmly, "and they were invited to it."

Verne Anderson, in his moose sweater, clapped an arm around Althea and bent so close to her gray curls that for once his whisper did not carry.

"Yes, yes," she nodded tearful and brave. "I will. I understand."

"Atta girl!" he gave her an affectionate slap and hopped into the back of Lund's car. "Come on, Tevy, and sit in here with me and Martie. That's where the fun's going to be."

"Would you like me to drive, Mr. Lund?" asked Mart. "The Trail's a little hard, the first time you go over it at night."

"Don't you drive coming back, Mart!" ordered Mrs. Fitts. "I know what the Harbor Bar's like on a Saturday night."

Rose Dallam left her sister's side and came forward, her hands squeezed tightly, an anxious frown pulling her brows together. "Wint," she said in a tense voice, "can't you drive us back? You don't drink."

Tevy gave a disgusted laugh. "Rose, you're being very funny."

But Roger Winton looked down seriously at her worried eyes. "I wouldn't want to drive anybody else's car, honey," he said. "Everything will be all right."

"I promise to be completely sober," Lund told her, smiling. "I'll limit myself to one weak beer."

"Of course," she turned to him gratefully. "I don't know why I …"

"Because you have sense," he said. "Thanks, Mart. I'll drive. Who's going to sit with me?"

Tevy laughed again and the gay note seemed a bit forced. "I've already been invited to sit in back, thank you. By one man. Are you going to invite me, too, Mart?" Sweeping up her tiered and flowered skirt in both hands she stepped in beside Verne Anderson.

Mart said nothing but he took his place at Tevy's left, as Winton, saying to Rose, "Let's …" held open the front door.

"Do we take the mail to town for Mrs. Fitts?" Anderson reminded Lund.

"Here's what was in our box," Mrs. Fitts held out a small packet of letters and cards, secured with string. "I just took them out and tied them together. The bus don't run on Sunday, so I'd be obliged if you'd stick these in the letter-drop outside the post office."

"I'd be glad to," said Lund sincerely; slipping them into his pocket. "Good night. Good night, Mrs. Sharon."

Althea did not answer. Like some superannuated WAC of 1898, she stood at stiff attention, an effect not without interest to Lund.

Well, they all interested him; what they did and what they said. Tevy's arrival and her greeting of Mart; a slip of Anderson's tongue made on the day they met; the assent to a small untruth. Tonight, the Senator's case neared its close. By watching and waiting could he, Lund, still discover ramifications of the plot, recognize accessories, living or dead, and establish beyond question the evidence against them, before his bird took flight?

On this night drive through the narrow, winding woods, the five in his car were doing very little for him. Beside him Rose Dallam sat almost silent, her hands folded in her lap. Occasionally she said something about the night scene to him or to the equally quiet Winton, erect with arms folded, not touching her.

From Tevy and her companions babble rose and fell, kidding, passing cigarettes and candy, a little horseplay—a good deal of it about haunted lumber camps and dead bodies. Now and then there was a touch of common social life, as when Lund said he was out of cigarettes.

"For the sake of clarity," he said, as Tevy leaned over his shoulder with a cigarette and Rose held up the car lighter, "I'm going to call the

Dallam girls by their first names."

"Have you got a nice name, Mr. L.," asked Tevy, "for me to call you by?"

"Eric."

"The older Dallam girl likes it," said Rose.

"Call me Verne," urged Anderson.

"That's a cheesy name," said Tevy, "but 'Andy' is cute. —Hello, Roger."

Winton turned his head toward her. "I prefer to be called 'Wint.' "

"I can see that you might," she said pertly.

He did not answer.

When Lund at last stopped his car at the dark front of the Petit Port post office, it was Winton who got out with the packet of mail and pushed it through the slot in the door.

A quarter-mile beyond the town the neon sign of the Harbor Bar made red streaks on the gravel and empty beer cases that surrounded it. The oblong block of cement, neat enough from without, smelled thick within of slopped beer and of people not at their best. Pink and green paper streamers were looped to the ceiling and dangled loose behind the bar amid the nudes of remembrance advertising. The bar was strictly for beer but a couple of women in wide-seated pastel slacks and hair just out of a week's curlers were giggling their way through the crowd to a side room, carrying bowls of ice cubes to their men folks.

"My God!" said Winton. "This isn't for Rose."

"It's for Tevy!" The tall girl stood beside him on the threshold. Her blond hair free of the pirate scarf was tied up in a short fluff at the top of her head and cut in a thick fringe over eyebrows which, sharp, short and darker than her hair, were the only feature showing kinship to Rose. The short sleeves of her black peasant blouse puffed out from arms rounder and fairer than her sister's, and the deep-peaked neckline framed delicate childlike skin where color flushed suddenly as she looked into Winton's shadowed eyes. Looked direct, for she was nearly as tall as he.

"You should save your oaths for the worst. Please be brave!" She was laughing and also pleading. "Here it comes!"

Summer residents slumming at the Harbor Bar were wont to say that you just never knew what instruments would be in play and that was half the fun. Local people accepted what they could pay for, but would have preferred Spike Jones. What they got tonight was a violin, an accordion, and a trombone, each entering far enough apart to make its wry individuality clear.

Winton's words were drowned. He put his arm strongly around Tevy's waist and pushed her into the crowd of couples heavily catching the rhythm of a polka.

"You and me, Rosebud," Verne Anderson light as a bouncing ball whirled her almost off her feet and away, her skirt of gold ombre plaid billowing and the amber band on her right wrist flashing with his pumping hand.

Mart was already at the bar exchanging cordial jibes with three or four fellows of his own age, and Lund, making his way among the dancers, ordered beer for them and stood aside, drinking his own. When he was sure that the Dallams and their partners had noticed him during several tours of the room, he unobtrusively left hot noise for the darkness of the North Shore road and the vast coolness of the lake.

"Hi," a familiar voice spoke out of the shadows into the bright path from the door. "I was thinking some of you folks might be down for the dance. Is Anderson with you, the fellow who had the chill yesterday?"

"How are you, Gregg?" Lund was cordial. "Anderson's inside, dancing with Rose Dallam. Want me to get him for you?"

"No, no. I'll do it when the tooting stops. 'Tisn't too important. I've been checking over my report on that drowning and saw he was the only one of you people I didn't ask to try to identify the body. I thought I'd get him to step over to the undertaker's and have a look. God help the poor guy. Edith's getting awful high."

"Do you know anything more about her?" asked Lund.

"Less." The sheriff sounded low. "She isn't a Duluth resident. The address she gave the car rental service was in New York City. Be seeing you."

Two minutes' walk along the highway brought Lund through a rustic arch carrying the lighted sign "Kiskiwiska Resort. Deep-Sea Fishing. Inner Spring Mattresses," and to Pete Larson's cabin among the pines.

"Here's the lot, Rik." Larson spread the Midaywin letters on the table. "Six letters by Mrs. Fitts, four turning down tourists, two grocery orders. And this."

Lund, filling his pipe, looked down at a white stamped envelope, addressed in small, sexless writing to Miss Emily Mary Walker at Middleshire House, Central Park South in New York City.

"Not a print on it," said Pete, "nor on the paper."

On the official stationery of Camp Midaywin the same careful handwriting said:

> Dear Emily: That Government job you were interested in has come through. Your interview will be at nine o'clock any night you can make it, next week, at the East Side office. I will be very interested to learn how you make out.
>
> Yours,
> Kitty

"Okay," said Lund. "That's the dope we need at the New York end. It should be easy to pick her up at the hotel and follow her to the Senator's on East 81st. Not smart operators, Emily and friend."

"I hate to tell you, Rik, about how smart we aren't here, either," Pete Larson's boyish face was grim. "There was a mess in the post office, yesterday, when your party was in there. The postmaster gave his clerk the Senator's letter to hand out, as we'd arranged, but he didn't check right off—they had a number of people wanting to register mail, and writing isn't the postmaster's highest skill. The clerk remembers all right that he gave the letter to one of the Midaywin people who asked for personal mail, as well as the resort bundle. Those people were Mrs. Sharon, and Winton and Rose Dallam who came in together."

"That's that," Lund drew moodily on his pipe. "Either woman could have claimed it for herself, for Winton or Anderson, for either of the Fittses, or for Mart Bryan. Later on, Mrs. Sharon dropped an envelope addressed to Mrs. Alberta Dahlquist, maybe for me to see. Check on it."

"Yes. Here's what I have about the arrival of the Midaywin people." Larson recited carefully. "Rose Dallam drove her Lincoln into the Pettyport Garage on June 29th and took the Wilderness Express, an hour later. Mart Bryan went up to the resort on the first of July. Anderson was next, about noon on the 7th, and you got there that evening. On the next day, July 8, about two o'clock, a big Cadillac with a New York license drove up to the Wilderness' office, and a middle-aged man and woman, described by the bookkeeper as 'high-ups,' deposited Mrs. Sharon and the pink luggage and drove off. Mrs. Sharon didn't buy a bus ticket, just checked the bags and went over to the Lighthouse Hotel. Half an hour before bus time, she came back in the shirt-and-shorts outfit and insisted on hitching 'for adventure.' The driver saw her in various vehicles on his way up the Trail. Later, as you know, Mart picked her up with the Command car.

"Roger Winton arrived in Pettyport that same afternoon, Wednesday the 8th, on the Greyhound that connects with the Wilderness. The seventeen resorts on the Trail are listed on the Wilderness ticket. Winton asked the driver about several of them and finally chose Midaywin."

Lund said, "So we go on from there. I won't be down tomorrow night, Pete, unless trouble breaks. It would look too suspicious for a quiet type like me to be seeking the joints of Pettyport again and on a Sunday evening. I'll be down early Monday morning. We need a copy of the June 25th issue of *Manhattan*. Let's hope the local library subscribes. Rose Dallam has a story in it, signed with her own name. It seemed to interest the bunch."

"If I can get hold of it before Monday morning, Rik, I'll call you, and—" He broke off, as Lund raised a warning hand.

A loud rap sounded at the cabin door. "Phone call in the office for Mr. Larson," a woman called.

"Coming." Pete left the cabin. "That," he announced on his return, "was my friend the sheriff. I mean my friend. I like the guy. He thought I might be interested to know that Verne Anderson didn't recognize an old acquaintance in Edith Brown. Anderson didn't seem disturbed. After he got outside, he retched a little but so did Gregg."

"You two got together on fingerprints?"

Larson nodded. "It had to be done the hard way. The skin was so shriveled that I got the coroner to dissect the finger tips. Lucky she was a large woman; they fitted over my fingers all right. The prints came out fine. They match some on the sedan. I've sent off the formula to the Identification Division. Here's a copy of the formula, Rik. You might need it."

"Anything new on Mrs. Frank Johnson of Cambria, N.Y.?" Lund pocketed the slip. "The lady who owns a 1940 Dodge."

"Not yet."

Eric Lund knocked out his pipe. "And now we'd better go show some interest in that dance!"

During Lund's absence, the crowd in the Harbor Bar had thinned but the atmosphere was no less thick. Both orchestra and dancers had lost something in rhythm, gained in noise, and over all now was more than a tinge of discord.

Lund's eyes searched the room. "Pete, look around the outskirts for Anderson. I'll stay here."

Again he ordered beer at the bar and returned a welcoming nod from Tevy Dallam. She was dancing with Mart Bryan, held tight against his navy T-shirt, her fringe of bright hair flopping against his forehead, her black yellow-flowered skirt, sleek over the hips, flowing out wide in descending tiers as their steps wove and interwove. Arms held at shoulder level, their hands palm to palm, made changing patterned circles around their heads. Although their movements were slow against the raucous bumping music, they managed to look extraordinarily energetic and young.

Lund was not the only witness fascinated by their gyrations. He heard several comments of "Monkey business," and Rose Dallam's eyes persistently followed Mart and Tevy as she and Roger Winton moved around the floor, with a slow grace not inspired by the toots and whines. These two were doing what, in Lund's youth, had been called a fox-trot and might still be for all he knew. The deep cowled neck of Rose's gown revealed, for the first time that Lund had seen, a remarkably lovely bosom, and Winton without losing his lordly air, was giving beauty its due. He had, Lund thought, an indolent sort of distinction, dramatized by strong features and a bold black brow. If the face were fuller, healthier, with no shadows beneath the eyes, would the distinction be less?

"The Sugar-Foot!" Pete Larson let his twenty-five years, red hair, and engaging pug nose momentarily overcome the seriousness of his job and his essential nature.

"I did hear 'Sugar-Foot?'"

"The dance your friends Bryan and the tall Dallam are doing. Our Verne is sitting in the side room at the left. He's undoubtedly been spiking his beer. He's nice and quiet. You won't have any trouble getting him home, if the passengers don't object to snoring."

Lund nodded, "Pete, my boy, how much longer would it be natural for an old man like me to hang around this joint before I take the kids home?"

"Not too long. Rose Dallam looks about ready to sing 'Good Night, Ladies.' She can't keep her eyes off her sister."

But at that moment, aware perhaps for the first time of her own jealous glance, Rose turned her head and laid it deliberately against Winton's down-bent cheek.

Simultaneously Mart's motions took on more tortured curves, and at Tevy's laughing response he swept her into the more decorous path of Winton and Rose.

"You wonder how they can dance at all to that music," said Lund. "At least, the tune's so old even I can recognize it."

"I'd like to try the 'Sugar-Foot' with Tevy Dallam," murmured Pete sadly. "Get her suspected, Rik, and assign me to her case."

Tevy's strong slim fingers flat against Mart's wide left hand, oscillating nearer and nearer her sister's orbit, suddenly collided with Roger Winton's ear.

"Look where you're going," he cried out in a blaze of anger far too hot for the offense, accidental or real. He stopped dancing but still held Rose close against him.

"I should look?" Tevy broke away from Mart. "Where do you think you're going?" Her clear loud voice stopped more than Winton. A circle of delighted dancers gathered round her as she continued.

"Both of you are walking around in your sleep." Her face was flushed crimson and the puff of hair at the top of her head loosed from the black ribbon fell against her neck. "Shall I wake you up?"

"Hold it," said Mart, hanging on hard to one wrist, but his blue eyes backed her up.

"Yeh, fellers. Come on outside and go to it. Show 'em you can fight." A huge broadfaced man in a sweaty plaid shirt started a shout that was echoed by the crowd. A woman giggled and another started a beery, hysterical scream. The big moment hoped for each Saturday night at the Harbor Bar had arrived. Would it peter out in the usual half-hearted fiasco, a blow or two exchanged only because of egging, or this time would a little blood really get shed?

Accordion and violin had stopped; only the trumpet snorted as a tall young man with red hair and a determined chin walked up to Tevy. "This is our dance, isn't it?" he asked with no uncertainty.

Her angry eyes turned from Winton to Larson's pleasant, firm face. For an instant, then, she became fully aware of the crowd and of what she had done to bring them close to her. With a little murmur of shame as well as gratitude, she pulled her fingers from Mart's and as the orchestra, commandeered by a quiet word from Lund, reassembled its sounds, she put out her hand and fell in step with Pete Larson.

Somebody whistled, somebody catcalled, but in a minute the crowd was dancing or back at the bar. Mart Bryan, Winton, and Rose Dallam stood together against the wall, Winton still white with fury, Rose holding herself stiff against a fit of nervous trembling. Suddenly Mart laughed.

"This is really funny. You and me twice in one evening, Winton. Over what? Do you know? I don't."

"Don't you?" Roger Winton began haughtily. He looked at Rose's pale face and tight-pressed hands and then out on the floor where Tevy, unsmiling, was doing a high-grade 'Sugar-Foot' with Lund's resourceful friend. "Possibly you don't," his tone modified. "Perhaps I don't either."

Lund, joining them, heard him with relief. "Here are the keys to the car, Mart. I'll bring Anderson along in a minute."

"Have we got time to get some hot coffee at the joint next door? Rose needs it." Mart touched her tense arm. "Come on. You coming, Winton?"

"Lund may need help." He turned into the side room where Anderson had spent his happy evening.

But it was Tevy that Winton escorted to the car. He tucked her into the far corner from the already somnolent Anderson, and settled himself between them. In front, Mart Bryan's arm lying along the back of the seat slipped gradually around Rose Dallam. She let it stay, and after a while, they too slept.

Alone, alert at the wheel, Eric Lund thought briefly about his Janet on the night, long ago, when her fingers had first touched the scars about his lips, but as the ghostly pre-dawn began to lighten the long road through the woods, he thought mainly that he had already started another day. A day of delicate work.

eleven
SUNDAY. JULY 12

A high wind rose with the dawn and at midmorning was whipping Lake Midaywin into whitecaps. Around the little cabin on Bear Cub Bay poplar leaves pattered noisily and cedar boughs rubbed and creaked. The chipmunks and squirrels were in hiding, not trusting themselves in the open glade where the gale drowned out the sound of possible enemies.

The noise of the wind, however, did not disturb a wandering black bear. Big as he was, he could never arrive anywhere in complete silence, and that size was also his protection; for although he was only a yearling he was already the biggest thing in the woods. At present his mother had a new cub, but instead of staying at home to express sibling rivalry by clawing his little brother, he had gone forth to set his teeth in some nice garbage.

The nicest garbage can in Camp Midaywin was Rose Dallam's. It was the oldest with, therefore, the most far-reaching aroma and with the most ill-fitting lid. With a brush of a paw it was off, and when he stood up and stirred the contents he pawed up two items which at this season he considered most satisfying, a sticky jam jar and the dregs of a can of green peas. When these had been licked clean, he upset the garbage can and in a spirit of good clean fun strewed the ferns and wild roses with chop bones, fish heads and bread papers. Then he made off up the hillside.

The removal of the lid and the overturning of the can had not been quiet operations and that is why Rose and Tevison Dallam woke up far earlier than they had intended that Sunday morning.

So, at eleven o'clock when Eric Lund strolled down the lakeside path, they had already consumed a great deal of coffee and orange juice, and eight of Mrs. Fitts' rolls, and Tevy had broken a screw in the tone arm of Rose's phonograph. Before the accident, however, she had five times played the record of Purcell's "Dido and Aeneas," and learned the Dirge so that she could whistle it loudly and accurately except for fluffing the final repetition of *Remember me!* which she obstinately pitched too high.

She was giving it another try as Lund came into view, and he heard the high note hiss and break at the moment he caught sight of Rose in her dark green beach coat, staring down at the dirty remains of the bruin picnic.

"Mr. Lund! I didn't expect to see you for hours," she called.

"Old man with bad but regular habits," he told her. "So you've had a bear."

"Are they always such messes?" She set the can upright and stooped for a banana skin.

"Usually, so I've heard. You seem to have survived the night handsomely. Here, let me straighten this out for you. I'm more the type."

"No," she protested. "Oh wait. I'll get the work gloves I use when I carry in the kindling. They're your size, not mine."

As soon as she had turned the corner of the cabin, he bent suddenly beneath a cedar. The handful of carrot peelings he had retrieved he threw ostentatiously in the can but a small object, gritty with coffee grounds, disappeared into the pocket of his leather jacket.

"Hi, Eric!" Tevy was coming now with Rose, looking gay in a very feminine bathing suit of apricot sharkskin, the short skirt showing a soft citron lining with each gust that tossed her bright hair.

"Are we the only survivors of the orgy?" Rose wanted to know. When her beach coat blew apart, it revealed the green and white striped swim suit, brief and businesslike. Her hair, he noted, was nearly as neat as if the day were windless.

"Not a sign of Anderson or Winton."

"And our young friend Martin?" asked Tevy.

"He's driving Mrs. Sharon to church in Pettyport."

"Who's Mrs. Sharon?—Oh, I remember. The Granny-girl."

"In the Command car?" Rose suggested.

"I think Anderson yesterday offered the Dodge. The Fitts family of course is on deck. Mrs. Fitts fed me with the usual overabundance. Mr. Fitts is washing up and toddling to the piano after every third dish to compose something worthy of lyrics by a *Manhattan* author."

"That slays me," said Tevy, and looked at Rose who pressed her lips tight.

"There goes the last scrap," Lund flung a soup bone into the can and pounded down the teetering top.

"Are you good at everything you do?" asked Tevy.

"Aren't you very good at flattery?"

"Well, what I mean is, I and my giant paws cleverly smashed a small but vital part of my sister's phonograph, so I wondered if you'd be good in that emergency."

"Tevy," he said, "you see a small-time lawyer who is just a frustrated mechanic. I love to monkey with things like that. Want me to do it while you swim?"

"Any time," said Rose. "If you'd really like to try."

"Yes, really.— What I came for was to ask you two if you'd care to come to my cabin at about six for a drink. Mrs. Fitts tells me you've ordered dinner at the lodge at seven. I'm asking the rest of the gang."

"We'd love to, wouldn't we, Tevy?"

"You know it. Thanks awfully. I love you even if you can't fix the phono. We're going up to lie on the float at the camp and get a tan. It's too windy to swim much."

"You don't mind if I look at the machine while you're gone? I'll probably have to come back some other time with the right tools."

Some other time, when they would again be on the lake, and he would have the chance to return what he hoped to remove right now. So far, he had incredible luck. Would it hold?

Inside the little cabin, he looked with quick discrimination for anything likely to contain letters. Except for scarlet pajamas bunched on one bed and a large pair of huaraches in the middle of the floor, the room was in order. The red-checked curtains, pulled back from the cupboard shelves showed only dishes. A trunk was under one bed, suitcases piled neatly in a corner: therein, of course, anything could be concealed. An orderly pile of letters lay on the single table. But at the picnic Rose had told Althea she would have to hunt. On the floor beside the typewriter stood a light metal case, its dimensions not much greater than a sheet of manuscript paper, and Lund chose to begin there.

The unlocked box was half filled with folders and he took them out, laying them one by one on Rose's bed, his back to the cupboard wall, keeping windows and door within his view. The first two folders held a few scribbled notes; for a novel, for a couple of short stories. Between the third and fourth lay a wad of paper. Lund smoothed out a letter, written in a firm feminine hand. Although it was obviously not what he directly sought, he registered the contents on the photographic plate of a memory trained for that exacting purpose.

Saturday morning.

Rose, my dear,

> Your father has been sitting on a bench under the cherry tree for the last hour while I, drippingly, pulled greenery—weeds, I hope, not onions. More than once he talked about you and the North Woods where he spent those wonderful strenuous summers long ago. It pleases him to think you wanted to see that country of his youth.
>
> He is very much the same, I think. Some days he has more pain

than others, but I can tell that mainly because of increased irritability. It is such a comfort to know that you and I feel the same way about him.

Tevy doesn't. And we can't wholly blame her. For your father isn't easy to live with, and while she knows he suffers, she is, I'm afraid, beginning to feel it's his own fault. After all, she was pretty fine about everything, eighteen months ago. For so young a girl.

There is something I greatly fear. Perhaps I'm imagining it but it seems to me that when she refers to that blight of our lives, I see a small halo of martyrdom rising behind the head of Saint James. This is a dangerous moment for such glorification, but at no time could I take it. And it could kill your father.

There's no reason for you to be a sister to Tevy, but nothing would help your father more than her removal for a few weeks and in your care. Could you bear it? She's so restless that I'm sure she'd jump at the chance. And it might be fine for you to have a companion your own age. Poor child, I always talk to you as if you were my contemporary, and you're only three years older than Tevy. Rose, please, I hate to ask you to do this but I am terribly concerned.

With my love, dear,

Elizabeth

It looked to Lund as if Rose, following Tevy's surprise arrival had hastily—and wisely—stuffed this into the manuscript file.

Even the most careless reading of the legal documents, letters from directors and trustees filling the next two folders would yield the information that the charming, democratic Miss Dallam was the sole heir to one of the greatest estates in America. The last thin folder contained a letter of acceptance from *Manhattan* for a story called "Profile of a Hero" and two sheets of folded paper, the first a plain typing sheet creased to fit a long envelope, the second club-size, and bearing the name of a New York hotel.

Two fan letters, Althea Sharon had said. Well, here they were.

In the upper right corner of the typewritten missive, someone had noted with pencil: 'Ans. 2/7.' This presumed an address which must have been destroyed with the covering envelope; for there was no heading, not even a date, on the letter Lund was now regarding:

Miss Thorn Dallam:

No sweeter name for a gal who goes under the skin with the pen point! Not ink in that pen. That's acid, sister. Or is it cold blood?

Seriously—very seriously—I admire your impersonal style. And your success.

I'm a regular reader of *Manhattan* but I haven't read you before. You're new. You're terrific.

Me, I'm just bad. Long time try, no time sell. I'm no colleague, but how about a bit of advice out of pure kindness of heart? (Or have you one?) Anyway, please answer me this. Is a literary agent indispensable for a beginner? Thanks and I do mean I'm grateful to Miss Dallam.

Yours,
Philip Carter

The thing, to Lund, sounded young, but it was a youthfulness that could be imitated: from life, from the movies, from magazine fiction.

The second fan letter, also annotated 'Ans. 30/6,' was hand-written in a well-bred but almost impersonal script, such as a librarian might use. Glancing from heading to signature, Lund whistled softly.

Middleshire House
Central Park South
In the City of New York

26 June

My dear Miss Dallam:

I have just finished reading your little story "Profile of a Hero." I am old and, I am *proud* to say, old-fashioned. The emphasis you put so *firmly* upon the value of *true character* was a great and unexpected comfort to find in so flippant an organ as *Manhattan*.

Perhaps I should confess that your name interested me somewhat more than did your tale. Are you by chance a descendant of Richard Dallam who came to this country from England in 1690? He was a lawyer, I believe, and married a forebear of mine. I should so like to know where any scattered branches of the family may be flourishing.

So often I think of the words of the great Daniel Webster:

"There is a moral and philosophical respect for our ancestors which elevates the character and improves the heart." Don't you agree?

Most cordially,
Emily Mary Walker

With perfect care Lund refilled Rose Dallam's file. The two letters Mrs. Sharon wanted were in his pocket as he turned to the phonograph on the table. Either or both of them could be quite what they seemed to be; people wrote letters like that every day. Or either or both could be a hook to catch the present address of Rose Dallam. If so, whose hook?

If either letter was false, the writer or writers, if now at Midaywin, would be eager to regain possession—particularly following Mrs. Sharon's announcement of their existence. Eager enough to cut through a screen door in the night.

And what about Althea Sharon herself? She wanted the letters. She could also want them back.

Swiftly Lund turned to the phonograph, dug out the broken screw with his penknife and left the cabin. He did not, however, quit the region. At the left of the small dock, almost hidden from cabin and path by the low hanging cedar boughs was the rocky boulder projecting into the lake. Lund walked out on the dock, turned and looked toward the boulder. This, now seen at the dock's right as he and Rose Dallam had seen it from their boat, marked the deep water from which the girl had made her dreadful catch. Along the granite top, close to the water's edge, a pine tree clung.

The path beside Rose's cabin was depressed below the level of the little house. A peeper standing there could see little of what went on within, but at night, mounted on the rock, one could get a clear view over the low intervening cedars into lighted windows. For the moment Eric Lund was not worrying about motives for such spying or their possible connection with the Senator's blackmail; he was just looking around.

He stepped up on the rock, and with his back to Rose Dallam's house gazed down into deep brown water that might conceal a woman's handbag containing small identifying articles, even a name that was not Edith Brown. To drag the lake was not his job—thus far.

He stood motionless, listening. Sounds of laughter from the bathers far up at the camp float came to him, but there were no footsteps near. He pivoted toward shore, forgetting the rock-borne pine, and felt a deep-scraping blow on his shoulder. Torn white shirt, red slit in skin, and above them a branch, tough, sharp, raw from a recent break.

Someone shorter than Lund, standing where he stood, turning as he had turned, could have gotten a nasty blow from that bough, could have tumbled stunned in darkness into the deep hole, could have drowned without a cry. Could have. No evidence that it had happened.

Eric Lund went back to his own cabin, there to devote the rest of the day to photography and to the preparations for his cocktail party, the purpose of which was other than to ply suspects with liquor.

The Fittses refused Lund's invitation, Mrs. Fitts because she had dinner to prepare, Mr. Fitts because of the look in Mrs. Fitts' eye, and the same blue marble censor may have decided Mart that there would never again be so perfect an hour for filling wood boxes.

To the other five Lund was an assiduous host and bartender, carrying drinks from his compact kitchen in tall glasses not the property of Camp Midaywin. It was a dressy party and for a while dull. Roger Winton drank a coke that blended beautifully with his brown tweed jacket and café-au-lait flannels, and with the suntan that had begun to warm his pallor. Sipping bourbon mixed to Lund's specifications, Anderson, his nuzzling moose sweater topping a white shirt, and Althea Sharon in a peasant-print dirndl and organdy drawstring blouse of tourist Salzburg in the 'thirties, lolled and perched side by side on the sofa.

The two were on their second drinks and Lund was reaching for Tevy Dallam's empty glass when he heard Anderson ask Althea, "How did you enjoy our Rosie's wee fan letters?" The fat lower lip was pinched as if it still bore an aftertaste of Saturday night.

"Fan letters?" Tevy's free hand swirled the heaven-blue and white ruffles that foamed over her ankles. "Fan letters for Rose? Whatever for?"

"Didn't you know your sister's a writer?" Anderson's tone was a taunt.

The fingers on Tevy's glass were suddenly rigid. "You do manage to have everything, don't you, Rose!"

"Oh dear," Mrs. Sharon began a plaintive bleat. "I haven't seen those letters yet. You promised ..."

Rose Dallam seemed to be studying her bare brown knees. "I can't find the letters." She was wearing a finely-made playsuit, shorts and high-collared shirt of white linen, with a tight-sleeved scarlet bellhop jacket. In spite of Tevy's long skirts, she looked the lady of the two. "I had quite a hunt just before we came up here. I guess I must have used them for kindling."

"How mean!" sobbed out Althea. "Now I may never see a real fan letter."

"There, there, baby," Anderson patted her arm. "You wait till you publish your adventures, and I'll write you one you'll want to frame. And so will Wintie."

"Will you," asked Tevy, "Wintie?"

But Winton didn't hear her. With passionate concentration he was looking at Rose, who had turned her head from the group toward the blue windblown lake.

Tevy relinquished her glass to Lund and her long fingers clasped her knees. She raised her voice. "Wintie, how do you like my sister's profile?"

Everyone was looking at her now and Anderson gurgled, "He loves it."

The wings of Roger Winton's nose widened angrily but his voice was cool. "I like everything about your sister."

"By the way, Tevy," said Lund, "I got the screw out of the phonograph. I think I have one in my kit that will fix you up, as soon as I locate my smallest screwdriver."

"Oh, thank you, Eric," Tevy spoke with exaggerated charm. "Henceforth we can play my sister's favorite song. I could sing it for you now."

Rose stirred uneasily on her chair and took a drink from her half-filled glass.

"No," said Tevy. "I'm better as a whistler." Clear, true, and high she began to pipe the tune that Lund had heard Rose singing low in the boat. "*Remember me. Remember me, but ah, forget my fate!*" Now it sounded gay, and strident; suddenly on the highest note it broke and stopped.

"Fluffed it again!" said Tevy. "I think I'll just tell you now how my sister's favorite song begins. *When I am laid in earth* … but," her smile for Winton seemed fixed in bright paint, "I wouldn't count too much on that if I were you."

Anderson laughed loudly. Winton went on looking at Tevy.

"Roger, would you like to marry my sister?"

Winton's head jerked slightly back as if he had received a blow. His eyes for a moment seemed to Lund desperate and lost. Then, whirling around gracefully, he bowed low.

"Rose," he said, "will you marry me?"

Rose Dallam was on her feet, standing at the cabin door. "Thank you, no." Her words were lighter than her tone. "I have a prior engagement. To burn my little sister at the stake. I'm going out now to gather faggots." She waved back Winton's forward stride. "No accessories, please." The door closed behind her.

But almost at once it was opened again and by Eric Lund. Whatever drama he might miss inside the cabin was of little value compared with the loss of the glass that Rose was carrying away.

When he got outside, she had taken the few steps to the lodge path and there encountered Mart Bryan.

"Hello," he heard her say, "how about a drink?"

"Okay." Mart took hold of her wrist and guided the glass to his lips. He looked up, swallowed quickly, and said, "Hi, Mr. Lund."

"Come in and have a fresh drink," said Lund, taking the glass carefully from Rose. Her cheeks were flushed but her hand was steady and so was her smile. Good girl, he thought, she's already got herself in hand.

"I can't. I've still got to fill Sharon's wood box. Here," he turned shyly to Rose, tugging at his hip pocket. "I thought maybe you'd like to take a look at this. It's the summer school catalogue of the 'U.'"

As the thick pamphlet emerged, something slim and bright came with it and fell to his feet.

"Uh-oh," Mart stooped for it. "I forgot I slipped that in my pocket. It's Winton's knife."

The cabin door opened quietly and Tevy came hesitantly down the path. Eric Lund, the only one to notice her, thought there were tears in her eyes. Then she took a determined stride forward. "What have you got there?"

"Winton's knife. Isn't it a beauty?" It lay flat on Mart's palm, a hunting knife, keen, broad-bladed, finely balanced. "I had to cut a wedge for one of his screens. I'd left my knife up in the bunkhouse and this was lying on his table. I must have stuck it in my pocket without thinking."

"And what are you going to do with it?"

"Give it back to him. What do you think!"

"I want it!"

The determination in Tevy's tone made Rose glance up sharply from the open catalogue.

"What are you going to do with it?" Mart demanded.

"Just what you were, of course." She closed her hand over the hilt.

"I don't fool around with a knife as sharp as that." Mart let her have it. "I'd better get going."

"Rose," Tevy went over to her sister whose head was again bent over the University bulletin. "Rose," she repeated. "I'm—sorry." She slipped her arm around the small straight shoulders and again Lund saw tears in her eyes.

"It's all right, Tev," Rose closed her pamphlet. "Let's go to dinner. We'll see you at the lodge, Mr. Lund?"

"And thank you," Tevy called, "for giving me such a nice party to spoil!"

Tall and blond in her soft blue gown, Rose's brown head just reaching her shoulder and Rose's slim red-clad arm around her waist, Tevy moved away along the woodland path, and as Lund watched them go, he saw the yellow light of early evening glint, now and again from Tevy's swinging right hand which still held Roger Winton's hunting knife.

twelve
MONDAY. JULY 13

"Hello! Rik?"

Leaning against the kitchen wall of the lodge, Lund answered the casual voice of Peter Larson.

"Swell day," Pete was saying. "I'd like to try a little trout fishing this morning. Yes, brook trout. If you're just hanging around, why don't you drive down and meet me at the Pine River bridge?"

"Well, thanks, Pete," Lund spoke along the twenty-party line, over which not more than half the subscribers were breathing audibly. "I'm not much of a trout fisherman but Anderson did all right, Thursday."

"How about ten o'clock? I'll throw some things in the car you might like to read. An old *Manhattan* and two or three biographies that aren't too bad."

"They will be much enjoyed." Eric Lund hung up the receiver and twisted the tail of the old wall phone with satisfaction.

Rose and Tevy Dallam lay prone on their small dock, bare toes dangling over the lake, heads propped on elbows just within the shade of the poplars by the shore. Rose was reading the University catalogue. Tevy was eating the chipmunk's peanuts.

"There's a beginning course in psychology," Rose said more to herself than to Tevy. "I don't know whether they'd let me into anthropology class, my first term."

"Why do you want to take that stuff?" Tevy generously tossed a snip of peanut toward an advancing chipmunk who fled in terror. "It isn't as if you had to do anything."

"I should do nothing? I should know nothing?"

"Oh, I suppose it's more fun to do something—part of the time anyway. You could be a model as easily as I can. Lots of filthy rich girls do things like that. At least, they do in the comics. There aren't any working for our agency. But you really could."

"What about you? You don't just want to go on this way, do you?" Rose spoke shyly. "Tevy, when I get my ... when Grandmother's estate is settled, you and Elizabeth are going to be independent. Dad can't stop that. Then you can do what you like. What—what do you want to do,

Tevy?"

Tevy rolled over on her left side, her disheveled blond head resting at the edge of the dock. Just beneath her chin, in a tiny backwater, a huge frog was supporting his neck on a half-submerged twig.

"I want to have a good time. I'm finding out it's hard to do."

Rose's voice was small and hard. "Dad would rather have had a good time, too."

"You think Dad's perfect, don't you? You don't have to live with him." Tevy grabbed the twig and overturned the frog. "It's like living with an iron rod or a marble pillar. I know he's the soul of honor, but what did it get him except a terrible beating? What good actually did it do anybody?"

"It's possible that, in the last eighteen months, not quite so many people have died."

Tevy did not speak or turn her head. In an otherwise rather frightening silence Rose could hear the buzz of a sawyer beetle boring through the wood pile. She sat up, timidly holding out a package of cigarettes.

"Want to smoke?— He hasn't been such a wonderful father to me, either, Tevy. If he hadn't been completely stony about having promised my mother to leave me always with Grandmother, I could have lived with him, and Elizabeth would have been swell to me, and you would really be my sister."

Tevy, half-turning her head, put out a hand for the cigarettes. "But," she said, "you wouldn't have had—all the money."

Rose looked into hostile eyes. "Have you really cared so much about that, Tevy? You want a good time. How much fun do you think it was, living in hotels with Grandmother and playing bridge with her old cronies from the time I could sit up to a table? It wasn't any more fun in Cannes or Cairo than it was in Swampscott or Pinehurst. And you know I loathed St. Prisca's and the hounds."

She lay down again on the dock, her back to Tevy's, breathing quickly, counting the ripples that flowed toward her like meshes of bright gold wire.

"You remember that Christmas?" Tevy spoke in a different manner, older, bitterly amused. "You don't know what I told Jim East about you. It's the way I felt about you then. It's funny."

Rose did not move, and Tevy went on, "I said my half-sister was the filthy rich granddaughter of Mrs. Edgar Warren Bridge. I said you were old, kind of, a stick-in-the-mud who just wanted to sit at home with the family. I said, 'I like her, but you wouldn't.'"

Rose went on staring down into the water where on the brown

bottom a dozen fallen trees lay drowned.

"I said it was funny," repeated Tevy. "All the men are crazy about you now."

"The Sweetheart of Midaywin," murmured Rose. "I'm Verne Anderson's Rosebud."

"And Scarface Eric Lund's and Mart Bryan's and Wint's."

"Tevy," Rose leaned over the dockside and gave a vicious tug to a hard-knotted yellow lily, "where did you know Mart?"

"He says I never did."

The lily head snapped off in Rose's fingers, the bright short petals broken apart. Ashamed she dropped them slowly back upon the water, turning her eyes from the bare ugly stalk still rooted in the lake.

"Do we have to be like this?" she asked gently.

"No," said Tevy, calmly. "We really don't."

"Let's get away from all these damned men. We could go down to Petit Port tomorrow morning on the Wilderness and pick up my car and go on to Fort William or anywhere you'd like."

"We could," Tevy stretched and sat up. "But this is still today, and I think here comes something we have to do about it."

Down the steep path from the highway to their cabin door a man was descending. For a moment after she recognized Winton, Rose did not stir.

"Right after lunch," she said, "I'm going on a long walk, and alone."

"Huh!" said Tevy.

"It's a four-mile hike through the woods to North Star Lake. I'm ..."

Roger Winton strolled slowly toward the dock, saying in a languid, faintly insulting tone, "I want playmates."

"One will do," Rose got up and started toward the cabin. "Tevy's getting herself a canoe after lunch. You could go along and keep her out of Hag's Nook."

"No, thank you," Winton drawled. "Where are you going, honey?" he came to Rose. "I'm coming, too."

"Oh no! I'm going to get dressed for lunch. You and Tev go on up to the lodge and I'll be along in a few minutes."

"I like these—clothes." His fingers just touched the bare skin between her belt and the high midriff.

"So do mosquitoes," said Rose.

"She's going on a long, long walk through the woods," Tevy explained. "Just Rose, all alone with the bugs." Head flung back, hands in pockets, she was smiling as she had on the night of her surprise arrival.

Winton barely glanced at her. His hands clasped Rose's elbows and with a fierce low intensity he said, "I'm going with you. You know I will. Don't you? Don't you, darling?"

Rose pulled away from his half-welcome clasp. "I presume you will," she said.

"I shall. I will." He laughed. "Meantime, I'll do everything you ask. Come along, little sister," he beckoned to Tevy. "Let's go climb up in our highchairs and tie on our bibs."

"Aw-wight!" With exaggerated baby obedience, Tevy scampered to his side, but in the lift of her brows, the tilt of her lashes, as she glanced from Winton to Rose and back again, there was a slow teasing insolence that did not belong to a child.

"Martin, you've got everything straight?" Mrs. Fitts slapped down the green eyeshade that was her symbol of driving to Petit Port and prepared to mount the Command car. "You pick out the best seventy-five-pound canoe for Tevy Dallam and then you take Mrs. Sharon in one of the boats over to Collins Island, and don't forget to bring their boat back. Give every door and screen a good going over. I don't want a word of complaint out of the Collinses when they come up to the cabin, next week. Mrs. Sharon can 'explore' the island while you're working around. Take along a bottle of 6-12 for her insect bites and some mercurochrome. She's bound to skin those bare legs on the rocks."

Mart, she thought, looked sulky, a little because of taking Mrs. Sharon but more because he'd just seen Rose Dallam turning into North Star Trail with that Winton. Mrs. Sharon was droopy, too, and probably for the same reason. She was tucking a notebook into her pack-sack. Not another thing in that sack, Mrs. Fitts guessed.

"Averill!" she barked him back from a daft gaze at three mounds rising on Tevy Dallam's chest. "Look here at me! You're to keep house."

The Dallam girl laughed. "Don't go crazy, Mr. Fitts! The central object is functional, but not nature." She pulled through the neck of her tight black T-shirt an orange of remarkable symmetry and size. "I've already got my pockets full. It'll be hot and thirsty on the lake."

Mr. Fitts gave a futile little hitch to his precarious pants. "Yes, my dear," he said to his wife.

"Well, that takes care of everything for you four. I'll get going."

A fifth, however, she had not foreseen. Out of the undergrowth between the car and the woodpile, there now waddled, with hair like a frantic slattern and the face of a cretin pig, an individual of that race frequently described as the stupidest thing in the woods. Seeing the four monsters in his path, his dull eyes grew dense with fear and he kept on going at his fastest possible pace, which was appreciably slower than a walk.

"Oh, oh!" cried Althea Sharon, and then in a high shrill note, "Oh! Oh!

Oh!"

One step took Mrs. Fitts to the woodpile, one hand grasped a stick and brought it down straight behind the porcupine's nose. With a little "snouf!" the creature flopped and died.

"They kill the trees. Dispose of it, Mart," said Mrs. Fitts, got into her car and drove away.

"Poor little porky," old Averill knelt beside the suddenly shrunken body. "It's such a natural animal." He put a finger into the half-open muzzle. "See the orange teeth."

"O-range teeth?" Althea asked throatily, bending beside him. "This is an adventure, isn't it?"

"For the porcupine," Tevy Dallam laughed. "His last."

Mr. Fitts looked at her with dislike. "It was a brutal blow," he said in an angry voice.

"I'll take him now, Mr. Fitts," Mart reached down for the tail and made for the woods. Back almost at once, he said in a tone not unsuitable to the right-hand man of Mrs. Fitts:

"Come along, Mrs. Sharon. I can't wait." And started for the dock.

Althea Sharon turned to Averill Fitts' rough gray head, still bowed over the spot where the porcupine had lain.

"Mr. Fitts," she said softly, "I think it was horrible to kill it."

"Do you?" He looked at her with a sweet, somewhat toothless smile.

"I do," her blank black eyes now included Mart's retreat in the total picture of brutality. "I shall not go in that boat!" she said spunkily. "I shall go up to my own dear cabin and write down every word of this for my adventures."

Too saddened at the moment to appraise her leaps up the slope, Mr. Fitts turned to his tasks. From within the lodge he pantingly transported the most deeply cushioned chair to the edge of the highway, set the door ajar so that the west breeze blowing through the lakeside windows would fan but not really strike him, and slopping himself all over the seat, he drew from under the cushion a book dearer to him than to less sensitive hearts. Prolonging the anticipatory moment before opening its spotted old cover, he looked about him at the clichés of nature: the bees around the flowers and the butterflies in the dust. He heard cries from far out over the lake "crazy as a loon." Some of them by loons, Mr. Fitts discriminated, others imitations by Miss Tevison Dallam.

Sighing at the pretty girl's lack of tenderness for dead nature, and for the whole coarse reality of life, he turned to page one of *Heart Throbs*.

Verne Anderson stretched and yawned on his bed. His sunburn made him feel sleepy and a little sick, and anyway, he might as well relax while he could. In just a day or two, when he had thought things out, he'd be pulling out of here. The old Dodge, he hoped, would get over the Wilderness Trail this time without kicking the gravel up into its own guts, and that would be its last trip; that is, with him at the wheel. A new car, something snazzy, maybe even a Lincoln like the Dallam girl's, and then, after a little, the kind of girl to go with the car. But not Rose Dallam, nor even Tevy; he knew his kind of girl.

Picking gently at the scab of a mosquito bite on his pudgy arm, he thought for a sorrowful moment of Rose, and the business that might have been. Perhaps someday?

Too dangerous. Anything about women was dangerous. They got jealous over everything and ruined the works. Still, it was lonesome, doing business without a woman, tougher than he had expected.

The spot where the scab pulled off was bleeding a little so he padded on flat fat feet to the bureau to get cotton. Through the window he could see Lund rowing down toward the Dallams' place to fix the phonograph, as he'd said. Anderson wished he'd thought of that one himself, but he hadn't, and anyway it didn't have much importance now. Lund was a simple sort of a feller, smart enough in his way, but you couldn't make deals with him. Just the kind of a feller you'd expect to find in a place like this, and damned if he wasn't about the only one here who was.

"I like it here." From the Collins dock Tevy flung out her arms toward the wide sweep of Midaywin, rippling in the mild west wind. To her left a dozen islands stood out sharp and green; to the right, past the length of Collins and the shores of Mystery, the blue expanse slowly narrowed through the mile-long approach to the Dark Arm.

"Look as long as you like," said Mart, "but if you want me to shove you off, it'll have to be now. I've got to get to work."

"Mart," she whirled to face him. "Listen, Mart...."

"Yeah?"

"I—want to ask you something."

"Yeah?"

"Mart, do you—are you in love with Rose?" Seeing his face stiffen, she went on quickly, "Because if you are, it would be awfully—convenient."

"Oh?" he said. "For who?"

"For—Rose."

"You wouldn't mean for you?"

"Of course not! You see, well, I think you'd be just swell for her. You'd be awfully sensible about her money. And decent. I don't want Rose to get a dirty deal in life. She's too innocent."

As he still stood rocklike, she added, faster, "I should think it would be convenient for you, too. After all, if you're going to college …" He was moving now, coming toward her, and the hands at his sides knotted in hard fists.

"Did you ever stop to think what could happen to a girl like you?" It was a very quiet voice; all the fire was in the blue eyes. "Plenty could happen. It could happen right here today."

The North Star Trail was not a road. From the moment they left the highway, a few rods opposite the Honeymoon cabin, and passed the scarlet chest that held equipment for fighting forest fires, Rose and Roger Winton were in the woods. Over a path soft, now with moss, now with anthills, they moved through deep green, the color broken only by gray boulders and white birch logs cut and piled when the path was made.

Ferns met over the path, sometimes as high as Rose's breast. She pushed them gently aside, liking their rough touch and the sunny aromatic smell that lingered on her fingers. She loved this short strip of cedar woods with a rare white streak of birch, and just ahead, the sudden birch grove with bright blue between the trees which could be lake or sky. But how did she feel about the man who walked behind her, a little too near and much too quiet?

Well, she thought, he isn't going to seduce me on a rock or an anthill. And certainly not here!

They had arrived at a small slimy pool surrounded by white rocks. Roots of four fallen pines, thick and hairy with earth, hung over the rocks, resembling a group of dirty old mammoths joined like Siamese quadruplets, and all thirsty.

"God!" said Winton.

"Mosquito Eden. Here's the 6-12. Rub it all over your neck. Don't miss a crack."

"You do it for me?"

"I haven't the Nightingale touch."

He handed back the bottle, and as she buttoned it into the pocket of her green jacket, his arms came around her, pressing her back against him.

"What kind of touch have you, honey?" he laughed against her hair. "Aren't you ready to show me?"

"No," she said, and was surprised and glad that her voice was so cold.

"You didn't come out here with me to take an eight-mile walk." His cheek was brushing back and forth against her forehead. "You came out to love me. Didn't you?"

"I did not." She gave an angry pull clear away from him. "I came to walk, and walk alone. I didn't ask you to come. I didn't want you to come."

"Oh no?" His eyes, dark and mocking, laughed at her. "Oh yes! I know what you want. But you aren't quite ready to admit it. You can't be quite honest yet, can you?"

She bit her lip, facing him, too angry to be afraid.

"Go along," his eyes taunted her. "Do your eight miles alone, if you've got what it takes!"

She turned away then and started toward North Star, hearing his voice, soft now with meaning. "When you get back, honey, I'll be waiting. On the chance that you might want—to see me, as much as I want you."

Then his footsteps sounded behind her, quicker and fainter, and when she at last looked back, he was out of sight.

Alone with her anger and with the painful conflict he had aroused, she walked on and on, tripping over a snarl of roots, bruising her ankle on the teeth of small rocks, jumping aside just in time to avoid the unformed smear of a bear. She passed small lakes half-seen through the trees, descended a sharp hill between the grapelike leaves of thimbleberries starred with bland white blossoms, and toiled hotly up a high ridge, jeered by a flippant red squirrel.

At the top she came for the first time to a strip of virgin cedar, with strong, green-black boughs and trunks in gray intricate folds. She took a deep breath, and the heat left her, the anger and passion and the jealousy she had hated and feared when she had first thought of Tevy at Midaywin. For this hour at least in peace Rose walked forward between the great trees.

Althea Sharon opened her notebook and picked up her rose-pink pen. The day was almost gone and she hadn't written a word. But it had been a very restful afternoon and she felt so relaxed.

And now how should she begin? So many adventures you simply couldn't describe in detail, particularly not if you really yearned to be published in the *Atlantic* and the *National Geographic*. And perhaps this wasn't really an adventure; it happened too often and to quantities of people.

She pushed the pink pen through her mussed old curls; her eyes, not quite so blank as usual, pulled closer together as she thought....

The pen came down to the notebook and Althea began slowly and very clearly to write:

Today for the first time in my life, I have seen a murder. I had never before beheld a murdered corpse.

She stopped there, reading over the sentences and wondering if the second was true.

thirteen
MONDAY NIGHT. JULY 13

The canoe was drawn up on the Dallams' dock, an orange peel clinging to a rib, a black-and-white pirate scarf flung down on a kapok pillow: gay like Tevy, careless like Tevy.

The cabin was empty and so neat that it was impossible to believe that Tevy had recently been there. No shoes on the gray-painted floor that looked cool and blue in the late afternoon light; no smell of sweet spilled powder to overpower the sun-warmed cedars now making a soft gloom around the windows; no hollow in the red and green blanket where it was Tevy's way to flop flat the minute she entered the house.

Rose, coming back to the quiet room after her rough walk, felt the enticement of her own smooth bed. Alone here for the first time since Tevy's arrival, she wanted to lie with her face in the pillow as she had lain four mornings ago: before Mrs. Sharon's red hat had bobbed through the trees; before Verne Anderson had popped in with his leers and his references to *Manhattan*; before she and Roger Winton had paddled lightly over the lake and he had said as lightly, "Darling, I love you." Before a dead woman had risen from the depths of Midaywin.

But there was something she must do while she was still alone: destroy Elizabeth's letter which, if read by chance, would hurt and anger Tevy. Yes, there it was in the file case, just as she had wadded it awkwardly, the night of Tevy's sudden appearance. As she pulled out the ungainly ball, a thin folder it had held erect flopped over and spread apart. Lifting it, too, for realignment, she recognized with mild surprise the two folded sheets that slipped between the covers. The fan letters, the note from the futile old gentlewoman and the brash explosion directed to Miss Thorn Dallam.

Fine hunter I was yesterday, thought Rose, dropping the letters back into the case and snapping it shut. Tevy had been watching then, amused and curious, as she laced the blue ribbons of her sandals between her bright-painted toes, and Rose very conscious of her stepmother's letter, must have riffled too hastily through this very folder.

Over the open lid of the stove she set a match to the balled paper, and in the intense quiet listened to the tiny crackle as the flame spread toward her fingers.

Suddenly a sharp short sound broke the stillness. A crack like a .22 shot. Almost at once there followed a thud and then a splash. Her heart pounding, Rose rushed out to the dock and strained her eyes toward the opposite shore of Lake Midaywin.

No one was visible on land or water. The leaves were fixed in motionless air but above a rocky cove where a small poplar had stuck obstinately to the thin soil, there now stood only a gray stump with a long white gash.

She sped back to the cabin for her field glasses, and returned to train them on the frightening shore.

Not far from the rocks a long U of ripples began to form on the flat lake. Something like a long stick was moving steadily forward, and as her focus sharpened, she saw the black nose that propelled it. The beaver, smart little beast, had gnawed the poplar through at just the angle to send it crashing into the lake and was now bringing it across to add to his timber she had already seen on her shore.

"What in hell are you looking at?"

Winton's voice broke into her delight.

"Oh! Just a minute, Wint. I thought I heard a shot and …" She went on admiring the beaver.

"When?"

"When what?"

"Oh, for God's sake! When did you hear the shot?"

"But I didn't." She lowered the glasses and turned to his angry face. "There wasn't a shot. It was the beaver."

"Make sense!"

"The beaver," she repeated patiently. "He gnawed down that tree over there. See what he's doing with it now."

He gave a quick look through the glass. "Cute," he commented without enthusiasm. "So Tevy's back." He gestured toward the small litter in the canoe. "How was your walk?"

"All right." The reminder of their parting sharpened her tone. "Wint, have you seen Tevy around the lodge or anywhere?"

"No.— Rose," he did not try to touch her but in his deepened tone and the fatigue of his face there was a plea she had to hear. "You know how I feel about you. Can you forgive the crudity, this afternoon?"

"Yes," she said rather stiffly.

"Thanks." The life had suddenly gone out of his features which now wore the languid look of the night he had arrived. He turned from her and with no other word climbed up the bank to the highway.

Watching him go, Rose felt rejected and lonely. She hadn't, she was sure, wanted a repetition of the scene on the North Star Trail, but neither did she enjoy being "my half-sister" who was old, kind of, and just liked to sit at home waiting for Tevy.

The first hour of that waiting was the shortest of the four that began with the crash of the beaver's tree. It was fairly easy to pretend that this was another golden July evening like those of a week ago, to go through the small pleasant performances of chipmunk feeding, a letter to her father, a swim. Dressing, she chose the gold shirt that Mart liked, and the second hour went less well, as she prepared the salad and sandwiches for two that might be eaten by one, and tried to evade any thought or feeling about Tevy's interim diversions.

Soon after seven she heard the Wilderness Express rumble up the grade above her rooftop. Now Mart would come with the mail. Mart and probably Tevy. When they come, she assured herself, I'll be kind, I'll be gay, I mustn't show that I care. And do I really? During the third long hour, she gave herself several answers, none entirely honest, ate a little supper and drank a great deal of black coffee.

Then darkness came, the forest darkness with the myriad small tensions. Tonight, on Mystery Island, a booby owl set up the weirdest of all moans, and now Rose, abandoning all pretense, paced the narrow cabin, fingernails digging deep into her folded arms. What ought I to do? What ought I ...? She still shrank from intruding on Tevy's fun, but for the first time she began seriously to face a nameless worry. Had something happened to Tevy?

It would be smarter to go up to the lodge, to get a bitter bracing pill of Mrs. Fitts' personality or to swallow the sweet old-fashioned nostrum of Mr. Fitts' music than to sicken here with her own fancies and the owl's ghostly whine. She set off, then, along the hidden path by the lake, to find the answer to her fears, carrying a pretended reason in her hand.

The familiar lighted lounge of Midaywin seemed strange and aloof as she stood blinking in the doorway, and so did the people gathered in two small groups. Mr. Fitts' coarse gray hair was flung back in creative confusion as he groped along the keys of his battered upright, with Mrs. Sharon in dirndl and ruffles curled girlishly in a wicker chair beside him, and writing big black words on a pad of yellow paper. Lund, Anderson, and Roger Winton were seriously playing bridge with Mrs. Fitts.

"Your sister's missing?" Mrs. Fitts didn't like the interruption. "Well, Mart isn't here either."

Verne Anderson laughed, of course, and Mr. Lund asked if Rose wouldn't like to take his hand. Wint, deep in the strategy of the game, spared her a vacant smile.

"Did Tevy have dinner here?" Rose persisted gently.

"Redouble. No," said Mrs. Fitts.

"But she was here an hour ago," Althea Sharon volunteered. "We saw her, Mr. Winton and I."

"I didn't see her," Winton corrected in an abstracted voice. "I thought I heard her whistling."

"Oh she was, right outside the window, and I saw her, too. You know the way she did at Mr. Lund's party?" Mrs. Sharon's puckered lips emitted a fair imitation of Tevy's disaster with *Remember me* … "It was about half past eight, just before the others came in and they all started playing bridge."

"Thanks," said Rose.

"She isn't a very thoughtful little sister, is she?"

"I brought you that stuff you wanted." She held it out ungraciously. "Those fan letters. You can have them if you'll promise not to look at them now. They're too silly for anyone to see but you."

"Oh I promise," Mrs. Sharon clasped them, not at all offended. "I won't open them till I'm all alone in my wee bed tonight." For once her eyes didn't seek the men.

Without saying good night, Rose went out to the dark Trail. Back alone to my own wee bed, she murmured, and did not find it funny. The tension of the long waiting hours rose up in a hot bitter wave. Tevy impudently whistling, mocking her with the song that had once touched off Rose's pity for Tevy's own fate. Tevy laughing, Tevy dancing the 'Sugar-Foot.' Tevy and Mart.

For the first time in her restrained life, she felt the words running along her nerves: I can't take it. I can't take it. Quickened by anger, her steps fled over the road, stumbled, turned off sharply at a path.

She was halfway up the stony slope to the bunkhouse before realization stopped her, breathless and shamed. She, Rose Dallam, had been about to spy on her sister, to play Peeping Tom at her lovemaking.

If they were in the cabin, if they had seen or heard her … Above her in the moonless night she could barely discern roof and walls, soundless, and—could she hope?—eyeless.

And then into her moment of weak trembling relief there burst the sound of whistling. Not Tevy's and not from above. Strong, masculine, mounting steadily towards her. Rocks and underbrush cruelly bordering the path, Mart's house above her, and a few yards below, swinging a towel at the white streak of his bare chest, Mart himself. She sank down on the rough ground, her face burrowing helplessly into shaking hands.

She heard him stop and jerk out, "Who's there?" and then he was beside her on the ground, drawing her to him, holding her defenseless. "Rose," he said, lifting her face to his, and then more urgent, "Rose."

She did not pull away as she had from Winton. Her arms went round his shoulders, and feeling the cool skin grow warm beneath her hands, she found the one word she needed, "Dear."

A moment later she gave a sharp moan.

"Did I hurt you?"

"Not you. Just a rock under my elbow!"

"And you're sitting on my wet swimming trunks. What a way to love."

"It's not too bad a way," said Rose, getting up.

"Come on to the bunkhouse and I'll change." He pulled at her hand. "What's the matter?"

In the second of broken contact the reason that had brought her here stood out harsh and clear. "Where," she asked coldly, "is Tevy?"

"Tevy? I don't know. I haven't seen her since early afternoon."

She brushed off his encircling arm. "She isn't up there?"

"In my bunkhouse? Are you crazy?"

"I asked you if she's there."

"You're coming up." His arm came back with no gentle grasp, pushing her ahead of him up the slope and over the sill.

"Take a good look," he snapped on the swinging bulb. "Don't forget to crawl under the bed."

"Mart," tears started on her cheeks and her hands mussed her hair more wildly than he had done, "Mart, I'm sorry. I don't know why I ..."

The light went off and they were together again. "Crazy," he repeated against her cheek. "I don't even like Tevy."

"Don't you? Oh Mart, I ..."

"You what? You what?"

"I—love you."

"That's okay with me."

But when he drew away from her and went to the darkest corner to dress, she knew that something was far from right. For if Tevy had not been with Mart, where was she now? Except for Mrs. Sharon's glimpse of her, whistling on the dark road, no one seemed to have seen her for hours. Why had she wandered about, hungry and alone?

"Mart, I've got to find Tevy. She may be hurt or—in the lake."

He said soberly, "We'll look around, as soon as I've done one more odd job for Sharon."

"I've done a nice little job for her tonight," Rose said. "At last I've given her the fan letters."

He made no response. At the foot of the slope he said, "Wait for me here," and went off toward the lodge. She didn't know how long she waited, the cloak of her new warmth pierced now and then by anxiety for Tevy. Around her in the bushes were soft animal sounds and around her neck and ankles were sharp insect stings that punctured romance. Out on the road the mosquitoes thinned, and she began walking slowly toward the camp buildings, thinking with the happy unaccustomed thrill of companionship: We'll find Tevy, Mart and I, we'll find her.

She reached the lodge, now in complete darkness, and still Mart did not appear on the Trail. Again she waited, standing by the mail box, slapping at the mosquitoes, feeling tired and thirsty.

The pump, she knew, was just behind the poplars, close to the cabin that stood empty between Verne Anderson's cabin and the lodge. She could get a drink without fear of waking anyone and be back on the Trail in a minute.

In the light of the stars she found the line of the path leading to the pump, her feet feeling ahead for unexpected roots or rocks. What finally stopped her dead was soft. She stood over it, fearful, and from the ground there came a low moan. As if, she thought wildly, she had trod on the booby owl.

She knew she must stoop and touch it, and finally, she did. Around the soft mass her feet had encountered was a layer thin and stiff. A shoulder in an organdy sleeve. She felt the curls, the neck and bodice, the folds of skirt, the arms flung wide, the empty hands. The heart, she thought, was beating and there seemed to be no blood.

As Rose got weakly to her feet and started toward human help, one further point, small and irrelevant, registered in her dazed mind. The fan letters were gone.

fourteen
MONDAY NIGHT. JULY 13

In a wide-armed rustic chair before his cabin fireplace, Eric Lund also was thinking about letters; letters and their writers. The chair had deep cushions to pad exhausted fishermen, but Lund sat erect, abstractedly rubbing the bowl of his pipe against his palm.

Just letters? Or the Documents in the Case, potential Exhibits numbered A to Z? The extortion letter sent to the Senator; the Senator's reply, withheld until Lund and Larson could reach and await its arrival in Petit Port; Rose Dallam's fan letters from the impudent Philip Carter and from Miss Emily Mary Walker, the genteel lady addressed by her

Midaywin correspondent "Kitty" as a somewhat rougher character: these pieces of the puzzle Lund had secured in the ordinary way of his profession. Chance and a hand, careless or frightened, had flung him another piece via a garbage can and a large black bear. A faint smile curved the mouth that Mrs. Sharon found sinister as he recalled a small soggy leather case, holding a card smeared with red.

Tonight in the city of New York, while he sat by the fireside in the silent, close-pressed North Woods, agents might now be closing in on Miss Emily Mary Walker who could be almost any kind of person, even an old lady with a quiet passion for genealogy. Soon, he too must make an arrest, but he still hoped that time or a lucky break might hand him all those involved or prove decisively that, at the Midaywin end, one criminal had worked alone.

Turning a screeching reamer around and around in the bowl of his pipe he considered the sketchy biographies Peter Larson had collected, beginning with Petit Port knowledge and opinion concerning Averill and Ida Fitts. Mrs. Fitts was a city woman but people had almost forgotten it. Twenty years ago she had come to the North Shore as housekeeper for some high-ups from New York who owned a big show place. After a few summers they tired of it and left. She stayed and got married.

Averill Fitts? There were several like him in Petit Port as there are in all towns on the fringe of the wilderness, where life, an endless economic struggle to fishermen, lumbermen and resort owners, seems a pure and simple idyll to the urban misfits with small independent incomes. Of the local quota, some painted, some wrote, some sat. Averill Fitts played the piano a little, drank a little, and received from the more austere and energetic members of his family a small regular allowance, a privilege Mrs. Fitts was said to have assumed at marriage in exchange for a loan equal to her life savings. So Camp Midaywin was built, and with their combined contacts and her smart management, everything, including Averill, flourished for many years. Then the buildings got old and so did Mrs. Fitts. The place was up for sale. The Fittses went South in the winters, and the last year they didn't open at all or even come back to Petit Port. Nobody seemed to know just where they were, all that time. People were surprised when they came back late this Spring and fixed the place up in a hurry, but didn't want to be listed with the Tourist Information Center. And in spite of their age and the size of the camp, they hired just Mart Bryan.

Mart Bryan, the fine American boy, looked you straight in the eye, and if his own eye was hard, that meant strength of character, and if he was close-mouthed, that was reticence ...? Lund slightly shook his narrow head. Born in Petit Port. Oldest son of a widow. Five years ago graduated from high school—which not too many local boys did. Resort worker, guide, garage helper while he was in school and afterward in Duluth, and then he's gone off ("around Chicago or somewhere in the east, Cleveland or maybe New York"). He came back to Petit Port on the 30th of June, and the next day went to work at Midaywin.

What was wrong with the record? Nothing, perhaps, but Martin must now be added to the others,—Verne Anderson, Winton, Mrs. Sharon—who, in time if not intent, had followed Rose Dallam to Midaywin. Mart had come two days after Rose's arrival. Had he trailed her there? Had they already been friends, or had he traced her through Tevison? By the girl's own words, spoken the night she had arrived, on the half-lit dock, Mart under another name had known Tevy in another place. And, eighteen months ago he could have been involved in the enigmatic Dallam trouble which seemed to have been especially Tevy's. He could have been anywhere—including prison.

Each of these four people had shown a strong ambivalent interest in Rose, which, in spite of overtones of desire, jealousy and frustration, could be solidly based on the estate of the late Mrs. Edgar Warren Bridge. But only those persons functioning in the Senator's blackmail case now nearing its end were of active importance to Eric Lund.

He rose to fling another birch stick on the fire and reached to straighten on the stone mantel the leaning photograph of his wife and child. This was the first case in which he had used his private life for a screen, and that, perhaps, was what made the characters he had to deal with seem meaner and dirtier than usual. On the other hand, it was rare to come across in his work a person he could imagine as a friend of Janet's, and he felt that way—with reservations—about Rose Dallam.

In all the present darkening confusion, Lund saw Rose as victim. Tevy was a potential troublemaker; trouble was made for Rose. And yet, there were two things: one she had done, one she had not. She had not made a clear choice between two men, and she had published a little story in *Manhattan*.

"Profile of a Hero"! A man who had departed from his home town with a royal sendoff had returned, expecting a comparable welcome, and what he got was cold isolation. A year before he had been fairly convicted and sentenced for an unnamed crime. Because community opinion concerning the seriousness of his offense differed vehemently from the State's, he had departed for prison a feted hero. But by a quirk of human nature, the town now saw him in a different fashion. The important fact was that he had been in prison; the reason why didn't matter. He was an ex-convict, wasn't he, and you don't invite ex-convicts to dinner …

Less naïve than most men, Lund did not believe that all fiction is autobiography. Rose Dallam did not need to have known her hero, to have suffered a like humiliation, nor to have witnessed such social irony. But intense feeling, controlled and whittled down, had, he was certain, led her to write this bitter tale.

She had looked completely vulnerable tonight, standing on the edge of the game in which even Winton had been too absorbed to give her much attention, putting the excuse of the letters into Althea's fluttery hands, and then going off into the darkness with the jealous suspicion of her sister and Mart.

The Dallam girls, Lund thought as he crossed to the open door: Tevy, grabbing, gay or defiant, for every lure; Rose, the prestige fish. Would either of them be part of his catch? Arms leaning lightly on the door frame, he stood smoking and listening to night sounds, until there was joined a small human cry, "Come! Please come!"

After a quick step backward to pick up the powerful flash and check the time, he was out on the path where Rose was running blindly toward the light.

In front of Anderson's cabin, he met her and with a steadying hand on her shoulder, heard her short quick words.

"It's Mrs. Sharon. Just off the path. Near the first empty cabin."

"Show me," he said, flashing his torch in a wide arc ahead.

"A little more to the right."

And now the light traveling beneath the black cedars fell like a flame over white ruffles and a pinched upturned face.

Lund dropped to his knees beside Mrs. Sharon's supine body. If she had tripped on a root she shouldn't have been spread out like that. He lifted a flaccid wrist in his right hand, studying her bosom in the torch's strong beam. The white organdy blouse, loosed from the tight dirndl bodice, was bunched up toward her chin, and in the folds, at the base of Mrs. Sharon's shrunken neck, lay three dry pine needles.

He raised his head, listening, looking to the spot where Rose Dallam had shrunk into the dark. Her cry for help would have reached more than himself. Already footsteps were pounding forward from the lodge and a light shone out from Anderson's window.

Quickly he again bent over Mrs. Sharon. His long deft fingers slipped beneath her head, turned it, parted the gray curls damply matted at the base of her skull. A groan shuddered from her body.

"Get out!"

A torch strong as his own swung into Lund's face. "Take your hands off her or I'll shoot."

Behind the blinded Lund, Rose Dallam cried out, "Oh, no!"

His hand still cradling Mrs. Sharon's head, Lund spoke quietly, "Just lower your light a little, Mrs. Fitts, so that we can both get a good look at this."

For an instant, eyes smarting, he waited. Then the light descended upon the scalp between the parted curls and rested on a small star-shaped wound, reddish brown at the edges.

"Blunt implement. Broke the skin," said Lund, and looked up at the long barrel of Mrs. Fitts' Colt. "Someone hit her and she fell on her face. Then she was turned over and left spread out like this."

"You were here first," said Mrs. Fitts. She did not lower the pistol.

"No," said Lund.

The door of Anderson's cabin opened loudly, as Rose said, "I found her."

"You!" said Mrs. Fitts, and gave a harsh laugh.

"I thought," Rose's voice shook, "that it was Tevy."

Verne Anderson's round pale head peered over her shoulder. "Who is it?" He could be frightened or merely vague with sleep.

"Mrs. Sharon," Lund told him, and the face moved back into darkness. "I'm going to carry her into the lodge," he announced to the Colt.

"Take the damned thing, Averill." Mrs. Fitts stuck out her right hand to the rear.

"Oh my dear, I …" floundered Averill.

"You've got it. Mr. Lund, you bring her to the left-hand bedroom beyond the lounge. I'll have the bed ready when you get there." She gave a hard stare into the shadows. "The rest of you come along. I'm going to get to the bottom of this business and quick. You here, too, Mr. Winton?"

"Need some help?" Roger Winton came up to Lund as he rose with Mrs. Sharon in his arms.

"Better alone. Thanks."

When her lacerated head settled against him, Mrs. Sharon moaned faintly and stirred. She was slim, but nobody is light, and it was with a heavy tread that Lund walked the path to the door of the lodge, held wide by old Averill. Rose Dallam, following, gasped out details of her discovery and Winton answered with soothing murmurs. Anderson made no sound.

Across the kitchen where a tea kettle already stood over heat, and through the half-lit lounge, Lund carried his burden to the room where Mrs. Fitts helped him ease it down to a wide white bed.

"Bad?" Her face was stiff with anxiety.

"I doubt it. But keep her here and don't move her till morning."

"Doctor and ambulance can come up then from Pettyport if we need them. I'll use compresses now and give her a sleeping tablet left over from Averill's last pleurisy. That head's going to be sore when she comes to."

"I'll get the compresses ready for you, Mrs. Fitts," Rose Dallam said.

"No!" Mrs. Fitts' word was an indictment. "No one is to leave my sight. Except Averill. You," she looked up from the pillows her harsh hands were gently arranging to relieve the pressure on Mrs. Sharon's raw scalp, "you know where everything is."

For the first time since Lund had met him, Mr. Fitts did not at once scuttle off at her bidding. He stood, staring at his wife, a dazed and comic figure in a wide-open old raincoat and pajamas, eyes glassy, mouth ajar, and when his hands sought and fumbled with the drawstring of his pink pants, it wasn't to secure them but to hide the trembling of his fingers.

"Ring out the cloths right," said Mrs. Fitts without looking at him.

"Yes," he said and went, but did not add the habitual "my dear."

Looking closely at Mrs. Sharon's squeezed eyelids, Lund stated an opinion he had held for some minutes. "She's conscious," he said and watched not Althea but the others, standing back from the foot of the bed. Anderson, half-closed eyes fixed on Althea's face, was pushing his index finger in and out of his chin. Winton watched over Rose Dallam with an expression as protective as the arm he held around her shoulders. The girl showed strain, the bones of her cheeks sharpened, teeth visible between pale lips. Before long, Lund thought, she's going to burst out with something, and he was sure that, like himself, she was keenly aware of the two who were missing, her sister and Mart Bryan.

"Mrs. Sharon. Mrs. Sharon," Mrs. Fitts was repeating slowly and distinctly. "Mrs. Sharon, can you hear me?"

"I—I ..." The eyelids relaxed. "My head—something—hurts."

"Just swallow this." Mrs. Fitts held a pill and a small glass against the quivering lips. "You'll feel better right away. You've just got a little crack on the head."

Supported by Mrs. Fitts, Althea Sharon let herself be raised slightly, moaned, swallowed, and opened her eyes on the three grouped near the foot of the bed.

"Mr. Anderson!" she cried out in a stronger voice. "Oh Mr. Anderson, you'll take care of me."

There was faith in the croaked plea and pain, and from it. Verne Anderson backed away as if he had been struck. His pasty face turned red and he lifted a fat hand above his eyes as if to shade them from her bright trust.

"Huh," said Mrs. Fitts, settling Althea among the pillows. "We'll all take care of you. That is, all but one of us will. Who hit you?"

Althea gave her a dead black look. "I—don't—know."

"What happened?"

"I—I was just going—going to the pump for a drink of water. And I heard a—a wee sound and I turned my head just a little and— That's all." She closed her eyes. This, thought Lund, was a more serious job of acting than she had done on the night the bear broke in.

"But you saw somebody," declared Mrs. Fitts. "Didn't you? You saw who?"

"Just something black like a person. I don't know who. Oh, my head!"

"Tall? Or short?"

"Not too tall."

"Tall as Mr. Lund?"

Mrs. Sharon opened her eyes and gazed at the criminal scars. "No," she said with regret. "Medium."

"That could be any of the men," said Mrs. Fitts grimly.

"Or," said Mrs. Sharon with sudden strength, "it might have been that big, hulking girl."

"Tevy!" The exclamation was Winton's.

Rose Dallam took a quick step toward the bed.

"Wait," Lund commanded with an authority that checked her. "Mrs. Sharon," he spoke gently. "Someone came up behind you and knocked you down. Then while you were out, the letters Rose gave you were taken from you."

Her hands flew to the ruffles at her bosom, fumbled, and fell away. "No, oh no, Mr. Lund!" She did not look at him. "I didn't have the letters with me. I—I'd already taken them up to my cabin and," she was speaking very slowly now, "I read them there and then I tore them up and burned them. Rose said, you know that they were just silly. She didn't want them. Nobody would."

"That'll do for now." Mrs. Fitts put herself between Lund and her patient. "No one's to bother her again tonight."

No one seemed inclined to do so. Lund's attention had quietly shifted to the other three. Anderson's and Winton's faces might be expressing complete indifference, or in Winton's case, faint amusement. Color high in her cheeks, Rose Dallam, ignoring the mention of her own letters, seemed burning to raise a different issue.

"Put it by me on the floor, Averill," Mrs. Fitts ordered her husband who now entered gingerly balancing a tray of kettle, cloths and basins. "The rest of you get out while I undress her and fix her for the night. Averill'll have the gun and see that none of you leave the lounge till I get through and come out there. And," her voice grew harsher and loud, "that especially means you!"

In the doorway to receive this blast with apparent bewilderment, stood Mart Bryan.

"And keep Tevy Dallam there, too. Averill, the gun's right beside you on the nightstand. Don't act so scared of it. You know you're a good enough shot when you want to be."

"What goes on here?" demanded Mart.

"You'll know. I'll tell you or you'll tell me. Now, Mrs. Sharon, let's get you comfortable."

"Goodnight, Mrs. Sharon," Winton gave the injured woman his rare charming smile. "We'll all do our best to find the brute that hit you."

"I'm sorry you were hurt," murmured Rose, "but I know Tevy didn't do it."

"Of course not, honey," Winton soothed, and led her toward Mart, Averill and the gun.

Verne Anderson laid his round hand over Althea's twisting old fingers. "You're quite a gal," he said.

"Oh," she quavered, "thank you. Will you—would you stay with me till I fall asleep?"

"Sure," he agreed good-naturedly.

But Mrs. Fitts shook her head. "Mr. Fitts'll sit here while we all have our talk in the lounge. You trust him, too, don't you?"

"Yes," admitted Althea Sharon, faintly.

Eric Lund was the last to leave these two women who had unexpectedly become so important to him. For Mrs. Sharon was now part of his case and Mrs. Fitts by her driving questions was helping him mightily—and would doubtless continue to help him—in the business he could not yet openly pursue. He stood for a moment on the threshold of the lounge where two small lamps threw shadows under the low rafters. Old Fitts was putting the softest chair across the main entrance and himself gently into the chair, not quite forgetting to point the Colt toward the big couch in front of the fireplace. Winton relaxed on one end of it, Anderson slumped at the other, each lighting a cigarette and watching a tense little scene between Mart Bryan and Rose Dallam.

"Never mind about Mrs. Sharon now," Rose had Mart's arm in a tight grip. "Everybody's looking after her. But what about Tevy? Where's Tevy?"

"I don't know, Rose. It's just as I told you."

"Mart!" She shook his arm. "Where were you? What were you doing all that time? I waited and waited."

He put his hand over hers and held it still. "Doing just what I said I had to do."

She looked at him doubtfully and he looked straight back. "Yes, you told me." Her voice sharpened. "'One more odd job for Mrs. Sharon.' That's what you said you had to do."

"Oh?" He stepped back from her. "And you think I did it with a rock or a piece of lead pipe?"

"Oh, Mart, I ..."

"Okay, you aren't sure," he said, and turned away.

The girl stood motionless while he picked up a newspaper from the mantel, took it over to the couch, and sat down between the other two men, the paper spread out before him. Then, like a child, she crept into the nearest chair, feet tucked beneath her and small head pressed against the cushion.

On a hard bench nearby, Lund regarded her with interest. Whether or not it was related to the slugging of Althea Sharon, someone should concern himself with the problem of Tevy's absence. And if there was a relation, then Tevy also was his business. The obvious motive for the attack was the securing of the fan letters, and any letter signed Emily Mary Walker was distinctly his affair. He had not seriously considered Mrs. Sharon as a part of his case, but if she were an innocent bystander, why knock her out to get the letters which any of the men, Mart, Winton, Anderson, could have had for a caress or a bit of cajolery? Unless there was something in those seemingly inane pages that the writer did not want her to see. Of course, she had said she had read them, but that was open to doubt.

But if Althea were actually involved in the plot? Then her general woolheadedness might be considered a hazard and the letters a danger in her hands. Frightened and in pain, she had lied for someone; the letters had not been burned; she had been loyal, perhaps, to the one who had struck her down.

How many in this room were also afraid tonight? Mart, concealed behind the peach-colored sport sheet? Anderson, with his head against the back of the couch and eyes closed? Roger Winton, leaning forward into the light, his dark eyes fixed on Rose Dallam? And Rose? Lund knew he should no more exclude her from potential fear of apprehension for the crime against Mrs. Sharon, or from the criminal's habitual shrinking from any approach of the law, than he should rule out old Averill Fitts in his pink pajamas, nodding over his pistol by the door.

Until Mrs. Fitts came into the room, no one moved or spoke. She wasn't quite so light on her feet or so quick as usual, but not a pin in her hair had slipped nor a line of her hard raw face. After all the hours of cooking, serving and nursing, starch still rattled in her white dress as she went direct to her husband, motioned him toward Mrs. Sharon's room, and put the pistol down on the center table.

"We're through with the radio thriller stuff," she said. "I'm not a policeman. I'm interested in just one thing. One of my guests got hurt."

She turned to Rose Dallam and demanded, "You want those letters of yours for any reason?"

"No, I never did," Rose sat up straight in the chair. "I want to find my sister."

"All right," Mrs. Fitts ignored the second remark. "Then I've got just this to say and I mean it. Every one of you get out of my camp by nine o'clock tomorrow morning."

In the complete silence that followed, her eyes darted from one to another, among the lights and shadows of the low room.

Winton looked toward Rose with a wild and tender hope that might well be visualizing two people driving down the sunlit shore of Lake Superior in a Lincoln convertible, but Lund knew that at least one person viewed an immediate exodus from Midaywin even more blackly than did he.

"So you don't want to leave," said Mrs. Fitts. "That's very interesting. You'll all get your money back, and a first-class breakfast even if I'm up all night. Or would you rather I called Pettyport and invited the Sheriff to join the party?"

"The Sheriff." Rose was on her feet, straight and determined as Mrs. Fitts. "If Tevy …"

"You don't know she isn't back in your cabin now," Mrs. Fitts broke in. "You don't know she hasn't run off after some other boyfriend."

Mart Bryan threw down his paper and said slowly, "Do I go, too?"

"No." Her smile was broad and unpleasant. "You'll stay, and you and I will have a showdown."

"Let's have it now."

For a moment she hesitated. "'Where were you at eight thirty?" she asked, "when Tevy Dallam was wandering around the Camp? Where were you when all the commotion over finding Mrs. Sharon was going on?"

Anger or fear made Mart more quiet, more direct. "Where was everybody else before Mrs. Sharon was found?"

"Yes, any one of you could have done it." She smiled and smiled at them. "If you had the strength. And a little skill."

"Where," said Mart, "were you?"

She started, her smile dead.

"Anybody," Rose cried out, "could have knocked down Tevy, too. She may be lying in the woods now. She may be hurt. A lot worse than Mrs. Sharon was."

Eric Lund got up from his bench and stood in the center of the room. "We'll find your sister," he said. "Shall I call the Sheriff, Mrs. Fitts? Or would you rather do it?"

Mrs. Fitts measured the strength of the long Nordic face. "I'll call him," she said.

fifteen
TUESDAY MORNING. JULY 14

Along the Wilderness Trail blanched and bloodless between gray trees, men hunted for Tevy Dallam. In the strange light of the three o'clock morning, the checked shirts of the boys from the State Conservation Camp and the spotted back of a dog stood out bold but colorless. From miles north of Camp Midaywin to a mile south, they probed the bushy ditches, sometimes calling the name of a girl they had never known.

Through the water of Bear Cub Bay a paddle swished close to shore as Elmer Oftedahl, the trapper, searched the shallows along the treacherous drop-off.

The forestry boys, the guides, the resort owners, Smith, the summer resident with his dog; all these were the neighbors rallying to the cry of "Lost Person" over the party line. They were the second wave of hunters; the third and official group would come later with the sheriff of Midaywin County and the Coast Guard crew bringing ominous ropes and hooks from the Lake Superior station at Petit Port.

The worried intimate group that had first sought Tevy throughout Camp Midaywin, had known by midnight that she was not there. While Averill sat by the slumbering Althea, Mrs. Fitts and the four other men combed the woods and paths with flashes, and covered every corner of the cabins and outbuildings. Rose, wrapped in a white hooded coat, moved quietly among them, her tension evident only in her low repeated calls of "Tevy!" Winton was often near her, gentle and considerate. Mart worked doggedly, thorough and sure, within a silent wall of anger. Awkward and nervous in the darkness, Verne Anderson collided with them all.

Hunting through night woods, Eric Lund had not been able to check the movements of his fellow hunters, to know or to guess with reasonable assurance who had preceded him into the empty cabin farthest from the lodge. Tevy was not there, but something else was; in this house, long tenantless, he met a faint wave of heated air. Lund opened the door of the airtight stove, throwing the beam of his torch upon a mess of smoking paper. Removing the crisp black fragments for the crime laboratory's hopeful reconstruction, he had little doubt that Rose Dallam's fan letters had now been burned.

When he had rejoined the group, Mrs. Fitts was saying wearily, "There's nothing else to do but wait for daylight," and they had all agreed and gone down to Rose's cabin to drink coffee and look for any answer to the questions of where was Tevy and why. Lost, injured, drowned? Or had she voluntarily and secretly left the camp?

"But she wouldn't have gone in shorts and that old black jersey!" Rose was certain. "And without her purse. No, Mr. Anderson, that's mine. Tevy's is the big red one. Thanks."

And when she had taken out the contents one by one, the cosmetics, the checkbook, the green wad of bills, it didn't seem likely that her sister had set out for town.

No clothes were gone from hooks or luggage. The apricot bathing suit hung on the line by the woodpile, and every Midaywin boat was accounted for. It was almost unbelievable that Tevy should have attacked to get the fan letters, and in any case, she was the only person who didn't know Mrs. Sharon had them. Unless, of course, she had listened at the lodge windows long after Mrs. Sharon had glimpsed her in the dusk.

Like Mrs. Sharon, she could have been attacked. By whom and why? Rose had said she couldn't imagine; no one else had said anything.

Each hour Mrs. Fitts' face showed deepened apprehension of the shadow that hovers over all resort owners in the North Woods: the fear of accident to a guest. A careless step on a slippery dock and the dead fall to a jagged submerged rock. A short adventurous wandering from the trail, a tumble over timber, a broken leg, and long hours of pain, bleeding, torture by mosquitoes and flies.

At last they took Rose back with them to the lodge, and now, while Mrs. Fitts made gallons of coffee and fried a dishpan of doughnuts for the volunteer posse, and while the Midaywin men caught fragments of sleep, the girl, small and cold in her white coat, dozed in a chair by Mrs. Sharon's bed.

The gray light on the lake was turning to pale yellow when Althea opened her eyes wide and struggled up to her elbows to stare at Rose.

"What are you doing here?" The hoarse whisper brought Rose erect in her chair.

"How do you feel, Mrs. Sharon?"

"Oh, all right, really." The veined hand touched the back of her head. "It's sore and I'm still sleepy. Where is Mrs. Fitts?"

"She's getting breakfast for a lot of people who are hunting for my sister. Tevy is lost. We've been looking all night."

Mrs. Sharon slowly studied the girl's small, anxious face. "You're worried, aren't you?"

"Yes. Almost anything could have happened to her."

"Come close," whispered Mrs. Sharon. And as Rose reluctantly bent over the bed, "You need help," she breathed. "You need someone you can trust. So I'm going to tell you a tremendous secret. There is just one person here you can rely on. Mr. Anderson."

"Mr. Anderson?" Rose nearly laughed.

"Hush. I can't tell you why. There's too much at stake. But go to him. He can see you through any trouble."

"He doesn't give quite that impression. I think I'd rather trust Mr. Lund."

"That's what's so clever about Mr. Anderson," Althea's conspiratorial croak went on. "I think Mr. Lund is really a very dull man. In spite of those scars."

"But you told me he was terrifically psychic," Rose took up the topic, humoring her.

"I don't think I said that." The old eyes took on their blankest look. "I never thought it."

Turning to the wall she feigned a sleep that had become real and noisy when Lund stood tall in the doorway and beckoned to Rose. Beside him in the lounge was Bill Gregg.

"I understand, Miss Dallam," the sheriff looked down at the brown felt hat in his hand, "that you haven't seen your sister since yesterday afternoon."

"Not since right after lunch. At two o'clock, I think. I started for a walk and she was waiting for—for Mart to get her a canoe."

The blue eyes flashed at her. He hadn't missed the hesitation before his nephew's name. "You went to walk by yourself and your sister was going canoeing alone?"

"She said she was going alone. But she went off with—Mart. I—Mr. Winton started with me."

Gregg nodded. "The doctor's out in the kitchen. He came up to see this Mrs. Sharon. He'd better have a look at you, too. Give you a sedative or something. Then maybe you can get a little sleep. After that I'll talk to you."

"Can I go back to my own cabin?" Rose asked. "I'd rather be there in case Tevy … if you find my sister."

"We'll find her. Mrs. Fitts is going to quit and go to bed for a while, if I can force her there, but there's a lot of neighbor women coming in to help out. How about one of them coming down to stay with you?"

"I'd rather not—have a stranger."

"Rose," Lund looked down at her kindly, "would I do? I can see that you eat something and then sit on the porch while you sleep."

"Yes," she said. "That would be … Thank you. I'll see the doctor, and then I'll be ready to go with you, Mr. Lund."

As the two men stepped out to the Trail, the sheriff said in a low voice, "I'm sure grateful for your cooperation, Mr. Lund. You fellows know how to get the stuff. How are you, Martin?"

Uncle and nephew, meeting on the road, gave each other cautious greeting. "Okay," said Mart. "Do you see what I'm seeing?"

Back and forth, circling above the half-dozen trucks and cars now parked around the lodge door, two large black birds swooped, flew into the woods, returned again, uttering raw portentous cries.

"Honest-to-God ravens?" asked Lund.

"Yes. After the porcupine Mrs. Fitts killed yesterday." Mart pointed to the hillside, then added, "I hope."

"Here's Rose," warned Lund, and saw the look, half-pleading, half-hostile that passed between the boy and the girl. She had had a shock and she was right to trust no one, and Mart had yet to explain that curious absence last night.

Back in her cabin among the cedars the signs of shock grew less. The cold beads of sweat left her forehead, and as she bit politely the toast and bacon Lund prepared for her, the fixed anxiety of her face changed to a younger, softer look. He did not talk to her until the second cup of coffee brought a little color to her cheeks.

"You're good to me," she said. "I hate to be such a trouble."

"I like to cook," he said, "and I'm not allowed to at home."

"You said something like that about fixing the phonograph. Don't you ever want to be thanked?"

"How did the phonograph work?"

"I haven't tried it."

"Let's see." He got up. "There's a record already on the machine."

The machine was working fine. The twang of the harpsichord came true and clear, and not a word was blurred:

> *… Darkness shades me:*
> *On thy bosom let me rest:*
> *More I would, but Death invades me:*
> *Death is now a welcome guest.*
> *When I am laid in earth….*

Eric Lund shut off the proof of his mechanical ability, not proudly. Rose Dallam had drawn a quick breath but now, with a nice feeling for his state of mind, she said, "Mr. Lund, you know I haven't seen those baby pictures yet."

"Well," he said falling gratefully into the pattern she had set, "it could be done now. I'm ashamed to say I have them on my person."

"No," she said, bending over the snapshots he put in her hand, "you aren't ashamed. Not of that beautiful child."

"You really like children, don't you?"

"Yes. I've been crazy about them ever since my little sister was born."

"You weren't a very big sister at the time, were you?"

"No, only three. But I didn't see her very often. Tevy's my half-sister. She was like a beautiful big doll that you're only allowed to play with on Sunday or your birthday. And Tevy's mother let me do everything for her, help give her a bath and a bottle. You know."

"Papa Lund knows. When you and Tevy grew up, didn't you see her more often?"

"Less, because my grandmother was quite old and she kept me in Europe most of the time. But I still like Tevy, awfully, Mr. Lund. She hasn't been … You haven't seen her at her best here. Tevy's had a rotten time."

Again she turned to the photographs. "I suppose those curls just grew?"

"Hand those over," ordered Lund. "You've done your duty by the Lunds. Now, have a cigarette and give me a chance to compliment you on your own creation. I've been reading 'Profile of a Hero.'"

"Oh," she said. The hand taking the cigarette shook slightly.

"It's damned good. And for a girl of your age. I'm just a lowbrow without any idea how writers work. You'd been pretty close to the stuff you were writing about, hadn't you?"

For a moment she didn't answer. "Not really," she said at last. "The story itself, what happened to the man when he got out of prison, I invented. I thought of what would be the most awful thing that could happen to a man like him, and I decided that would be it."

"But the parties before he went to prison were real?"

"They were real. But the man wasn't. That is, I didn't know him."

"You wrote about him as if you hated him."

"I did," she said, "but I didn't know him. He was Tevy's trouble. And, much more, my father's."

"He was someone Tevy didn't hate?"

She shivered slightly and reached toward the white coat hanging beside the bed.

"Lie down and cover up with the blanket," Lund said. "I'll sit here till the sedative does its work. Or on the porch if you'd rather."

She climbed obediently on the bed, tucking the pillows high under her head.

"Please stay. I want to tell you about this thing, now I've started. It wouldn't be fair to Tevy to stop. If she—when she comes back. Nothing about it is her fault."

"Do you mind my pipe?"

"Oh no," She had the look of one anxious to lay a burden on a broad impersonal mind. Lund had thought it might come out that way.

"I'll have to begin," she said, "with my father. He's a lawyer, terribly honorable and a bit stiff. Elizabeth, my stepmother, is wonderful, warmhearted and the only person who could ever tease Dad and make him like it. Three years ago, Dad had a touch of TB. His lung healed quickly, and the family went to live in a small town where the climate would be mild. He was getting along well. He wasn't practicing law, of course, but he was almost ready to.

"A year ago last Christmas," her voice grew tight, "my grandmother let me visit them. The house was in the country. Snow and pines all around—greeting card stuff. We made cookies and hung wreaths. The town, about three miles from Dad's house, was a whirl, all kinds of parties and Tevy went to them all. I could have too, but I didn't. Because it was so exciting for me just to be living in that kind of house and feeling it was my home. No wonder Tevy told Jim East I was an old stick-in-the-mud. I thought nothing could hurt people in a place like that. I couldn't have thought more wrong."

"You need a light," said Lund, holding out a match.

"Yes," she inhaled. "I suppose there are hundreds of towns like that one, where a half-dozen families can break all the laws that exist. You know, do seventy down the main street without an arrest, and if they get drunk and start breaking up the place, the tavern keeper has to smile and smile and help them home in the morning. That type of young hero was taking Tevy to a dance one night. It was a dinner dance but at eleven o'clock he hadn't showed up and Tevy went to bed mad.

"Dad and Elizabeth and I were sitting by the fire. The bell rang and Elizabeth went to the door and Dad was just behind her. I didn't see or hear what happened. But they told me as soon as he went. He asked for Tevy and he was swaying. He had a bottle and offered Dad and Elizabeth a drink and said it was all right about Tevy. And then he drove off. A mile down the road there had been an accident. A car had skidded and overturned across the highway. A woman was dead. Another car had stopped to help.

"Someone saw our hero coming at eighty plus and ran out swinging a flashlight. He came straight on and killed that man and two more.

"Naturally he wasn't hurt at all. His car overturned ever so gently and sobered him up so perfectly that he was able to remember to take the bottle with him when he strolled into town. Everybody who wasn't already dead was too busy collecting legs and eyes and collar bones to notice his departure.

"So nothing would have happened to him in that town, if it hadn't been for Dad. Grandmother ordered me to New York by plane the next day. I wasn't a witness and neither, of course, was Tevy. No threats of ostracism or death could keep a man like Dad from telling the truth. So Mr. J. East went to prison, after the parties were over. Then Tevy got the ostracism and Dad nearly died."

"Was Tevy," asked Lund, "in love with the man?"

"I don't think so. Elizabeth was sure she wasn't, just cocky about being his girl of the moment. Tevy stood up for Dad all through the trial and for quite a while afterward. But you see, two of Jim East's cousins were in her class. So during her whole last term, the girls wouldn't talk to Tevy. That's too much to take when you're eighteen."

"Or eighty. What happened to your father?"

"Several things. The hero's friends driving past the house all night, honking their horns. Then a wheel came off Dad's car. Finally, one night, he was beaten up—by persons unknown. He's been an invalid ever since. Perhaps he would have been anyway; maybe the TB would have gone into the bone without any such injury. The family moved to Westchester after that, and Dad isn't easy to live with. So sometimes Elizabeth is afraid that Tevy is reversing the role in this sordid little drama and making the manslaughterer into a martyr."

"He was sent up for manslaughter? What degree?"

"Involuntary. The least you can get. He's out already."

"Has Tevy seen him?"

"I don't know. She hasn't talked about him—really—since she came. We've hardly talked at all together. I wondered, when I was waiting during last night, if Tevy had used my invitation as an excuse to get away and join him somewhere. But of course that's crazy. Why come way up here? She had plenty of money to go straight to him."

"I'd also doubt," said Lund, "that she'd be welcome. After all, her father sent the guy to prison."

"Yes, I said it was crazy. It couldn't be true. It mustn't be true! It would kill my father. And I couldn't bear it for Elizabeth."

"Rose!" Lund spoke sharply. "Come out of it. You've taken your real troubles like a man. Don't go to pieces about the one you've invented."

"I'll try not to." She swallowed. "I'll stop. But things have been so mixed up lately. Things and people."

"Such as?"

"Mrs. Fitts asking me if I didn't know Mrs. Sharon in New York." The drug was dulling her. "Mart insisting that Roger Winton came here to be with me. And Tevy …" She stopped.

"Tevy announcing that she was an old friend of Mart Bryan's?"

She looked down at her hands folded on the gay blanket.

"Where did they know each other?" Lund asked.

"Tevy wouldn't tell me."

"But Mart would."

"I haven't asked him, I didn't think of it when … If I had, would he have told me the truth?"

Eric Lund stood up and pulled the blanket over her shoulders. "You're half asleep," he said. "Get going the rest of the way. I'll be right outside if you want anything."

"You'll let me know if Tevy …"

"If there's any news, good or bad. I promise."

On the small screened porch, he sat smoking, his eyes turned from the lake and the Coast Guard boat that dragged for Tevy in waters where so recently the body of Edith Brown had floated. He thought of Rose's story, of the far different case that had brought him to Midaywin and still kept him here, and again of the suggested relationships of all these seemingly separate people. Who had known whom and where? Who would lie about it? Who would tell the truth? Well, all of them would have a chance, this morning, to tell it; not to Eric Lund but to Bill Gregg, sheriff of Midaywin County.

sixteen
TUESDAY MORNING. JULY 14

"Nope, I didn't seen her anywheres." The driver of the Wilderness Express shook his shock-head with regret. "I've been looking all the way down from the border on account of the alarm about her being lost. Gosh, I hope nothing's happened to that girl."

"You liked her," said Sheriff Gregg, looking up at the lank young figure on the seat of his circus chariot.

"Oh sure, any guy would. She has what it takes. Good kid. But out for a good time. She seemed like she could take care of herself pretty well." He gave his cap a bewildered tug. "Now if it had been that old cuckoo out of a clock that hitched up the Trail, two, three nights before—. Well, I'll be looking for her all the way to town. Guess we'll have some rain."

A scarlet blot in the gray morning, the mail truck headed for Petit Port. Hand on straight hip, the sheriff surveyed the terrain of Camp

Midaywin. Low clouds hung over the red roof of the lodge, and from the kitchen, whiffs of coffee and clatter of dishwashing women blew south toward the car park, the pump and the hidden line of cabins. Not hidden behind much, the sheriff observed. The small poplars and cedars between them and the road gave a feeling of privacy and kept out highway dust, but they weren't dense. A man could step through them at any point, easy and without a sound.

"Damned filthy birds," he cursed the crude caws above the trees, as he crossed gravel and opened the main lodge door.

"Hello," he said to Averill Fitts drowsing on the settee by a smoking fire. "Pretty tough for you and your wife. You never had trouble here in twenty years."

"No," agreed Averill sitting up sadly. "No. My wife never wanted to take these girls. Nor any girls."

"She didn't, eh?" Gregg gave an effective poke to the fire. "Why'd she take them?"

"Because …" Averill groped through his hair. "Well, she asked the first one, Rose, a tremendous price of an aged cabin, thinking she'd refuse it. But Rose Dallam is a very innocent sort of girl, and they tell me equally wealthy. Since she was here—paying such a rate—Mrs. Fitts felt she had to let the sister come, too."

"Sister the same type?"

A snag of tooth showed in Averill's smile. "Tevy's a very taking girl. But somewhat wanting in tenderness."

"Tenderness to her sister? Or to the men?"

"To the dead," said Mr. Fitts.

"Oh?" said the sheriff. "Who's dead around here?"

"A porcupine," said Mr. Fitts. "Tevison Dallam laughed. Then she went off in the canoe with Martin."

"When was all this?"

"Yesterday afternoon. Shortly after two o'clock. And that is the last time I saw her. I heard her, though. All the way to the Narrows, mocking those most dignified birds, the loons. Such responsible parents."

"You didn't see her come back? Or hear her whistling last evening?"

"No," said Averill. "Last evening was particularly peaceful and relaxed, full of music. And," he stiffened his body, "so was the entire afternoon. For two hours or so after my wife left for town—two-fifteen, I should say, until four o'clock—I sat in front of this building, reading a most enrapturing book. Have you ever perchance encountered *Heart Throbs?*"

"I haven't read anything," exaggerated Gregg. "And what did you do after that?"

"I read within doors. It had become a little warm along the Trail. At a quarter before five, I went to sun me on the dock, and there at five I was discovered by my dear wife."

The sheriff nodded, his eyes fixed on old Averill, whose hands began to fidget as he continued his offered alibis.

"And while catastrophe overtook our sweet, sensitive Mrs. Sharon, I was in bed slumbering."

"Dead to the world, eh?"

Averill's thumbs suddenly hooked through his belt. "No," he said. "I think that is a slight misstatement. I must have been merely dozing. For I could hear Mrs. Fitts typing in the adjoining office. All the time. Until Rose Dallam called for help."

"Thanks, Averill. You've been a big help," said Gregg, and left the frightened old liar whom it was not yet the moment to break down.

"It's a terrible thing for Rose," Roger Winton's unhappy shadowed eyes turned slowly from the boat dragging along the lead-colored water inshore, to Gregg, smoking beside him on the Honeymoon steps. "If Tevy drowned, like the other … She was drowned?"

"Edith Brown? She was drowned. The doctor found plenty of water in her stomach."

"Have you found out anything else about her?"

"That she gave a fake New York address to the car rental agency," Gregg grunted. "The town had to bury her yesterday."

"Nice little country you have here, until something goes wrong."

"This is no kind of country to fool with," Gregg said. "We should have the Dallam girl soon, unless she ran away, and even so…. What kind of a mood was she in, the last time you saw her?"

"Tevy? That was at lunch yesterday. I thought she seemed perfectly natural." He flicked open his lighter and held it out to Gregg. "She had had her irritating moments, needling Rose and everybody else, but not yesterday."

"And after lunch?"

"I had a date with Rose. To hike to North Star Lake. When we went off, there was a whole bunch near the lodge, Mrs. Fitts and Fitts and Mrs. Sharon and Tevy. And," he added, "Mart."

"You away from Camp all afternoon?"

Winton shook his head. "Rose was, but after we'd gone a short way, I came back."

"You did?"

"You consider that your business? Rose and I … Hell, corn is the shortest way to say it. We had a so-called lover's quarrel. I released my brakes too soon. It gave her a jolt. She told me to walk home."

"Do you happen to remember what time you got back to the Trail?"

"Around half-past two."

"You didn't see Tevy Dallam around? Or anyone else?"

"No, but I wouldn't have. The North Star Trail begins right opposite this cabin, and I came straight here. To lick the wounds." He smiled slightly at Gregg. "And then I began to worry about Rose."

"You were in your cabin when Tevy came back to camp?"

"I'm afraid I worried myself into a sound sleep." The long lashes drooped in self-mockery. "But when I woke up, about five, I went straight to Rose's cabin. She was at home and so was Tevy. That is, she had come off the lake. I didn't see her, but the canoe was on the dock, with some of her trappings in it. I was only there a few minutes. Rose …" The slim fingers opened the collar of his dark red shirt. "I was forgiven," he said rather bitterly, "but Rose was somewhat more interested in a beaver, so I left, like a six-year-old kid."

"Neither of the Dallam girls showed up at the lodge for dinner?"

"No. Rose didn't always, before Tevy came."

"But Tevy was around after dinner."

"Apparently. We were going to have some bridge, and I went out in the kitchen to get a drink of water. Probably the whole crowd has told you what I heard."

"Mr. Lund told me."

"We'd all heard that performance before. From where I stood by the sink, it sounded as if Tevy were on the road near the other wing, outside the office. Mrs. Sharon, who heard her better than I did, was at the lounge window nearest that corner of the building. The others were over at the lake side of the room, setting up the table and getting out the cards, and Mr. Fitts was at his piano."

"You didn't actually see the girl."

"No. It was beginning to get darkish and I wasn't right at the window. I called to her, 'Fluffed it again, Tevy,' or something of the sort. I wish now I had gone out."

"And you were all in the lounge together until Rose came up at nine o'clock asking for her sister? And something about letters?"

"Oh God, yes," said Winton wearily. "Sharon was always asking for them and Rose was promising them and then losing them. Women who write!"

"They're not for you?"

"Not Althea, the antique fay! Rose has published one short thing—a story in *Manhattan*—but she's through with writing."

"So you were all together all evening. Except Rose."

"Rose?" The voice that had so calmly discussed the missing Tevison shook slightly. "No, Rose wasn't there, but don't try to make something out of that! Somebody else wasn't accounted for. The fellow who went off with Tevy in the canoe, and who didn't show up when Mrs. Sharon was knocked out. How carefully have you investigated Mart Bryan?"

"I'm investigating him," said Gregg.

"You might want to ask Miss Dallam a few questions," Winton suggested. "She and Mart had unkind words last night in the lounge. When he finally showed up, a half-hour or more after we found Mrs. Sharon, I think Rose had reason to wonder where he'd been, and Mart thought so, too."

"That's a lead," Gregg got up from the steps. "Thanks for talking so frankly." Under a small pine straining out of a rock by the cabin porch, he stopped. "One thing more. How would you describe Tevison Dallam?" You, his look implied, who have known a lot of women.

"She's a big handsome girl," Winton answered. "A little reckless. Out for fun. You see a lot like her. You play with them quite a lot. But, to continue the frankness, afterward you don't remember much about them."

"Well, it's a little hard to describe," Verne Anderson poked a thoughtful finger into the cushion of his chin. "Tevy was quite a gal. A little more my type than her sister is. But not enough. See what I mean?"

The sheriff nodded.

"Gosh, I wish I could think of something to help, Mr. Gregg. Those two poor kids. But I didn't see or hear a thing. Right after lunch I came back here and slept most all afternoon, from two o'clock or so till Lund woke me up to go fishing. I had a bad sunburn and a bunch of mosquito bites and I didn't feel so good. Then he and I sat out there by the entrance to the Narrows fishing for walleye—and getting them, too! Until we came in for dinner at seven o'clock. We saw Mart rowing home from Collins Island alone, and I guess that's about all."

"That checks with Lund's account."

"As for Mrs. Sharon's bop on the bean," Anderson lowered his feet from his cabin table and trotted over to the mantel for cigarettes, "you know that, too. We all left the lodge at the same time, Mrs. Sharon and Winton and Lund and me. She went across the road and I saw her start up the bank to her cabin. The three of us came along our path and I left them first, having the nearest cabin."

"Yes, Mr. Lund told the same story. Thank you, Mr. Anderson."

"Listen, Bill Gregg," Mrs. Fitts set coffee in front of him and sat down squarely on the opposite side of the kitchen table, "I sent for you because one of my guests is missing. Stick to that. It should take all your time."

"We're doing what we can," he said. "Two planes are up now and you know the rest that's going on." He knew the anxiety she suffered, but that wasn't all. "I understand your old boss went through town last week Wednesday."

Her hand on the coffee pot tightened but she did not lower her eyes or reply.

Okay, we'll take that up later, he thought. "How were things around here last night? Was everybody acting about as usual?"

"Yes," she said impatiently. "Except they didn't talk so much at dinner, probably because they were eating more. I never fried so many pike in my life. Two of the men had been out fishing for hours, but Winton ate just about as much, and Mrs. Sharon had two big plates full."

"They strike you as pretty much the usual run of tourists?"

"The men? It's funny. Anderson and Lund look like a hundred I've had here in the past, and I've had some Wintons, too, but still these are kind of queer."

"How queer?"

"They don't say a word about their business. Most men bore you stiff with how they sell refrigerators or fire insurance. Anderson and Winton tell you nothing. Lund does, of course, but I'm beginning to think that makes him queer. And he's the only one with a decent car. Even Rose Dallam left hers in Pettyport. She says," added Mrs. Fitts with spite, "it's because she's a writer."

"Writers and girls you can do without?" Gregg grinned at her.

"Rose Dallam is a decent sort of girl. I didn't have much trouble till Tevy appeared on the scene."

"Then fur flew?"

"Well, they're half-sisters." The stereotype satisfied her. "Jealous, of course. Rose has all that money but she's got an inferiority complex and don't think she's attractive to the men. In spite of having all the men till Tevy came. She couldn't make up her mind between Mart and Mr. Winton. They had a fight about her, Saturday, just before Tevy showed up. Rose didn't expect her so soon. Rose," she added irrelevantly, "isn't a bad shot."

"She was the one who 'found' Mrs. Sharon."

"Yes." Her mouth shut tight.

"Where were you at the time?"

"In the office making out bills. Averill was in bed in the next room. And sound asleep."

"Where," he asked, "was Mart?"

"You'll have to ask him."

"I shall. Your Mrs. Sharon is next on my list. Yes, I'll go easy on her, but the doctor says she's all right. What I'm going to ask her will be strictly part of my business. That's business that you, maybe, among others, elected me to do."

Althea Sharon was waiting for the sheriff. Her gray brushed curls reposed in a nest of pink and blue baby pillows, rose silk ruffles tried to soften her throat, and on the quilted satin coverlet over her knees lay open the book of her adventures. When she heard his step in the corridor, she let out a soft excited breath, ready to tell almost all.

For a moment the step did not come nearer. Bill Gregg was taking a quick look at the plan of Midaywin lodge. The short hallway, leading out from the north end of the lounge, served, he saw, a group of four small rooms: to his left and toward the lake a bath and the room occupied by Mrs. Sharon; to the right, with windows facing the road, there was first the office with typewriter, counter, phone, and post card rack, and behind it, a bedroom. Unlike the other rooms, this bedroom had a door opening on the strip of clover and petunia beds that lay between the house and the Wilderness Trail. The Fitts bedroom, the Fitts office.

Bill Gregg sighed and turned reluctantly to Althea Sharon's door. The disorders of a Lake Superior town he could deal with confidently—the traffic accidents and drownings, illegal slot machines, brawls—but the troubles the tourists brought with them into the North Woods were outside his way of life. As he marched in to face this specimen, he said, "Thank God for Lund."

"Mrs. Sharon," he announced in a level voice and before she could flutter out a greeting, "I'm sorry you were hurt. Sorry to trouble you. But I need your help. We haven't found Tevison Dallam yet. I hear you're the last person around here who saw her."

"Oh I am. I was. I will!" Althea gasped at this fine male type.

"Okay," he said. "Shoot!"

"Shoot? Oh," she laughed, "of course—tell you all about it. It was last night. Not really night. In the gloaming."

"What time?"

"After eight. A little."

"Just where was Tevy? How did she look?"

"It was right outside the window, the nearest window in the lounge to this hall. She whistled that thing about 'Remember me' and missed the top note. And then Mr. Winton called out from the kitchen, 'Fluffed it, again, Tevy.' She always did it most badly, Mr. Gregg."

"She was close to the window?"

"Rather close. And I'm sure she had that same insolent expression on her face that she wore the night she arrived. That's the way she looked when the skull cracked. It was such a brutal blow, Mr. Gregg."

"So," he said, "you actually saw Tevy Dallam hit you?"

"Wait, wait!" She wasn't listening to him, bending over the notebook, holding it away from her face. "Here is what I wrote! 'Today,'" she read with trembling fervour, "'for the first time in my life I have seen a murder.'"

"You mean what might have been your own death?"

She looked at him angrily. "Oh Mr. Gregg, don't please be stupid. Not mine. The porcupine's. Just one skillful blow. Tevy laughed. And those beautiful orange teeth."

"Tevy Dallam," Gregg interpreted with relief, "killed a porcupine."

"No, no, Mr. Gregg, you're still all wrong. Mrs. Fitts did it. She just killed the harmless little beast with one most accurate whack and then drove straight off to town. I'm afraid she lacks tenderness and she's just a little narrow-minded. But she's awfully kind to me, now I'm sick."

"Well," said Gregg, "after she killed the porcupine and drove off, what did you do?"

"I went straight to my cabin," Mrs. Sharon's voice suddenly became righteous and prim. "And there I wrote up my adventures. All afternoon."

"It must have been hard work," said Gregg.

"Oh, it was. Writing is fearfully hard, but few people appreciate it. Only very sensitive men like you. And Mr. Winton. The first time he saw me, almost the first minute, he said he could tell I was a writer. But of course he's very psychic. But then that Dallam girl ..."

"Tevy?" She didn't answer him. "Rose?"

"Both of them. They continually chase men, and they say the most shocking things to each other. Tevy forced Roger Winton to ask Rose to marry him in front of everyone at Mr. Lund's cocktail party. Rose threatened to kill Tevy. And then," she lowered her voice to name a blacker sin, "Rose ran out of the house and held hands with Martin."

"Martin?"

"Isn't he a sweet boy. We've had some lovely hours together, but I think he's been ... I hate to say seduced. And the next day Tevy got him, and Rose went off with Roger Winton."

"Uh," said Mr. Gregg.

"But I don't think that really suited anybody. Each of the girls wanted both men and just hated each other."

"Mrs. Sharon," said Gregg sternly, "last night Rose Dallam gave you some letters."

"Those silly things!" She tinkled.

"Someone hit you on the head."

"No," she spoke deliberately now. "That is wrong. That is what I said when I was still dazed. Now I'm all right and I know what really happened. I was going to the pump to get a drink of water and I ran into a tree. It was completely dark."

"Where are the letters now, Mrs. Sharon?"

"In the fireplace up in my cabin. I just tossed them in and then threw a lighted match on them." She gestured airily. "They were fan letters people had written to Rose. I only asked to see them to flatter the poor girl."

Gregg stood up, feeling tired. "You'd better get some rest now."

"Oh, I will. After I've written up some more of my adventures. I'm so far behind."

"Don't have too many more," Gregg warned her. "One of yours seems to have been a little risky. Aren't you ever afraid that they might be useful?"

"I never thought … Useful?"

"Useful to the wrong kind of people."

"No, it couldn't happen," she said simply. "My philosophy protects me. Good triumphs over evil. I can always select the good people from the bad."

"You're brighter than I am," said the sheriff.

"Everybody do his best to hang me?" Mart, elbows on knees sat on the edge of his bunk and grinned ruefully at his Uncle Bill.

"No crime's been committed here suitable for hanging—that I know of."

"When you do get wise to it, I'll be elected."

"The word's indicted," said Gregg. "Mart, I know what you've done to put your mother and the kids on their feet. You've been at it ever since you were in Junior High and a wave washed your dad off that ore boat. You've held good jobs and worked hard. What the hell are you doing here at Midaywin?"

"I thought I'd do something for myself for a change." Mart stooped to tighten a bootlace. "I've saved almost enough for a couple of terms at the U. Working at a resort I'd save room and board, and Mrs. Fitts was offering a fancy price."

"Why?"

"There's an angle. That's her business, and it hasn't anything to do with this mess. Anyway, I'm quitting August first."

"Okay, Mart. Now, what were you doing yesterday from two o'clock on?"

"Sheriff speaking?"

"Right." Gregg didn't return Mart's smile.

"Two o'clock? I was going over to Collins Island to open up the cabin and get it ready before the Collinses come up for the season. Sharon was to go with me. After Mrs. Fitts left, she balked and I didn't complain. Tevy Dallam had just rented a canoe. She suggested that we paddle over in it and then I wouldn't have an extra boat to tow home. I had to get the Collins boat out from under their house and bring it over to the Midaywin dock, ready for them. That's what we did."

"How long did Tevy stay on the island?"

"She didn't. She—stood on the dock a few minutes and left."

"Oh?"

"Yes. What else do you want to know? Everything I did in the next two hours?"

"Okay," said Gregg when Mart had finished. "If you did all that, your time was full. One of the deputies'll go over to the island and check. Now, when you got back here, Lund and Anderson saw you land soon after four o'clock. Go on from there."

A long list of resort chores came forth. At a quarter of five he had begun to ice the cabins.

"All of them?"

"Not Rose's. I met her on the road coming down from the North Star Trail and she said she didn't need any. I filled Winton's chest first. He was lying on his bed. Sharon was perched on hers. Anderson and Lund, of course, were out on the lake."

"And you didn't see Tevy?"

"Never, I tell you," said Mart hotly, "after she left Collins Island."

The usual course of evening jobs had been lengthened by Verne Anderson's awkward dousing of an outboard motor when he had taken it off the boat at the dock. Fortunately it had been chained, but Mart had worked for hours, taking it down and drying it out. Then he had gone for a swim.

"What time?"

"I came out around 9:15."

"Let's have the rest of it."

"I'm not boring you, Uncle William?"

"No."

"There's one little job I still had to do. I had to do it every night. Nurse girl stuff for Mrs. Sharon. Fill a Thermos bottle of hot milk at the kitchen and take it up to her cabin. And a bowl of ice cubes. Cubes. Chopping up her own ice wouldn't do for Madam's nightcap, and the only electric box is Mrs. Fitts'. Last night, Mrs. F. did me dirt. She'd turned the current off and the refrigerator was defrosting. No cubes. So after I heated the milk, I went down to the ice house and chopped up a bowl of stuff to look enough like cubes to be acceptable—maybe. Then I took the stuff up to Sharon's cabin. She wasn't there, as you know full well. I came back down and saw all the lights in the lodge and asked what all the shoutin' was about. You yawning, Bill, or are you going to hang me?"

"Where's the ice house?"

"South. Beyond the last empty cabin."

"You say you walked from this bunkhouse to the lodge kitchen and down to the ice house before Mrs. Sharon's body was found?"

"I didn't say so but that's what I did."

"Right after your swim?"

"I got dressed first."

Gregg's next question veered. "When you were in Mrs. Sharon's cabin, was there any drinking water in the place?"

"Huh? There was a full bottle of it in her ice chest. I noticed when I put in the bowl of chopped ice."

"You didn't notice the fireplace?"

"Sure I did. I cleaned it out yesterday morning and laid a new fire. Last night it was just the same. She hadn't thrown a scrap on the logs or burned a thing."

The sheriff nodded. "Mart." He looked hard at the young face so like his own. "What kind of a girl is this Tevison Dallam? What do you think's happened to her?"

"I don't know what's happened to her. That's straight, Bill."

"Yes?" said Gregg, waiting.

"What do I think of her?" His tone was angry and low. "When she turns up, she'll tell you, so I might as well do it myself. I told her to get the hell off the island, and if I heard she drowned on the way home, it would be a pleasure."

"Why?"

"I'll leave that for Tevy to tell to the sheriff of Midaywin County."

Gregg walked over to the door. "If Tevy Dallam doesn't turn up, Mart, it's you who will do the telling."

"I know that," said Mart. "To you and the judge."

"And to the jury," said Gregg.

seventeen
TUESDAY AFTERNOON. JULY 14

"I can't believe she was wandering around all that time. Wint, it isn't at all like Tevy."

"You're probably right," Roger Winton moved nearer to Rose at the edge of the Midaywin dock. "Mrs. Sharon is a hell of a witness. But I heard Tevy, too. Let me put this around you."

Beside her in the thin falling rain, he wrapped his windbreaker around her shoulders, holding it there, head bent, eyes anxious.

"No, Wint. You'll get wet. I have a coat on already." She shrugged off his hands.

"Honey," he said, "you know I'll do everything to help you. As soon as the other men finish lunch, the sheriff's sending the whole posse over the North Star Trail."

"Wint, could it have been faked?"

"What?"

"Tevy's whistle."

He nodded.

"Who?"

"Rose," he hesitated, "the only person outside the lodge was Mart."

She pushed the heavy hood away from her forehead. "He wasn't the only one," she said. "I could have done it!"

"Don't, Rose!"

"They've looked everywhere around here. She must have gone off somewhere after you heard her. It wasn't like Tevy to go off alone."

He put his hand on her shoulder, searching for warmth beneath the wet white wool.

"You think Mart took her off!" Her cry was angry, half-convinced.

"I think nothing. It could be. Anything could have happened. Rose, listen to me. Before Tevy comes back, I've got to tell you. What I asked you Sunday afternoon, I want terribly."

His vehemence shocked her out of herself.

"Marry me, Rose! You're the only thing I've ever really wanted in my life."

"Oh, Wint! Not now. I just want to find Tevy."

The circles stood out sharply beneath his eyes. "Yes. I've got to be off now. You'd better come inside the lodge."

But Rose stayed alone kneeling on the wet dock boards, her head against the keel of a canoe. She didn't want to think about Roger Winton; she didn't want to think at all, or to feel; only for a little while to look at the fine rain and the gray water and the blurred green of Mystery Island.

It didn't work. She couldn't forget Winton and the mixed, unhappy feeling she had about him and about everybody else. The romantic mocking figure of the day in the canoe; the short wild scene in the woods beside the stagnant pool; his anger and his cool apology while they watched the beaver push the tree across the lake; his quiet, considerate nearness throughout the past night. What did she feel about him? What was he really like?

And what about the others? Was Verne Anderson really clever and reliable, and Eric Lund criminal and dull? Was Mrs. Sharon to be judged by her clearer moments or by her most fuzzy? And below these lighter bewilderments lay a weight almost as heavy as her fear for Tevy: what about Mart Bryan? In the days before Tevy had come, and again, last night, while they had loved, she had been certain of the kind of man he was, straightforward, hard and honest. Then, while she had waited, confident that she would never in her life be quite alone again, he had deserted her. There had been time for him to knock out Althea Sharon, far more time to hurt Tevy Dallam—and perhaps a deeper reason, born in that place and period where he might have met and known Tevy.

The cold thought brought Rose erect and shivering away from the bleak water. Over the tilted rim of the canoe she faced the Wilderness Trail where men stood talking in a group. Eric Lund was there, long in a raincoat, and next to him, in blue jeans and leather jacket, Mart Bryan, who flung up his right arm in greeting and started toward her.

Watching him come, her eyes and mouth set rigid with distrust, though her cheeks flushed alive to his nearness.

"Rose, are you all right?"

She did not answer the question or the anxiety in his eyes. "Mart," her throat was dry. "Where did Tevy go when she left Collins Island?"

"She said she was going right back the way she came."

"Did she do it?"

"I couldn't swear to it. She headed for the Narrows but you can't see the channel from Collins' dock. And I went straight into the cabin to get to work."

There was a short strained silence. "You don't believe me, do you, Rose?" Mart said.

"It's a little difficult," her voice was small and tight. "It would be out of character for Tevy to leave you like that, especially when—" she wished that she had not begun this. "Because Wint was with me."

His straight stare did not help her, and she went on, hardly aware that Lund had joined them on the dock. "I can't believe Tevy was alone here in camp all afternoon and evening. What would she do? She doesn't like to read. She didn't go swimming. She didn't even play records. I've got some new hot jazz. She loves that, but *When I am laid in earth* is still on the turntable."

"The only time Tevy could have passed through the Narrows without being seen," Lund's matter-of-fact words came between them, "and paddled home to the cabin, was between three and three forty-five."

"How do you figure that?" Mart's attention was still on Rose.

"She couldn't have left the Collins dock before quarter to three? Well, from two-thirty till three I was rowing down from my cabin to Rose's, putting a new screw in her phonograph, and rowing back. From three forty-five till seven, Anderson and I were anchored in the Narrows, fishing. But during those forty-five minutes—three until three-forty-five—I was having a nap and Anderson says he was doing the same."

"Perhaps she never came home, Mr. Lund. If the canoe had drifted back empty could someone have seen it and just happened to pull it up on the right dock? No, that's crazy, but so is everything! Why is the plane looking for her beyond the other shore of the lake? Why is...."

"Because they're doing everything thoroughly," interrupted Lund. "They're dragging the lake, although there's no evidence of drowning. They're watching trains and buses and planes at Duluth and New York."

Rose caught a quick breath. "Hag's Nook! Tevy could have paddled home through Hag's Nook. It would have been just like her."

"Hey, what you talking about?" Mart checked her. "You mean the passage between Mystery and the mainland? The going would be tough but she could have made it, particularly yesterday with the breeze behind her. If she did try it, she got through. The canoe wasn't hurt any."

"But maybe she was hurt. She could be caught in that terrible dead tree. I told her to keep out of it, and so of course she wouldn't."

"Rose, stop," Lund ordered her. "The sheriff's men went through that channel. They searched the shore on both sides. I heard them report."

"Oh," she said, "but there must be some other wild place where she could—" The hysterical note left her voice. "I know where." She was quiet, very confident. "The Dark Arm."

"Tevy didn't know about it," declared Mart.

"She did." Rose turned abrupt to Lund. "You know we've all talked about the picnic. I'm sure we did on the night of the dance, and Mrs. Sharon was always throwing out hints of horrors. And yesterday at lunch, just before Tevy went off, Mr. Anderson was teasing Althea about bodies in shacks."

Lund nodded, watched her closely.

"I'm going to the Dark Aim. I'm going now."

Mart glanced at Lund and back at the girl's white, obsessed face.

"I'll take you," he said, and stooped to unfasten the chain of the nearest boat.

"No!" At Rose's absolute rejection Mart straightened, flushed and tense. "The sheriff had better— I'd rather ask him."

"I'll talk to Gregg," Eric Lund said. "Coming along, Mart?"

They went, and in this second interval alone, Rose thought only of Tevy. Hugging the white ulster against her breast she kept her gaze on the slim curving passage between the two islands, their rocks and pines softened and faded through the rain: Collins to the left where Tevy had parted from Mart; to the right, Mystery, long and slender, ending down the bay at Hag's Nook.

When Lund came back, Oftedahl, the trapper, was with him, light-footed and sure while he lowered the boat to the water, twisting his long neck in embarrassment as he mumbled to the girl, "I'm a deputy. You better sit up here with him," and moved a finger toward Lund.

"Anderson offered to come," Lund said, steadying Rose as she slipped down to the boat, "but the sheriff needed him in the office to help type some notes."

Mart came across the dock, carrying blankets and the heaviest Seahorse.

"Should we take food?" Rose looked only at Lund.

"I've got a flask," he said, settling beside her.

"Tevy had a lot of oranges with her," Mart spoke from the stern, his head bent over the motor, "and matches, too, for her cigarettes. She could have picked up some wood and kept fairly warm. Maybe she still had that knife of Winton's."

"Did she have it?" Lund asked Rose.

"No. She gave it back to him Sunday night after supper. He and Verne Anderson walked down the road with us to our cabin and I saw Tevy hand it to Wint just before the men left."

The motor started then, ending all talk. The rain, as they crossed the south end of Bear Cub Bay and passed between the submerged ledges of the Narrows, sank to soft mist, loosening the girl's tight nerves. She thought: I've brought all these people out on a mad whim. Tevy has run off to join Jim East, and the worst thing her old friend Mart has done was to fake the whistle, last night, so that she could have a long start.

But around the point of Mystery Island north wind struck the boat, whipping Oftedahl's wide hat brim and driving chins into collars. It was slow going along the island's length, and past that devil's dump of rocks and ragged branches. Ahead, black and imprisoning under today's low sky, waited the dense walls of the Dark Arm.

Suddenly Rose cried out and clutched Lund's wrist. Alone on a rock that marked the farthest outthrust of the shore, a poplar jutted over the lake. Something gray and dank dangled from the slanted trunk, like a swatch of T-shirt hung all night in the rain.

"A signal?" Rose was pointing. Her eyes entreated Lund to agree.

He brought his mouth against her ear. "A loose piece of poplar bark," he had to tell her.

Drooping, she saw the three black shacks appear, the gray stripes of lathing, the dull grass dripping around the dock. Mart cut the motor and there was only the quiet dip of Oftedahl's oars when Rose cried out again.

"Tevy!"

Brilliant in the dull day, in the center of the dock lay a strip of orange peel.

"It's hers. We left everything clean on Saturday. Mrs. Fitts insisted."

"Other people come here, Rose, not just from Camp Midaywin," Mart said, but he was interested and so was Eric Lund.

"Tevy!" she called. "Tevy! Tevy!"

There was no answer.

"The houses," she begged, as Lund helped her ashore. "If the plane didn't see her in the clearing, she must be inside."

"We'll look." Lund said to Oftedahl, pulling the boat up on the dock, "You and Mart go. I'll stay with her."

He took off his raincoat and tossed it on the ground. "Sit down," he told Rose.

The other men entered the horse barn. They came out again at once, and tramped through the weeds to the bunkhouse.

Crouched at the landward edge of the dock, Rose kept her eyes fixed on the ground, studying the safe inane details: an ant circumnavigating a twig, the pink under-petals of white clover bordering a rock. When she heard the bunkhouse door creak, she looked up fearful. Mart waved stiffly, Oftedahl shook his head. Then they both climbed the broken steps of the last shack.

She looked up at Lund lighting his pipe, and down again to the ground, her fingers running lightly through the clover. Then she saw the glint like a scrap of copper. She picked it up, a tiny cylinder open at one end.

"What have you got there?" Lund asked her.

She pushed it against the end of her finger, staring at the diamond trademark stamped on its base, at the dent made by the firing pin.

"One of our shells from the target shooting," she said listlessly.

"Put it back." It was a very quiet command.

Rose Dallam obeyed.

It was a long time before the men came slowly down the cookhouse steps.

"We went under the broken flooring," Mart said. "Nothing there."

"Now what?" asked Oftedahl.

Over Rose's bowed head, Lund made a small gesture with his pipe. "The old trail to Bear Cub Bay?"

The men's eyes turned in the direction of his arm. And so did the eyes of a large sleek raven posed some fifty feet away toward the woods, like a mortuary urn, on a dead stump.

"But Tevy didn't know about that path," Rose protested. "She wasn't with us when Mart told us. She couldn't have found it alone. She doesn't know a thing about the woods."

A look of silent agreement passed among the men.

"Give it a try," said Mart.

"Stay here, Rose," said Lund. "We won't go far."

So long as she could watch the three men edging along the shore, past the horse barn, around the dead end of the Arm where the old skid road broke the tree line, Rose found it easy to sit still. Now at the beginning of the opposite side of the bay, Mart vanished among the trees. Close behind Lund's high blond head, Oftedahl's hat and checked shirt faded into the woods. Then only a loud cross caw marked the direction they had taken. The crowding pines, the black, shut shacks, the terrible bright strip of orange; she could not stay alone with them. She got up and very slowly began to follow the lakeshore. Weeds soaked her cold to the knees. Farther on, raspberry vines bit into her ankles and tripped her flat. She got up, glad of the bruises that felt real and ordinary, meticulously picking brambles from her palms, making the task last as long as possible. Then above her, somewhere on the hill down which the lumber of that ill-fated camp had once slid to the ice of the Arm, she heard a light steady tap.

"Someone," she half said.

From the dense spot, impenetrable to her untrained eyes, where the men had disappeared there was no sign of life. Above her along the skid road the tapping went on. Should she call out?

Instead, she started up the slope. At the top, the green of leaves suddenly was gone. Brown, hollow and branchless, stumps and trunks stuck up against the dull sky, a ghost of a forest. Standing in motionless horror, she heard the sound again, striking hard and regular like a ghostly hammer against what once were trees. She saw great rectangular grooves cut into the sides of the trunks, niches without saints.

The sound stopped. Then as she stood breathless she caught a flash of color, and the tap, tap, tap resumed, almost at her side. Horizontal to a trunk and braced by a long stiff tail like an auxiliary leg, a black and white wood pecker continued to drill for ants, red head driving a beak fierce and precise into the dead wood.

From another stump over the devastated hillside, another woodpecker echoed the activity, making a natural success of the human failure that had driven the legendary lumberman to his death. Ghostly sight, ghostly sound, but Rose relaxed, and as she heard distant steps climbing the hill, she turned with a smile.

Eric Lund was leading the three men, Mart close behind, Oftedahl obviously lagging. Lund looked alert, ready for action. He did not return her smile.

"Rose," he said. "You were right about the Dark Arm. We've found your sister."

"Yes, Mr. Lund," she said, and knew before he had told her that Tevison was dead.

eighteen
TUESDAY AFTERNOON. JULY 14

For a moment Rose Dallam stood quite still, regarding Eric Lund with an expression of mild courtesy. Lund, cognizant of shock in many guises, waited.

"Tevy!" She choked and ran stumbling down the hill.

He caught up with her at the lakeshore. "Stay here." He held both her arms. "Don't go into the woods. There is nothing you can do for Tevy."

"Let me go!" She pulled hard against his hands. "I've got to know. If she's really there. If she's really dead."

"No, Rose," Lund stood firm. Mart, coming behind her, laid his arm over her shoulders. "Tevy is lying on the path, not far into the woods. Her body is completely cold. She has been dead for a good many hours."

The girl stopped struggling. "How did she die?"

"We don't know yet. We can't move her until the sheriff gets here."

She looked past Lund to Elmer Oftedahl, demanding, "How did my sister die?"

He hesitated, avoiding her face. "Seems like she was shot."

"Shot? Someone killed Tevy?"

"Looks that way, Miss Dallam."

She glanced from him to Lund, eyes wide and wild. "I thought she had run away to Jim East!" she accused herself. "Oh Tevy!" Her body began to tremble.

Mart said to Lund, "I'll take her home."

"Hold on a minute," Oftedahl came forward. "Don't forget there's been a murder. I'm in charge till the sheriff gets here. You aren't going off alone with the girl in the boat, Mart."

"We're going," said Mart flatly.

"No!" Rose, aware for the first time of his arm on her shoulder, cried out in fear. He stepped away from her, and Lund let her draw out of his own grasp.

"We're going. I'm taking Rose out of this place." The muscles of Mart's cheek and jaw tightened out all expression.

"I got a gun, Mart. I'd hate to have to use it."

"So?" said Mart. "Mr. Lund doesn't know the channel. Do you?"

"Not too well."

"Okay. You and I go with Rose, and Lund waits here for Bill?"

Elmer shook his head. "I can't leave him alone with the evidence any more than I could you."

"Then we all go and forget about …?" Above Rose's bowed head he pointed to the ravens again hovering noisily over the woods.

Rose Dallam laughed hysterically. "How to get the Indians across the river."

"What's that?"

"It's a game you play with matches."

Mart said, "We're taking off."

Eric Lund walked over to the deputy, holding out a small flat folder of black leather. "You've used good judgment, Oftedahl," he said evenly. "If you'll look this over, I think you'll agree that the sheriff would be willing to leave me here alone."

"Yeah?" Elmer regarded the open wallet with simple suspicion. "It's your picture all right," he admitted cautiously. "Department of Justice. Special Agent. That means the FBI?"

"Yes."

"Okay." Elmer handed back the folder, convinced.

Rose Dallam's face lightened with relief. "I was right about something," she murmured.

But Mart Bryan's voice was taut. "This isn't a Federal crime."

"One of our jobs," Lund told him, "is to cooperate with any law enforcement agency."

"Did you just happen to be staying at the camp?"

"Sheriff Gregg and I understand each other. I'm asking you in his name to say nothing to anyone about my status. It's important to all of you. Now get Rose Dallam back to Midaywin as fast as you can and get the sheriff over here."

They set off, then, to the boat, Oftedahl leading, Rose Dallam's plucky little head erect, her steps slower than usual but steady. She walked wide from Mart and did not once look toward his grim young face. Eric Lund followed them to the dock. Where three days ago he had sat idly playing middleman to their inarticulate love, his present concern was for a bit of copper and a twist of orange rind. He had no cause for alarm. Each person stepped as scrupulously around the bright peeling as if it had been Tevy's corpse.

When the receding motor had left him quiet and alone, Lund walked back toward the old cookhouse, eyes fixed half-idly on the grass, until he reached the fallen log where, on the picnic evening, they had toed the mark and shot. He took up the position, facing the peppered wall of the horse barn where, some thirty feet and more away, their target had hung. Very carefully then, he turned to the right, and walking an imaginary line at an estimated 110° angle from their line of fire, stepped off a distance of four feet. He stooped in the high wet grass, bending it back, pivoting slowly on his heels. There were shining bits of copper on the ground, two or three dozen of them scattered over a rough oval some two feet at its greatest length.

Lund nodded and stood up. From the concentration of ejected shells to the point from which they had been fired, distance and angle were correct for a .22 Colt. He retraced his path to the log and set off again, counting his steps, now walking straight out from the mark and direct to the corner of the dock, where the tip of his boot met the solitary shell Rose had discovered. Twenty feet, he should judge, from the spot where the picnic party had stood to shoot, and at a clear right angle from the line of fire. No possibility that it had been ejected from the automatic on Saturday afternoon.

Four feet from that single shell someone could have stood and pointed a gun toward a girl on the dock. The range would have to be close, if death had come from so small a bullet. A girl laughing, bright and defiant against the backdrop of the Dark Arm, stretching out her strong white hands to launch her canoe? Then the gun before her face, close to her side, and no escape....

Well, thought Lund, some imagination is a help in a job but not this much. For Tevison Dallam lay dead in deep woods on the far side of the Arm, and the empty shell at his feet, perhaps picked up idly by any one of the Saturday target shooters and dropped as idly here, or shot at any chance object by unknown hands on any preceding day of the summer, could never be evidence for the sheriff's murder case. Until Gregg came, Lund searched systematically for other ejected shells.

Bill Gregg arrived alone, worried, unhappy, ready to go at the job and stay at it until the end. Other men would soon follow him—the Coast Guard in their grim boat, the boy who owned the best photographic stuff in Petit Port—but he needed now a few minutes alone with Eric Lund.

"I kind of wanted to look the place over by myself," Gregg said, "and hear what you can tell me. I'll be grateful for any help you can give me, Mr. Lund. This is a new kind of a business for me."

"Anything we can do, we'll do, Gregg. We can't be sure yet whether this murder is tied up in any way with our case. There's plenty you and I can do for each other."

"Elmer says you think the Dallam girl was shot. Probably by a small caliber bullet. Some of the boys are checking firearms around the camp. I just had time for a word with Mrs. Fitts before I left. That target pistol, you know, that they were all shooting off over here on Saturday?"

Lund nodded.

"She keeps it on the top shelf in the kitchen dish cupboard. It's been there all summer till Saturday. Mart says he put it back up there when he carried the picnic stuff inside. Ida Fitts is sure she saw it on Sunday. Last night, I understand, she was waving it at her guests. Well, it was there today all right. Cartridge had been removed from the chamber. Ida thinks one clip of shells is missing but she can't swear to it. Of course, we don't know the girl was killed with a .22."

"It isn't the weapon an expert would choose for the job," said Lund, "but if any of our local amateurs were looking for a gun, Mrs. Fitts' certainly was handy. The Midaywin guests are in and out of that kitchen at all hours of the day."

"There's one way a .22 wouldn't be bad," Gregg followed Lund's lead toward the woods. "Nobody up here would pay any attention to the sound. Somebody's always target shooting or taking a pop at a partridge or some kid's wasting a shot on a porcupine. Beaver gnawing down a tree sounds about the same, too. We'll never be able to time the shot by what anybody heard. If it was a .22."

"Oftedahl and I didn't take time to hunt for shells around the body," Lund said. "Before I leave, I'll show you a shell I found at the dock, not near the target."

"Did the whole crowd shoot over here on Saturday?"

"No. Here, try some of my brand," Lund stopped to extend his pouch toward the sheriff's empty pipe. "Mart, Winton, Rose Dallam and I were the only ones who competed—none of us bad. Fitts is a good shot, according to his wife. You'd probably know about those two. Anderson made quite a point of telling me a couple of times that he couldn't bear to touch a gun. Which could be perfectly true."

"Do you think Mrs. Sharon could hit anything?"

"By mistake, sure. She's nearsighted but she could probably do all right with her glasses on. If her vanity lets her own a pair. I haven't seen any."

"I'll have to check it," Gregg sighed, "along with all the rest."

Now, as they pushed through the bushes that nearly closed the beginning of the path, the two men grew silent. For the first few yards, they stepped easily over a mosaic of roots and rocks chinked and smoothed by fallen pine needles and dead leaves. Within the woods that, from without, seemed black and threatening, the air was warmer than beside the rainy lake, sweet with cedar, cheerful with exasperated squirrel talk. They came to a heavy-branched jack pine, fallen across the way.

"This is where Oftedahl and I climbed over," Lund pointed to matted boughs.

"Mart, too?"

"No. Elmer told him to wait for us on this side. He would have made me wait, too, but I was already over. Look here." He pointed to raw twigs broken in another passage. "If the murderer came over the path from the Wilderness Trail, he might have done this. Or the girl may have crawled over here just before she died."

Not until they had crossed the tree did they see the body. Sixty feet ahead, the path dipped down into a small damp hollow. Here, where the top soil had washed away, exposing the red clay of a glacial moraine, the girl had fallen forward on her face. Her bare bent legs were toward the lake and the approaching men; her blond head, darkened by rain, pointed into the woods and toward the far Wilderness Trail. Around her neck the sleeves of the black jersey she had worn when she left Camp Midaywin were tied loosely, and between the yellow midriff and shorts, her back stretched naked and purpling. Falling, she had landed on her elbows, and as these had collapsed, the arch of her body had moved slightly to the side, revealing the bare abdomen and just above the tawny belt a small neat hole.

"She didn't bleed much," said Lund. "The red streaks on her arm and chest are clay."

In anger and pity he looked down on the dead remains of Tevy Dallam whose dominant charm had been glowing vitality.

Gregg spoke out of the same anger. "Why in hell would anyone want to kill a girl like that?"

"I wish I knew," said Lund. "For some reason that began long before she came here, maybe. She recognized Mart, the night she arrived. Rose is her half-sister; there could be trouble in that."

"How would you size up the two girls and their troubles about the men?"

"Frankly, I don't know." Lund, like the sheriff, had turned his back on Tevy's corpse. "The girls were jealous of each other, but I hadn't thought it went very deep. Rose had all the attention until Tevy came. Tevy is the type that wants all of it wherever she is. Rose, I should guess, would be happier with one man. The trouble was she hadn't made her choice. My money was on Mart."

"So we've got sex, too!"

"It's standard. Here's something you need to know, Gregg. The night Tevy Dallam arrived, she was alone in camp while we were all over here in the Dark Arm. About the first thing she did when she met us at the dock was to boast that she had prowled each cabin and knew all our secret vices. The only vice she named was mine. You don't kill a girl for revealing your weakness for pictures of your first child, but a general threat to expose secrets isn't a safe game."

"Why would she do it? What kind of a girl was she, anyway?"

"For money, power over somebody, hate … With Tevy it might have been just teasing, her idea of fun."

"Whodunit," said Gregg, smiling without mirth. "Who of that crowd knew about this old trail?"

"All of them. Length, destination, distance from Rose Dallam's cabin. Everyone knew all about it, except Tevy."

The Sheriff turned back to the girl's body. "After some fellow got her in here with a gun, she learned all she'll ever need to know."

"If she was shot here. She wasn't shot in the back."

"Huh? You think she could have been dragged in here after she was dead? The tree don't look as if anything had been dragged through it. She would be heavy to carry."

Lund looked down once more at the small terrible hole on Tevy's blue chest. Only a little blood colored the round rim. "Probably she was shot here," he said, "but with wounds like this, you can never be sure. If no large blood vessels are injured, death comes slowly. People have been known to walk distances, carry out plans, before they die of internal bleeding. It's possible that after the murderer escaped in her canoe, Tevy tried to get home by the only remaining route."

"But you just said she didn't know about this path."

"I know," said Lund. "But there is one way she could have found out. If she had arrived first in the Dark Arm, she might have seen her murderer come out of the path. If that happened, he—or she—would probably have told Tevy about the trail. I don't consider this a premeditated crime, Gregg."

"Unless a damned fool planned it and had awful good luck. You couldn't count on getting safe through Hag's Nook and to the Dallam dock without being seen."

"No," Lund shook his head. "Whoever met Tevy here or came here with her in the canoe, may have intended just to frighten her, and force her to some kind of terms. How good is your coroner, Gregg?"

"Doc does a good autopsy," the sheriff said confidently. "He'll have the evidence lined up clear for the jury—whether she was raped and when she ate her last meal. Doc knows how to get out a bullet without spoiling it. He gets a lot of experience in deer hunting season."

"What killed her and when. But who?"

Walking with care, Eric Lund passed to the right of Tevy's body, placing each foot on rocks and pine needles, avoiding contact with the wet path.

"If the fellow," said Gregg, following suit at the left hand, "has only planted a pair of footprints in this wet clay, we'll be all set. There aren't many places where it's on the surface in this part of the state."

"Not much of it here, either." Ten feet or so beyond the body, the path had climbed out of the hollow to higher, drier ground. "This is the end. No more clay."

Gregg, on his knees beside the path, said quietly, "Maybe it's enough."

Lund leaped the path and bent where the sheriff pointed. Where the first damp red patch appeared, a foot had been placed and quickly withdrawn. Only the toe of a shoe rested in the clay, and of that, no more than half had been pressed firmly, too little to tell the complete breadth. But for the portion not quickly withdrawn, there remained the clear imprint of a rubber sole.

"We could have something here," said the sheriff. "How to make the right kind of cast of these things I don't know."

"I could have the materials flown up here from our regional office," Lund volunteered. "What you want is a three-dimensional reproduction. You have to spray the imprint with some special quick-drying shellac, and then spoon some semi-liquid plaster of Paris into it. That will give you something solid to carry into court."

"That would be swell." Gregg straightened, listening. "I can hear the motor in the big bay. We better get back to the landing. Wait till I cover this up good."

With heads averted the two passed the body, their steps gradually quickening toward the open shore. Even the black deserted buildings were now a brighter sight than what had, so short a time ago, been Tevy

Dallam. Bill Gregg pushed his hat back from his forehead and said heavily, "If anyone came over this path and killed her after that whistle last night, Mart did it."

"If anyone came over it and killed her in the afternoon," Lund said, "she isn't dead."

"How do you figure that?"

"To get to this path from the Wilderness Trail, any one of our friends—and I don't think a stray tramp committed this murder—would have had to pass Averill Fitts, sitting in his chair on the road in front of the lodge. Mrs. Sharon was up in her cottage, Anderson in his, Rose Dallam and Winton had gone up the North Star Trail. And Mart, we know, was already on this side of Hag's Nook and The Narrows."

Bill Gregg, a sour grin twisting his naturally pleasant mouth, admitted the truth. "So after I clean up this mess over here," he said, "I go back to Midaywin and look for liars. Liars with red clay on their shoes. Beginning," he added harshly, "with my own nephew."

nineteen
TUESDAY. LATE AFTERNOON. JULY 14

But Bill Gregg did not carry out his plan. From first place on his projected list of interviews, Martin Bryan's name dropped to the last. For Mart had disappeared.

Elmer Oftedahl told the bad news to the sheriff on his return to Camp Midaywin. "I slipped up bad," he said, rubbing the back of his neck ruefully. "As soon as we got back here from the lumber camp, Mart took Miss Dallam to Ida Fitts. Nobody's seen him since. That was about two hours ago."

"Where's Lund?"

"He's gone, too. Somebody give him a phone message and he got in his car and drove off, right after he landed. Hell, Bill, was I supposed to hang on to him, too? I thought that FBI stuff was okay."

"It was," said Gregg wearily. "How many of the others are swimming across the border?"

"All six of them are inside and I'm keeping them there." Elmer pointed to the lodge where at each door stood a stiff embarrassed deputy with a deer rifle. "The girl's in a bedroom at this end. Ida's getting dinner, and Averill and that other dame are in the kitchen with her, peeling spuds. You can see what your other two pals are doing."

On each side of the big barred door to the lounge was a window, each framing a sour face. "Mr. Winton and Mr. Anderson don't like me today," said Gregg.

"They don't seem to be liking each other much either."

"Suspects usually don't. They suspect each other."

"I'll never forgive myself," Elmer said. "I knew Mart was a suspect, too. I meant to put him in there with the others. But when we landed, I was kind of confused with the girl's death and calling in the posse. And hell, Mart's your nephew, Bill. I've known him all my life. I got men out looking for him now, but Mart ain't a city girl. He knows this country."

"Keep looking. I've got to talk to these people. I'll be in the empty cabin next the pump if you need me for anything."

When he had shut the cabin door behind him, Bill Gregg sat down heavily in the nearest chair and pushed his hat back from the sunburned forehead now wrinkled out of resemblance to Mart's.

Everything we've got against the boy, he thought, means more now that he's taken off.

He considered all those things, taking short, quick puffs at his stubby pipe. Anyone could have done the Sharon business; he'd seen, this morning, how easy it would have been to slip through the poplar screen in front of a cabin, out to the highway, and back on the path behind old Althea, without a sound of progress reaching the three cabins— Winton's, Anderson's, Lund's.

For each of the Fitts couple there had been an exit without disturbing the other, and Rose Dallam admitted being on the road at the time of the assault.

He recalled what Lund had told him: Rose accusing Mart, last night, before everyone, of having done "one more odd job" for Mrs. Sharon; Mrs. Sharon's murmurs of "lovely hours" which would have looked different to Martin ... And throughout the evening no one had seen Martin around the camp. Or no one had let on if he had. If Tevy Dallam had died at the Dark Arm after the whistle had been heard by Winton and Mrs. Sharon, only Mart could have killed her.

Disregarding Mrs. Sharon's story, the last time the girl had been seen at Midaywin, she was leaving in the canoe with Mart. The last person to admit seeing her alive was Mart. He hadn't concealed the fact that they had had a fight. At the time that had seemed good to Gregg, but now the main thing was that as soon as her body had been found and Lund's profession had been revealed, Mart had disappeared.

I'll have to talk to the one who saw him before he took off: the sheriff shook his head, and sent a deputy for Rose Dallam.

Before the girl arrived, Lund knocked at the door. "I had to take a phone call about my case on the State Conservation Camp wire. We'll talk about it later." He looked as if he had liked his news. "Anything about Mart?"

"No. I'm going to question them all now. I'd like to have you stay," said Gregg.

Rose came into the cabin, pale, but with head held high and a slight courteous smile for the two men.

"Mart got out of the boat before it touched the dock," her low tired voice answered the sheriff's questions. "He practically lifted me out and hurried me into the kitchen. To Mrs. Fitts. Then he went away."

"What did he say to you when he left?"

"He didn't say anything. He didn't speak to me after we left—the Dark Arm."

"Did you think that was kind of odd?"

"Did I think …?" she repeated vaguely. Then, "No!" she spoke sharply. "I was thinking only of Tevy."

Yes, Lund thought, she is thinking of her sister and of who killed her. She knows it could have been Mart. That is all he means to her now.

"What did you do next, Miss Dallam?" the sheriff persisted gently. "After Mart went out of the kitchen?"

"Mrs. Fitts took me through the lounge and into the bedroom, not the one where Mrs. Sharon was. Across the hall. She gave me some of the medicine the doctor had left and a hot water bottle. I lay there for a while. Then I went into the office and put in a call for Elizabeth, for my stepmother. I told her about Tevy. Then I went back and tried to lie still until you sent for me."

"No one was with you during any of this time?"

"No."

There was a short silence.

"Rose," it was Eric Lund who spoke, "I'd like to ask you something about those letters you gave Mrs. Sharon. Do you remember where they came from? The post offices or the return addresses?"

Her brows lifted at what must have seemed irrelevance. "One was from New York, a hotel near Central Park. I don't remember the name. The other was from a man named Carter, and the address was Baltimore. Just General Delivery."

"Did Mart ever show any interest in those letters?"

"Mart? No."

"Did anyone else here at Midaywin ever ask about them?"

She thought a moment. "Yes. Verne Anderson did. It was the morning after Wint—and Mrs. Sharon—came. He was being very funny about my story in *Manhattan*. That's all I remember about it."

"Miss Dallam," Gregg resumed, "at any time last night before Mrs. Sharon was found, did you see Mart?"

The girl's mouth hardened.

"Did anyone see you after you left the people playing cards in the lodge?"

Her gray eyes grew dark and alarmed as if, for the first time, she realized that she could be suspected of her sister's death.

"It will help you as well as the sheriff, Rose," Lund leaned forward to light a cigarette for her. "We are all trying to find out how and when Tevy died."

"Yes, of course." Again she was the well-bred girl.

"You left there," said Gregg, "at nine fifteen." Plenty of people had told him that. "Mr. Lund heard you calling for help at 10:03. Where were you, Miss Dallam, for that three-quarters of an hour?"

She did not answer at once. She took a deep drag at the cigarette held in shaking fingers, and the sheriff, watching, let his pipe go out.

"I went on looking for Tevy," the words caught and stumbled. "I— All of you," she turned to Lund, "had suggested that she was with Mart. I went to his cabin."

Gregg held in his eagerness. "You found her there?"

"No. Mart made me hunt all through the cabin. To prove Tevy wasn't there. He said she hadn't been, ever. He said," she added intensely, "that he didn't like Tevy."

"Mart was in the cabin when you got there?"

"No. He—caught up with me before I got all the way up the slope. He had been swimming. He said we'd hunt for Tevy. He got dressed and we went down to the highway. He asked me to wait there at the foot of the slope until he did something for Mrs. Sharon." Her voice was clear and hard now and so was her face. She might have been seeing Mart sneaking up behind Althea, ready for an assault so much lighter than the attack on Tevy.

"How long did you wait before you started walking along the road towards the pump?"

"About fifteen minutes."

"Miss Dallam." All friendliness had gone from Gregg's face. "It didn't take Mart half an hour to show you your sister wasn't in his bunkhouse and to put on a few clothes."

A faint flush brought youth back to Rose Dallam. "But there isn't really anything to tell. We—loved each other. I didn't even dream that Tevy was dead." There were tears in her eyes of grief or of anger.

"Thank you, Miss Dallam," said the sheriff. "I won't keep you any longer."

She snubbed out her already dead cigarette and walked to the door. "And I have something to tell you," she paused, her hand on the bolt. "I have lost the key to my car."

"Since when?" asked the sheriff, interested.

"I am quite sure I saw it in my purse yesterday morning. This afternoon when I looked through the purse for the address book with my father's telephone number, the key wasn't there. Last night, after we'd been hunting for Tevy, everyone was in my cabin. My purse was on a table beside Tevy's. Those purses were shifted around a good deal while we were drinking coffee. Anyone could have taken the key. I have quite a powerful car, Mr. Gregg. Everyone knew that."

When she had closed the door, Gregg said to Lund, "Meaning Mart could be using it for a getaway. He could. I'll go phone the garage in Pettyport and get him stopped if he shows up there. Any chance she was lying about the key?"

"To throw more suspicion on Mart? I doubt it," said Lund. "I agree with you that she thinks he killed Tevy. She has reason to think so. But that didn't keep her from giving him an alibi by telling something she'd rather have kept to herself."

"Nine fifteen to nine forty-five. That ends any chance of an evening killing, at least by one of this bunch. Mart was the only one who could have managed it, and he couldn't, with this half-hour alibi right through the middle of the time. It also explains why he said he took an hour and a quarter to do what he should have done in a lot less time."

Roger Winton, like the rest of them, showed the night and day of strain. There were small nervous blotches on his high, finely shaped forehead and the irritation in his tone was sharp.

"Of course the sound could have been faked. I told Rose so when she brought it up. I didn't mention it myself because I thought the implication might disturb her."

"If it was an imitation of Tevy Dallam whistling, how, Mr. Winton, would you explain Mrs. Sharon's statement that she saw the girl?"

Winton jerked his head impatiently toward Eric Lund. "Ask him about the evening she thought she entertained two bears. I think he'll agree that she's a highly suggestible type."

"I agree," said Lund.

Mrs. Fitts brought Althea Sharon to the cabin, stood like a sentinel outside the door that Gregg firmly closed.

"Mr. Gregg," Althea said simply in her cracked old voice. "I'm ashamed of the things I said this morning about those two poor girls. It was horrible. I don't believe it was true."

"Mrs. Sharon." The sheriff held out a small leather folder. Like Lund's, it had a convincing official air, but it was smaller. In one corner was a smear of red. "Have you seen this before?"

"I ..." She peered at it, eyes squinted. "I don't know."

"Hadn't you better put on your glasses?"

"My glasses? I never ..." The two stern faces stopped her. "Yes, they're here in my bag." She opened the clasp.

"Were you wearing those specs last night, Mrs. Sharon, when you saw Tevy Dallam?"

"No, no I wasn't. I only need them for reading."

"Or for target shooting at fifteen paces?"

"Mr. Gregg," she pointed to Lund, "what is that man doing here?"

"He's helping me. Mrs. Sharon, are you sure you saw Tevy? Remember, there has been a murder."

She said weakly, "I'm not—absolutely certain. But," her gray curls shook in vindication, "I know I heard her."

"Mrs. Sharon," said Gregg, "can you whistle?"

"Whistle?" Then she understood and cried out, "Oh, no, no. I did hear Tevy Dallam. I swear it. I swear it."

"Thank you, Mrs. Sharon. Mr. Lund'll take you back to the lodge. When you go out, please tell Mrs. Fitts I'll take her next."

Her hand clutching the doorknob, she asked fearfully, "Mr. Gregg, on that little card in the folder—the red ... Was it blood?"

Eric Lund answered her. "It was tomato pulp."

"All right, Ida Fitts," Gregg held back any pity he might feel for the tired woman. "We've found your missing guest. Considering the way she was found, we'd better get everything straight."

She nodded. "I don't fool with murder."

"Where were you all yesterday afternoon?"

"That's easy to prove. You know what time I started for Pettyport. I guess I've got proof of where I spent most every minute there."

"Yes," said the sheriff, after he had written the list of stores, bank, and post office and the friends she'd met on the street. "It'll have to be checked, of course, but it looks as if you're the only person who had an honest alibi. For the afternoon, I mean. Nobody's clear of suspicion in the Sharon business."

"Averill and I told you ..."

"You didn't tell me there was an outside door to his room. Or that even if he was wide awake, you could easily have gone out through the lounge without his knowing it."

She stared at him, showing nothing.

"When Albert Sharon was in town last week, was it to bring his sister?"

"Yes."

"His very slightly goofy sister."

"There's not a thing the matter with her."

"Not enough to lock up, but enough to make her hard to take. What kind of a proposition did Mr. Sharon make you, Ida?"

"I suppose you have to know. There's nothing wrong about it. I'm not so strong as I was once. We haven't much to retire on. Mr. Sharon wrote me last winter and asked me if I'd take Althea off their hands for the summer, make this place look natural so she wouldn't think she was shut up anywhere—there's no reason why she should be—but not have many other people around, just run it for her."

"He paid plenty?"

"He could. I took the three men who were transients so it would look like a real resort. Rose Dallam was a mistake."

"Where did Mart come in?"

She set her jaw. "I aimed to give full return for the money. Mart's a sensible, good-looking fellow. It didn't do him any harm to add a little 'adventure' for the poor woman. He was offered high wages."

"But he wasn't told about this in advance?"

"No, and he didn't do much to earn his money, either. It would have been a safer way to spend his time than with the Dallams."

"That may be, Ida. I wish you'd told me this before. Elmer's coming now with your husband, so I'll ask you to go."

"Do you have to question Averill? He can't add a word to this."

Gregg said, "I expect to get as much from him as I have from you."

"I've been looking over my notes, Averill." The sheriff turned a page. "I was wondering if you'd like to change anything you said."

"I don't think so," Mr. Fitts' dewlaps drooped.

"Well, here you say you were sound asleep when Mrs. Sharon was hit, and then you say you heard Mrs. Fitts typing without a break."

"I did," said Averill loudly.

"Well, let that go. Fitts, somebody murdered Tevy Dallam, and I swear it was one of you people here. But if you did like you said—2:15 to 4 P.M., sitting in a chair outside the lodge, right on the highway—if you were really there all that time, no one could have got by you and I figure that, all appearances to the contrary, the girl is still alive." He got up and stood over the heavy crumple that was Mr. Fitts. "She isn't still alive. She was murdered. Are you going to tell me again that you spent the whole afternoon in that chair?"

"No." Large, unattractive tears formed in Mr. Fitts' eyes. "I didn't sit there long. Not longer than—about ten minutes."

"Where'd you go?"

Mr. Fitts blew his nose, the handkerchief over his eyes. "You had a 'peaceful, relaxed afternoon,'" quoted the sheriff. "Where?"

"At—I called on Mrs. Sharon."

"And stayed how long?"

"Until quarter of five."

"Did you look out of the window? See anybody down on the road?"

"We kept far from the windows."

"Mrs. Sharon'll tell the same tale?"

"Must she be asked?"

"I'm not interested in monkey business. Would you two prefer to be charged with a murder?"

"No. And it was not 'monkey' … Mart had been a disappointment. Althea really is most sensitive."

"And Mrs. Fitts had just killed a porcupine."

"No, no," Averill entreated. "You mustn't believe it. She would never kill a person."

"So you've been thinking she might have killed Tevison Dallam?"

"No, no, no," Fitts mumbled, "I only thought she—she might have hit Mrs. Sharon."

"That's why you changed your mind about being asleep? For God's sake, why would a smart woman like your wife try to beat the brains out of her chief source of revenue?"

"If she suspected what happened in the afternoon—she might." He spoke with fulsome dignity. "Mrs. Fitts is very fond of me."

"That's the story, Lund," Bill Gregg sprawled in the biggest chair. "Gosh, I'm all in. I thought I was tough, but all this worry—" He hitched his chair around so that he didn't have to look through the doorway into Lund's bedroom, where, row on row, neatly ticketed, stood the shoes from every cabin at Midaywin. Six more pairs still on the hoof, and a seventh to be added when they caught up with Mart.

Eric Lund, who hadn't slept much since Sunday night, poured a fourth cup of hot black coffee. "Several new stories," he said. "Murder after the whistle at eight o'clock seems to be ruled out."

"I'm ruling it that way for the present. Mart couldn't have done it and got back to Rose at around nine. Mrs. Sharon didn't see Tevy. So the whistle was faked."

"By any one of four people."

"Yes. Now in the afternoon, Averill wasn't sitting in the middle of the road, so anyone could have done the killing. Except Ida Fitts. She's got a real alibi. A half a dozen folks in Pettyport can swear to that."

"Anybody could have killed Tevy who could have operated between 2:15 and 4:45," said Lund. "Those are rough figures. This was no split-second job. All of us were around the camp dock between two and two-fifteen. Everybody was back in camp before five. There are two routes the murderer could have taken to the Dark Arm: from Bear Cub Bay by foot across the mile of old trail, since Mrs. Fitts swears not a boat or canoe except Tevy's had been in the water all day. Or through the Narrows and down the big bay. Mart and Tevy were headed that way at 2:15."

"I've been thinking about the time." Gregg said. "They would've had to stop at Collins Island and get Collins' boat, the one Mart brought back through the Narrows at four o'clock. Stopping for the boat and rowing down to the lumber camp would take about an hour. That makes it 3:15. He would have had to shoot the girl right away and start off rowing and towing the canoe. Back to the Dallam place through that bad passage would take a stiff half-hour to row at the best. Then after he'd planted the canoe on the dock, he'd have had to row back through Hag's Nook and down around Mystery Island and then come through the Narrows. That's where you and Anderson saw him at four o'clock. He could just about have made it. But he couldn't have done it and cut all the wood and filled all the lamps he claimed he did at Collins' place."

"You're checking that."

"Oftedahl will do it. Everybody trusts him. I don't want any yells about favoritism. I don't feel that way, God knows."

Lund nodded sympathy. "All the others would have had nearly an extra hour. Time to get to the Arm, time for trouble to develop, time to get back here and get set to be seen at five o'clock. Rose and Winton together. Either one alone after they parted. Averill and Mrs. Sharon together, since they're each other's alibi."

"That pair. Why?"

"The tryst didn't have to be in her cabin. How about those romantic shacks at the Dark Arm? Averill, her protector-hero, with a gun for show. All relaxed and lovely, and in walks Tevy Dallam, exploring purely on her own. Tevy wasn't the type to keep that kind of joke to herself, and Mrs. Fitts wouldn't have found it funny."

"Fitts would agree on that." A tired grin lightened Gregg's face for a moment only. "That's four of them, and five with Mart. I didn't see how Verne Anderson could have done it any more than you could have."

"No," Lund said. "He couldn't have gone to the Dark Arm and been back in his cabin where I woke him up at 3:45. However, he could have been working with the murderer. It was he who suggested we go fishing and he chose the time and place."

"You mean," Gregg spoke eagerly, "he could have been keeping you in the Narrows, out of sight of Hag's Nook and the Dallam cabin?"

"Yes. Or there because I'd be sure to see Mart at four o'clock. I have no reason to think that's so, Gregg."

"Well, I've got more reason than you have." The Sheriff put down his coffee cup and reached for his hat. "When I was questioning Anderson this morning, he made a little slip of the tongue. He's the only one who spoke about Tevy Dallam as if she was already dead."

"That isn't the first slip he's made," said Eric Lund. "The first time I talked with him, he made two of them. I told him I had located Camp Midaywin through a tourist bureau in Duluth. He said so did he."

"You knew the Fittses didn't list the resort this season?"

"Yes, I knew it," said Lund. "Then Anderson made a bigger mistake. I said something about Rose Dallam, that she wasn't the sort of girl you'd expect to find alone in a North Woods camp. He replied: 'I was surprised when I saw the place.' The place," Lund repeated. "The girl didn't surprise him at all. I suspected then he had followed her to Midaywin."

twenty
TUESDAY. EARLY EVENING. JULY 14

At the early-evening hour when the forests around Lake Midaywin are most green and quiet, a seaplane roared in low and alighted on the still water. Spray dashed up around the yellow fuselage and in a long V, the wake raced behind it as it taxied toward the dock.

"Hey!" The guards at the doors of the lodge yelled at one another, all running toward the shore, all pointing at a long, canvas-wrapped bundle lying on the dock. "Get that out of the way!"

Out of the kitchen, two ambulance men from Petit Port, doughnuts in fists, sped to their van backed down to the dock for loading, and behind them came Mrs. Fitts and her kitchen crew and the unguarded inmates of the lounge. Before the first hands had shifted the canvas bale, the Piper Cruiser was at the landing, and Pete Larson, swinging a briefcase, had stepped ashore and not on the body of Tevy Dallam. Among the drab deputies and ambulance men, Winton's rich red shirt, Mrs. Sharon's fluttery ruffles, Averill's harsh old hair, his wife's raw veined cheeks and starch-stiff dress, and the round white face of Verne Anderson mixed and mingled.

Rose Dallam, leaving the lounge with the others, had stopped at the edge of the Wilderness Trail, a small lonely figure in green, her back to the lively scene by the lake. It was she who first saw the men with Mart Bryan.

There were two men, one short, one tall, walking in heavy unison. On the crude stretcher they bore between them, Mart lay inert. The girl started toward them, as Eric Lund and the sheriff came out from the cabin path to the highway.

"It's his head," the bearers explained. "We found him back of a boulder along the North Star Trail."

North Star is a border lake, and the two, starting a half hour after Mart had last been seen, had made a quick trip over the four-mile trail to see whether he had attempted to take the boat, chained on the shore, for an escape to Canada. The boat was in place and so, for want of a better plan of action, on the return trip they had made a slow search of the woods.

"He was only a quarter of a mile from this road." The forward bearer surrendered his load to Lund and flexed stiff arms. "What a crack he got! Done with a rock, I'd say. Whoever done it wasn't playing."

"Put him right in the ambulance," said Gregg. His face and voice were expressionless. He went ahead through the grass, past the petunia bed, past the bright canoe rack to clear the crowd away. Rose Dallam walked close to the stretcher, her eyes on Mart's motionless form. Lund, at the stretcher head, saw that Pete Larson had already moved the knot of people to the far side of the dock, away from the ambulance, and had ordered the attendants to open up the rear.

"Get out your stretcher," Gregg told them. "Transfer him as easy as you can."

The ambulance men looked at each other. "What about that?" The driver pointed to the long roll of canvas on the dock. "That's what we come for."

"That," said Gregg, "can wait. Mart can't."

Rising from his knees after easing his end of the stretcher gently to the grass, Eric Lund took a quick look through the group. The Midaywin suspects were all there: Verne Anderson poking a thumb into a chin like clay; Mrs. Fitts with an iron arm about the shaking Althea; Winton's somber, shadowed eyes staring over Averill's bowed, averted head. No one spoke while the ambulance men made the swift expert transfer from the crude stretcher to their own blanketed litter. Rose Dallam slipped from behind Lund and knelt beside Mart. Her hand touched his unfeeling cheek where the small stiff hairs of the beard contradicted the fixed childlike look.

"We'll hope it's only concussion, not skull fracture," Lund said kindly to her. "If it is, he may be unconscious for quite a while, but he'll recover completely. And fast. He's a strong boy."

She said to the sheriff, "This means, doesn't it …"

"I'm not going to lie to you," said Gregg. "What has happened to Mart don't automatically clear him of your sister's death. Somebody besides her murderer could have done this. He could have been attacked by someone who thought he was responsible for her death. No one is free of suspicion yet."

The girl shrank back at these words, retreating, Lund felt, from Mart as much as from the Sheriff.

"You going down to Pettyport with us, Bill?" the ambulance driver wanted to know.

"No. Oftedahl is. He won't stir from the hospital till Mart is conscious and ready to talk. Then I'll be down." The crowd was drifting apart now, back to the lodge, away from the plane. Someone stumbled against the mummy-like body and in horror swore.

"Who's in the sack?" Peter Larson asked Lund.

"Tevison Dallam. Shot."

Larson's hard-trained young face showed nothing. He glanced toward the dock where the close figures of Rose and Roger Winton stood with Bill Gregg. "Sister of the murdered girl being comforted by a friend," he commented. "For further pictures, see section 2, last page. Take the briefcase, Rik. I'll stay with the sheriff."

For the next half hour, alone at his cabin table, Lund studied the full typed histories of the Dallam girls and their parents and of Averill and Ida Fitts. Mart Bryan's, covering two years of job wandering, was less complete.

The report from the Identification Division interested him even more. Monday—only yesterday morning—he had delivered eight sets of fingerprints to Larson in Petit Port to be flown to Washington. Six lifted from the highball glasses, one from the piano keys, the eighth from the glossy print of little Miss Lund. From Duluth Pete had brought the result of the search through the criminal and the non-criminal files of the FBI. Only two sets of fingerprints were known, but Lund was not altogether disappointed. His blackmail case was now clear and in addition he could offer the sheriff evidence of a motive for the murder of Tevy Dallam.

But it was the formula for a ninth set of fingerprints that most interested Lund, the same figures repeated four times, each instance carefully labelled with the place of origin: from a locker in a small-town high school, from a typewriter in a hotel on Central Park South in New York, from the door of a rented car, from the wrinkled skin of a drowned corpse—the formula that Pete Larson had handed Lund on Saturday night at the dance.

During the long call from the FBI office in New York he, Lund, sitting at the Conservation Camp phone this afternoon, had checked and rechecked the figures. A Special Agent taking the "Kitty" letter, with the appointment with the Senator, to Middleshire House, had found that Emily Mary Walker was a well-known employee. For three years she had been a summer mail clerk and typist; in the winters she was a school librarian in Cambria, New York. On Tuesday, July 7, Miss Walker had suddenly left her job pleading "family emergency," saying she would probably return. Everyone was surprised because the woman was so conscientious. What else was she? Forty-five, stout, glasses, good clear worker, very quiet, secretive "even about where she bought her clothes," jealous of the young girls in her office. Since she was expected to return, her typewriter still stood covered as she had left it.

In the closed school at Cambria, Emily Mary Walker had left distinct prints on door and shelf. No one in town knew her as Mrs. Frank Johnson, or had heard she was ever married, but they knew the old Dodge and the driver (stout, middle-aged, wore glasses, quiet). She was away a few days around Easter, said she'd been visiting a relative at some institution in the South, a sanitarium or something.

So this was Emily Mary Walker, winter librarian, summer hotel mail clerk, who as Mrs. Frank Johnson owned a 1940 Dodge sedan and as Miss Edith Brown of Duluth had rented the blue sedan to drive to her death in Lake Midaywin. A good quiet worker, the blackmailer of a United States Senator.

Lund put the documents back in the briefcase and opened his cabin door.

"Hi," Bill Gregg came up the path. "During the excitement around the dock, Mr. Verne Anderson got away."

"How far did he get?"

"Halfway to Smith's place. He was trying to thumb a ride on a soft-drink truck when we picked him up. He had the key to Rose Dallam's Lincoln in his pocket."

"Where is he now?"

"Larson has him in the last cabin up the line. You should see your old fishing partner now."

"I've been looking at him steadily through one of the longest weeks of my life," said Lund. "Right now, I'd like to have you come along with me while I have a stiff talk with Mrs. Althea Sharon."

Althea Sharon sat tense in the chaise longue of her luxury cabin on

the hill. She had been placed there politely, even solicitously, by Lund
and the sheriff, but there was nothing soft and congenial about their self-
contained faces. Perhaps what the sheriff said was true: Lund really
looked like an FBI man as he sat down at her desk and took a pen and
notebook from his pocket. "Your name?" he asked impersonally.

"Al—Althea Sharon. You know that."

The sheriff had remained standing. "Last Friday morning at the
post office in Pettyport, you asked for mail under a different name. That
is the name Special Agent Lund wants."

Her lips opened, closed, opened again. "Alberta Dahlquist. But I don't
use it. Really I don't."

"It's your legal name."

"Yes. But it's dull and not like me. I wouldn't use it at all except that
my alimony comes that way. And it's all the actual money I have. My
brother—my twin brother, Albert—pays bills, but if I didn't get that little
bit of alimony, I couldn't have adventures. He even forgot to leave bus
fare for the Wilderness Express. That's why I had to hitch. I didn't know
it was wrong to use another name."

"On the first night you were here, while you were in the lounge," Lund
said, "Mr. Winton came in. Now you've told people that, although he'd
never met you before, he called you by your name. Did he say, 'Hello,
Alberta Dahlquist?'"

"Oh, no," she laughed a little. "He knew it was Althea."

"Mrs. Dahlquist," Lund said sternly, "exactly what did Winton say to
you?"

"I'll try to remember." Her eyes, often so blank, understood his
implacable look. "I don't recall the exact order. He said I had the face of
a writer. Sensitive and flowerlike. Like a rose without any thorns. That
had to be my name."

"Go on."

"But that's all," she said. "That's it. Althea. Don't you understand? The
althea is a flower. Its other name is the Rose of Sharon."

Eric Lund's expression did not change. "You also asked for mail on
Friday morning under a third name. Not Dahlquist or Sharon. What
was that name?"

The woman's eyes went suddenly dead.

"The man who calls himself Verne Anderson," said Lund, "is now
under arrest for a serious crime."

"No, no. I don't believe it," she protested. "If the sheriff has arrested
him or if you have, you'll all be very much ashamed."

"Why?"

"Because," she said, "he's one of your own men. Mr. Anderson belongs to the FBI."

"He told you that?"

"He showed me."

"He showed you this," Lund held out the small black leather folder he had found among the garbage from Rose Dallam's cabin, opening it to show official printing and a name signed. The name was Frank X. Johnson. "That isn't an authentic identification, Mrs. Sharon. Look at this," he extended a second folder. "This is mine."

Althea Sharon worked her chin back and forward, her hand about her throat.

"Mrs. Sharon," Lund demanded, "what name did you give in the post office at Petit Port, last Friday morning?"

"Mrs. Frank X. Johnson," she gasped, "or Mr. Johnson."

"What else did 'Special Agent' Anderson ask you to do for him?"

"To—to stay home from the dance on Saturday night in case he needed to send me some secret message by phone."

So Anderson had been that mean. "What else?"

"To keep on trying to get Rose's letters. And to take them to him in his cabin, last night. I was on the way. Mr. Lund, he wouldn't have had to knock me down."

"No," said Lund.

"Mr. Lund, did he," she choked and then went on, "did he shoot Tevy? He said he couldn't shoot, targets or deer or anything. Was that to deceive us?"

"It could be the truth," said Eric Lund.

Verne Anderson, as the sheriff had suggested, looked a mess, pasty, sick, shrunk. Drops of sweat beaded his round baby forehead as he whined his eagerness to inform.

Lund stopped him short. "No deals. We know all you know about the Dallam murder. You've been scared to death ever since the girl disappeared. That was a dangerous slip you made to the sheriff yesterday morning. You were the only person who showed you knew the girl was dead."

"I didn't know it," Anderson quavered. "I didn't have a damned thing to do with it."

"It was Rose Dallam that brought you here." Lund ignored the obscene denial. "Verne Anderson, Frank X. Johnson, Edgar Walker, etc., you are under arrest for using the mails for extortion, and for impersonating a special agent of the FBI."

Anderson's slug fingers went up to his eyes, pulling off his glasses, hiding expression.

"You had lost your glasses on Friday morning," Lund said, "before your wife's body rose out of the lake. You didn't recognize her. That wasn't why you threw your fake identification into the garbage can as you went home along the path. The leather was wet but so was the garbage, and anyway no one would have seen it before or after it reached the dump if it hadn't been for a stray bear. You were willing in any case to take a chance, after Mrs. Fitts mentioned the sheriff was about to arrive. No reason to fear him or think he'd search you, but you've been beaten by the law more than once. You were afraid and not too bright, Anderson."

"I didn't have a thing to do with what happened to my wife. I don't know why the hell—"

"No, she shouldn't have come here. Her job was to make contact with the Senator in New York. We've found out several things about Emily Mary Walker. She was a respectable woman until she married a cheap crook. Older than you, better educated, and jealous of all young girls. When you added Rose Dallam as an element in your scheme, you added trouble.

"When you left prison with the knowledge that your famous fellow prisoner Dan Galloway was the illegitimate son of a public man, you couldn't hold down your greed very long. Your plan was pretty well worked out before your wife saw the June 25th issue of *Manhattan*. That gave you an extra idea. Pettyport was an address in the center of a big resort area. Lots of transients. Lots of people getting mail by general delivery. And always the possibility of more loot later on from the granddaughter of Mrs. Edgar Warren Bridge."

Anderson kept weak eyes on the glasses he was wiping on his sleeve. "I didn't know a thing about the Dallam girl."

"Rose Dallam answered your wife's letter on June 30," Lund reminded him. "On July 3, you wrote the Senator, naming your price for silence about Dan Galloway. The Senator is a fighting man. The possible loss of an election meant nothing to him in comparison with the conviction of a blackmailer. You left town, giving him your address as Pettyport. But I left first: We held up the Senator's answer until I had made contact. I picked you up outside the post office when you asked for the letter that hadn't yet arrived. I followed your car up the Trail, found out where you stopped, and came back here later that day."

"You put my car out of commission." Even now Anderson cared about that.

"It was convenient that your wife hadn't been able to raise the price of anything newer than a 1940 Dodge. So then we all went down and got the mail together. Of course, you told me you weren't interested in mail. You didn't show any interest that day. But the next night you did.

You reminded me to mail the Midaywin letters on our way to the dance. Then when that letter to your wife was mailed, and couldn't be retrieved, you saw your wife's dead body in the morgue. After that you had to think up another way to get the Senator's twenty thousand dollars. What you thought of, that night, was to get drunk."

"I didn't talk," boasted Anderson. "I'm not talking now."

"No, I am," Lund told him. "Ever since Wednesday evening, you've been anxious to get back that fan letter that Emily Mary Walker wrote to Rose Dallam. I think you cut Mrs. Sharon's screen door on Thursday night. After that you got her to help you. She was bringing you the two fan letters last night when she was knocked out."

"I didn't do that, I didn't touch her. I wasn't out of the cabin from the time you left me at the door."

"No? You were curious about that second letter Rose Dallam got, weren't you? What was in it, who wrote it, whether somebody was trying to cut into your pie."

"You'd kind of like to know all that, too," said Anderson.

"I do know," said Lund.

twenty-one
TUESDAY EVENING. JULY 14

In the little glade by the lake sun still lay bright on the red roof of Rose Dallam's cabin, but the dense trees pressing down upon it from the hillside, were darkening for the night.

On the clothes line tied from cedar to cedar dangled Tevy's apricot and citron bathing suit. Rose, walking through clover ankle-deep, pulled out the wooden pins, and folded the satin with shaking hands. Begging chipmunks followed her to the doorstep, the boldest of them running up her slacks with sharp importunate pricks.

"Peanuts later," she promised, brushing him off, and went into the house.

The sheriff had agreed that she should come back here alone. He had seemed almost to urge her to do so, saying something about packing up her sister's things to fill the hours of waiting. Waiting for what next?

Some of Tevy's things hurt worse than others: the black skirt sprinkled with yellow flowers in which she had danced the 'Sugar Foot' at the Harbor Bar; the red purse holding the wadded remains of the five hundred dollars Rose had sent for the trip. "Tevy," Rose could hear herself saying, "have you really cared so much about the money?"

The record from *Dido and Aeneas* she could put out of sight in the carrying case—but the words didn't easily hide, nor the refrain she caught herself humming and stopped and hummed again:

> *When I am laid in earth, may my wrongs create*
> *No trouble in thy breast;*
> *Remember me, but ah! forget my fate.*

On the road above, a truck rumbled heavily and gears shifted for the hill. The Wilderness Express is late tonight, she thought, and there followed a second thought, the nightly anticipation, now false and deriding: soon Mart will come with the mail. He would not come again. Tonight he might be dying; tomorrow, suddenly strong, he might be up and off—to prison because he had killed Tevy.

Turning her back on the window that looked toward the winding green path by the water, Rose gathered from night table and shelves the gay noisy necklaces, bracelets, combs that had accented her sister's life.

The screen door creaked and opened. Across the room Roger Winton looked at her, silent and dark.

"Wint," she called out in relief, "how nice of you to come. It was getting to be too grim here alone."

He crossed to her side, in the narrow passage between the two beds. His strongly modelled eyes focused black and heavy on her face. "We can be together now," he said. "Lund left camp a few minutes ago and the sheriff's off for Petit Port. His deputy phoned that Bryan is conscious and ready to talk."

"Oh, I'm so glad." She hadn't known that, even now, good news of Mart could mean so much to her.

Winton came nearer. "Glad? Rose, aren't you afraid?"

"No. Afraid of what?"

"Do you remember what the sheriff said to you this afternoon? Mart could have been attacked by someone who thought he had killed Tevy. Rose, did you do it?"

Tevy's copper bracelets fell to the table with a sharp clink. "No!"

"Can you prove it? Was Mrs. Fitts or anyone else with you all the time after you came back from the Dark Arm?"

"No," her voice was steady but very low.

"And you aren't sure there was a deputy on duty every minute outside the door to the office wing, Rose." He sat down on the head of her bed. "Darling, I don't care. No matter what you did. You mean everything to me."

The thought that she meant little to anyone else showed briefly in the girl's eyes, encouraging the desire already strong in Winton's.

"Come away with me now."

She leaned away from the demand of his eyes.

"No, Wint. Why should I? I haven't done anything wrong. I wouldn't go with you anyway."

His face was terribly white. "It's Mart. You love him."

"Yes."

"Even though he's killed your sister?" There was a queer taunting light in his eyes.

"No! But I don't want anyone else!"

She pushed past his outstretched feet, out of the tight aisle between the beds.

He caught up with her in the middle of the room. "Come with me whether you love me or not. Anderson's car is still in the park. We can pick up your car in Petit Port. We'd get married tonight. It would be safer for you."

She did not answer.

"Oh God, Rose I love you." His eyes were those of one who follows a lost hope. "Since I first saw you. Before I knew who you were."

"I'll never go with you anywhere."

He looked at the gray eyes, cold beneath her short sharp brows. "You mean that."

"Yes, Wint."

He laughed, and for the first time she was afraid. "I love you!— I came to Midaywin because I hated you."

"You didn't know me." She stepped away from him and he followed her toward the wall.

"Last June I got back home. I'd been away for eighteen months," he said. "I didn't have much to do at home except read. I read *Manhattan*."

"You're Jim East!"

"You're a damned clever girl. You guessed right. About the town's attitude. How did you know that everybody would turn against me just because I had been in prison? The week before I went, there were parties for me every night— How did you know?"

"I didn't know," she had to answer his demand. "I thought of the worst thing could happen to the kind of man I thought you must be."

"You and your damned father. When you answered that Philip Carter letter I wrote you and I found out where you were, I had something to do except sit around town. I had a purpose."

He came close, not touching her. "What was I going to do? Seduce you? Get your money? Rape? Hurt!"

She took a step backward and he followed till she stood tight against the cupboard.

"When I got here," he had an ugly smile, "the first thing I saw was that cheap blackmailer who calls himself Verne Anderson, grinning beside the bus. Do you know what that meant to me? I'm on parole. I had permission to come here but not to drink nor to drive nor to 'consort with criminals.' So he needled me. How fast I'd lost my prison haircut, alcohol and allergy, that damned thing you wrote. And you," the smile deepened, "asking me to drive you because I would be so safe. That was funny, Rose."

She leaned back against the cupboard, the shelves cutting into her shoulders.

"I had talked too much to Anderson," his self-disgust showed, "about all the Dallams. Even you. Although I didn't know much."

"I was old. I was 'filthy rich.'"

He seemed hardly to hear her. "I walked into the lounge, the first night." His eyes were vague, seeing it again. "I thought old Sharon was Rose Dallam and the whole thing seemed too easy to be worth doing. As easy as it was to knock her down, last night, before she could read that letter. The next day," he was again aware of the girl, "you were on your dock. I fell for you before I knew your name. I decided that was a good thing. Then Tevy came."

She couldn't keep from saying the dangerous words. "You killed Tevy."

He did not answer her directly nor move the last steps to her. "Tevy loved me," he said. "She protected me. She hated her father for what he did to me. The night she came here, she prowled the cabins. She saw something and then she knew I was here. When I came back, do you remember what she said? 'I thought we'd met before, but if that's your name, we haven't.' You thought she meant Mart Bryan. She wanted you to think that, but she was telling me that she wouldn't give me away. Not then."

His face darkened as he reached inside his coat. "This is what Tevy found. You're too frightened to see it very well, aren't you? But you've seen it before. It's the same knife Tevy took away from Mart. With my initials on the blade. J.W.E., James Winton East. And this also from my sentimental old man, 'Jimmie from Papa.' Unfortunately I didn't have time to use it on Mart."

Rose cried out as from a nightmare, "You killed Tevy."

"Somewhat by chance." He spoke almost lightly. "You see, she not only knew me. She inconveniently loved me. I thought things could be arranged by a long quiet talk in a romantic spot. We planned it Sunday night. After she had been poisonous at Lund's party. Mart's gun was only an accessory."

"You staged the quarrel on the North Star Trail." A hate equal to his was growing in her eyes.

"Yes, but I really wanted you. You needn't suffer from hurt vanity, my dear. But I couldn't make an arrangement with Tevy. She was not," he laughed again, "like Verne Anderson."

"Shall I tell you what I offered Tevy?"

"Yes!"

"To love her, marry you, get the money, divide with her. It wasn't an honest offer. I wanted you for keeps."

"Also the money."

He was not listening to Rose. Instead he seemed to be reliving the last scene with her sister. "She had an odd streak in her. She loved me. She was so jealous that she almost hated you. But she swore she would tell you everything. Not just my name. All the things I'd said."

"So then you killed her."

"I wasn't sure. After I shot her, she got up. When I looked back to shore from the canoe, she wasn't dead. She was walking along the path toward the woods. I came back here, not knowing if she'd turn up, and here you were, talking about a shot and a damned beaver."

He took a step backward. A fierce brightness burned the despair from his face. "Now I'm going to kill you. I know now." The knife flashed towards her. "That's what I've always wanted since I read 'Profile of a Hero.' I want you dead."

His left hand gripped her right shoulder, the whole weight of his body pressed her back into the cabinet. His right hand held the knife level with her eyes.

Held down by the hot inexorable weight, seeing nothing but his face blurred and doubled in front of hers and the slowly moving knife, she kicked at his legs, reached desperately for the dishes above her. Weakened by the past days of strain and grief, it was hard to struggle. Was it worthwhile? Suddenly she remembered. Mart was going to live. Mart hadn't killed Tevy.

She had strength enough to lift her left hand to the shelf above her head, to grasp a heavy glass pitcher, and quickly bring it down. But the knife was quicker. She saw the triumphant gleam in Winton's eyes and as she brought the pitcher down to his head, felt metal reach her neck.

The pitcher crashed far from the mark, and she too was falling, sliding down against the cabinet, crumpling to the floor. She tried to hold her eyes open, to meet Winton's to the last, but she failed. Darkness closed in.

twenty-two
AFTERWARD

On one of those summer afternoons in Petit Port, when the whole town seems filled with the shining blue of Lake Superior, Eric Lund stood at a hospital window. As he looked out over the bright oceanic expanse, he thought briefly of how on a recent night it must have looked to James Winton East, driven along the black shore to long darkness ahead. He turned away from the glare, and sat down beside the bed.

"Yes, it was the knife," Mart was saying. For twelve hours after the sheriff had trapped Wint with a lie, his nephew had remained unconscious. Today, his voice was weak but a healthier color had come to his lips and cheeks.

"I read what was engraved on the blade, Sunday afternoon," he told Lund: "But 'Jimmie' didn't mean a thing to me until right after we found Tevy's body and Rose said something about Tevy running away with Jim East. I thought about it, going over in the boat. Then I went right after him. I knew he was with the posse on the North Star Trail. I wasn't very bright."

"You were very lucky. Your Uncle Bill has talked to a couple of the men who must have come along the path just after East had slugged you. He came out from behind the boulder and joined them."

Mart's fingers moved restlessly on the edge of the sheet. "You're sure Rose is all right?"

"She is so right," said Lund, "that when I picked her up from under the mess of knives and broken glass and Mr. J. W. East, she apologized for fainting. As a matter of fact, the faint and fall deflected the knife. The sheriff had his gun trained on East. If Bill had let out a yell, East would probably have whirled around and dropped the knife, but he didn't like to risk Rose. So I tried the old FBI trick of jerking East up by the armpits from behind and kicking his feet out from under him. He went down like a sack of potatoes. Unfortunately, on Rose."

"Did you tough guys have to put Rose through all that?"

"Bill needed all the evidence he could get, Mart. The fingerprints identified East as someone with a motive. He had the opportunity to shoot Tevy at the Dark Arm. The footprint matched his shoe sole, and no other shoes in camp had a trace of that red clay. But that isn't very strong evidence for a jury. There shouldn't be much trouble getting a conviction after Rose repeats East's statements in court."

"She'll have to go through that?"

"She can take it. Remember, this is the man who crippled her father and murdered her sister." Lund smiled at the troubled young face. "Rose is fundamentally all right because she knows you are coming out all right, Mart. And because you didn't kill Tevy."

A faint red appeared along Mart's sharp cheek bone. "How did you first spot East?"

"Rose told me a story about her family. She'll tell it to you. And the fingerprints from Roger Winton's coke glass were identical with those of East."

"I still don't get what it was all about."

"I'll tell it fast," said Lund, "before your doctor kicks me out. Jim East was in a Maryland prison, serving a sentence for manslaughter and drunken driving. He was convicted fairly on evidence given by Rose Dallam's father. In the town he lived in, no one of his social class would have appeared against him and no one of a lower class would have been a formidable witness. The Dallams were outsiders of his own class. East bore a heavy grudge against his 'unfair' treatment. In prison he brooded and grumbled when he worked in the library with a blackmailer, Verne Anderson.

"Anderson was soon to be released. He saw East as a source of information about people of the class he would like to victimize but concerning whom he knew little. The most interesting thing he heard about the Dallams was Rose and her grandmother's money. East didn't care anything about Rose but he seems to have had total recall concerning all the family who had done him down. He was just repeating some stuff Tevy had told him about her half-sister."

Mart said, "I thought he came to Midaywin to see Rose."

"You weren't entirely wrong," answered Lund. "I'm guessing things went something like this. When Anderson first said to him: 'You could make something out of that. An oldish dame with money,' East wasn't eager. He was not a criminal in his own estimation. He expected to return to his old life when his short sentence was served.

"However, on leaving prison he had no nice reception in his home town—the inhabitants now considering him a crook because he had been in prison, not for the reason he went there. At the time when he had no job and no friends, he saw Rose's story in *Manhattan*. Rose had by chance or insight imagined the kind of situation that would give his type the worst hell, and it was the one he was in. The social favorite ostracized. East, madder than ever, remembered Anderson's suggestion, and started out to get in touch with Rose for whatever he could get out of her. He wrote her a fan letter in care of the magazine, she answered it, and he came, under a different name, to Midaywin.

"Anderson also saw *Manhattan* and had his wife Emily write to Rose in the character of an old lady. He didn't plan to blackmail Rose but he wanted to see if he could locate her and look over the chances for later blackmail of the only very rich person he had ever heard anything really personal about. He had intended to look up East after release and ask him to help cook up a Dallam deal in which East would be finger man. Now Anderson thought he had a chance to operate alone. When Rose replied from a remote camp near a much-used resort post office, Anderson decided to use Camp Midaywin as a hideout while waiting for his current deal to mature, and scout Rose for the future. When he saw Rose, he realized of course that his type could never directly compromise her, but he could watch for a possible false step. With you. Or, when East appeared, with him.

"Anderson wasn't surprised to see East at Midaywin, but East, the inexperienced and emotionally disturbed, was shocked when he met Anderson. He had forgotten all about him. For a while, they needled each other and then, after East purposely upset Anderson out fishing and then ostentatiously saved his life, they seem to have made a deal to keep out of each other's business. Anderson would stay away from Rose and East wouldn't interfere with any aspect of Anderson's extortion schemes.

"The blackmail Anderson was carrying on from Midaywin had a prominent man for victim who had come to the FBI. Do you remember the picture of the famous bank robber, Galloway, hanging in the Dark Arm shack? He was a stir pal of Verne Anderson. He's the illegitimate son of the man who would rather face shame in public life than pay blackmailers. He won't have to do either now. That's all the story. Except—" Lund's pause acknowledged death, "except for Emily Mary Walker."

"Did Anderson put her in the lake?" Mart asked.

"It doesn't look that way to me," answered Lund. "However it looked, I couldn't prove it. His denials check with what we know about times and places. Her personality—what we've learned from her associates in that school and at the New York hotel—fits with Rose's observation of her. A jealous aging woman, afraid of losing the man for whom she'd given up a safe, respectable life. Suspicious at the mention of a young girl, even remotely connected with this crime. She came up here to spy on her husband. I think that on the night Mrs. Fitts heard the splash like a dead fall into the lake, Emily Walker had followed the path she had seen Rose take in the afternoon. The big boulder beside Rose's dock is a good spot for overlooking the cabin, and a fall from there would have put the body right where Rose's fish hooks caught it."

"So it really was an accident?"

"I'd say so. We'll never know. But Anderson didn't want his wife to die. He needed her alive in New York to collect the extortion money. If he had met her at Midaywin, he'd have found an argument to send her back fast."

"It was an awful thing," said Mart.

Lund's mouth tightened. "She was a blackmailer. Don't forget that. Anderson hadn't decided what to do on his own, before Tevy was killed. He suspected East had murdered her and didn't want to be mixed up in it. He and East made one more small deal, when they got together in an empty cabin, during the hunt for Tevy, and burned the fan letters each had written to Rose. Then, when Tevy's body was found, Anderson ran away. Not far."

"And East took that crack at Mrs. Sharon? Why?"

"He wrote Rose a fan letter about roses and thorns, and then when he first met Althea, thinking she was Rose, he addressed her in the same corny style. Mrs. Sharon, if she had read that letter, could have spotted him. He was afraid of anything that would show he had previously known Tevy."

"The night Tevy came," Mart said slowly, "I understand now why she pulled that 'If that's your name' stuff. She was aiming it at East and pretending it was for me."

"She said some reckless things, that night," Lund got up and stood tall beside the hospital bed. "She had trouble coming to her. But she did not deserve her fate."

"Tevy wasn't a bad kid at that," Mart said soberly. "Even when I was mad enough to drown her, I had to admit that in her way she was trying to help Rose as well as herself. I'm not talking about it."

"Tell Rose someday. Tevy merits it. Good-bye. I've been here too long. And Rose is waiting to see you."

Mart's jaw tightened. "No. I haven't anything to say to her."

"Why don't you let her do the talking?" said Lund. "And forget about her money."

Rose touched Mart's limp fingers, dark on the white sheet. "Please take this. It's the key to my car."

His look questioned, did not yield. He said gruffly, "This is the first time I've seen you with a hat on. It makes you quite a stranger."

"I'm leaving by plane in half an hour," she said, "to take Tevy home. In a few weeks I'm coming back. Not up here. To the University, for the second summer term. If you're all right, Mart, will you drive my car down to Minneapolis? We could …"

He did not help her.

"Mart!" she was afraid she would cry. She laid her hand gently below the bandage on his head. "Your ears are as big as the doe's."

Mart pulled down her hand with surprising strength. "Take off that damned hat," he ordered. "Come closer. Now your hair is really going to get mussed."

Across the street at the gawky courthouse, Eric Lund shook hands with Bill Gregg and signed a receipt for his fishing partner, Verne Anderson. A fast new car with Pete Larson at the wheel was waiting in the alley. As Lund and his companion approached, hand in hand, two women rounded the corner of the building.

"I had to come," Althea Sharon croaked with excitement. "I had to tell you, Mr. Lund, how sorry I am that I misjudged you."

"Thank you," he said brusquely, moving his handicap awkwardly toward the car door.

"But my philosophy is still true. Good did triumph over evil. Only I got the good people mixed up with the bad." She scowled at the sullen face of the formerly extrovert Anderson. "Oh, Mr. Lund. I've got one question. I have to know so that I can write about it in my adventures. Where did you get those fascinating scars?"

Eric Lund helped Pete shove Anderson into the car and got in and slammed the door. Then he rolled down the window a little and said with weary kindness. "On the barbed wire fence I was blown into when I was six—one sub-zero day on the prairies. I froze there. A passerby pulled me off but not quite all of my face."

"How romantic!" squealed Althea, and fumbled in her bag for her notebook.

"Mr. Lund," Mrs. Fitts' grinning red face followed Althea's at the car window. "This is my question. About those baby pictures you were always showing around like a proud papa. Was all that just a disguise?"

"Like Tevy Dallam, you've found my secret vice," said Eric Lund. His face was as red as Mrs. Fitts', as the police car drove away.

THE END